united we fall

MAVE HATHAWAY

LOFTY WINGS PRESS

Cover Design by: Jess at brushtoblades

Map Art by: Mave Hathaway

Interior Art by: Amphi

Edited by: Maventhoria

Formatting: Lofty Wings Press LLC

Paperback ISBN: 978-1-970998-00-9

EBook ISBN: 978-1-970998-01-6

Published by Lofty Wings Press LLC

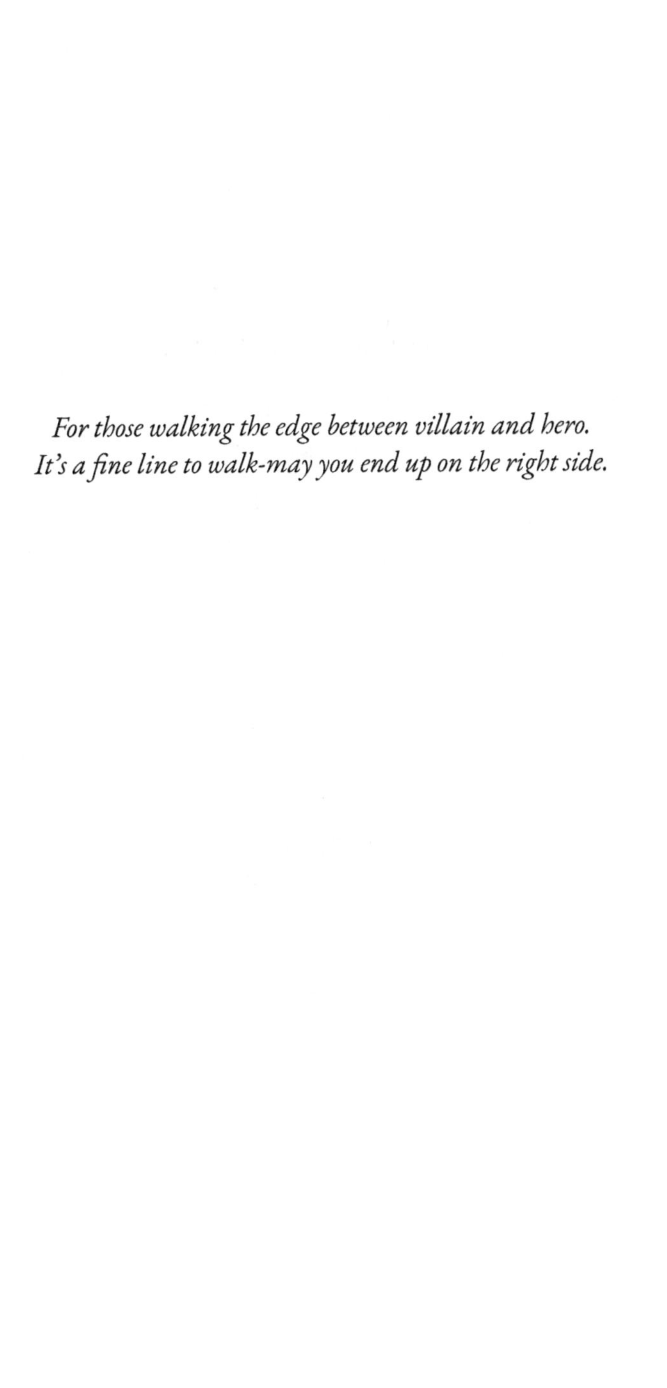

For those walking the edge between villain and hero.
It's a fine line to walk-may you end up on the right side.

trigger warnings

TIXDARR

The rumor amongst the Gods residing in the Void is that the mortals reading this are concerned about their own mental well-being. As the Lord of the Dead, I will never understand it. Regardless, here are the terrors you may encounter on the page, a mere sample of my specialties.

- Physical abuse
- Death
- Gore
- Eyeball-Searing

I shall see you at the end of this story, if you enjoy it. Do proceed with caution.

~ Tixdarr, Lord of the Dead

The Baelian Empire
Balthor
Dulvak
Dodsfell
Palion
Temple
Drakore
Longspire
Meltem
Fae

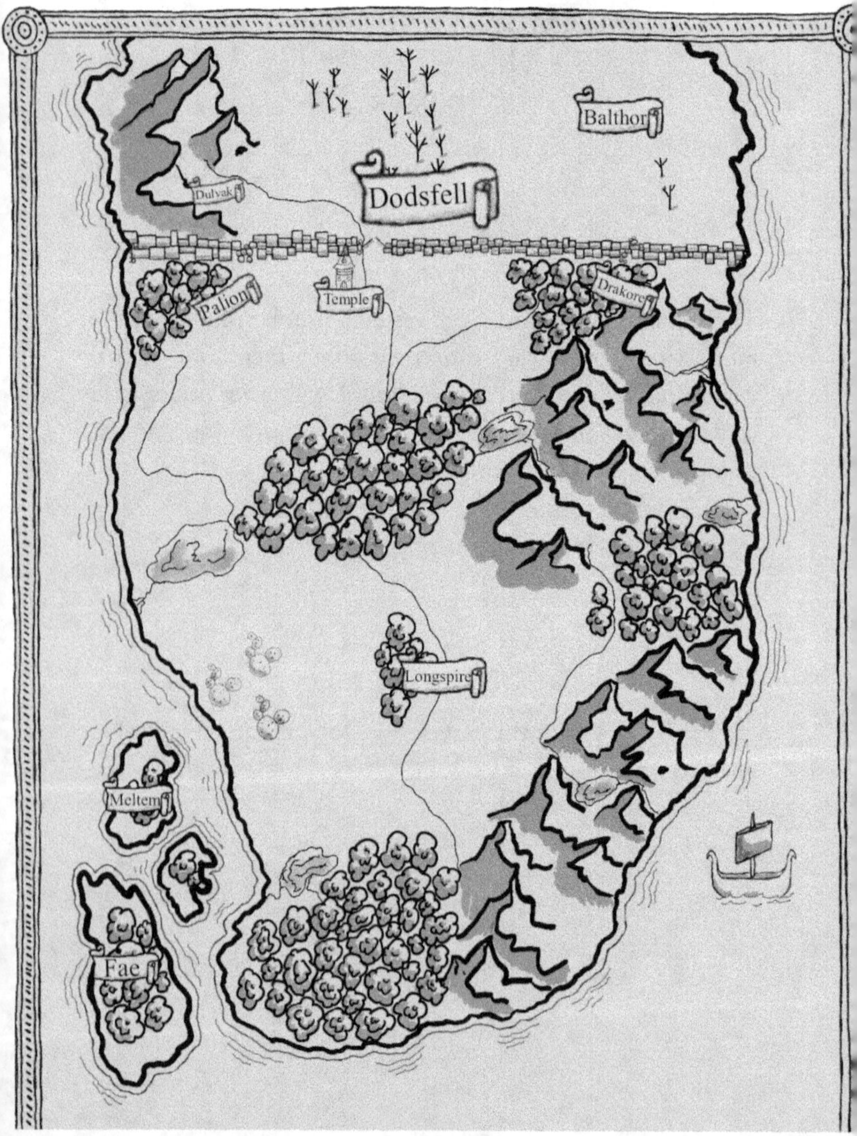

book blurb

Darling Mortal Readers,

It appears Lucian and Aurelia have finally been united. How touching. I am eager to see how my little minion has affected Lucian's perception of the beloved Princess. Will they find the common ground they so desperately need? Or will they crumble, allowing me to finally release the masses? War, after all, is better fought in droves rather than one on one.

~Tixdarr Lord of the Dead

THE ENIGMA OF TIME

the enigma of time

TIXDARR

Time passes differently for every being, living or dead. I hear rumors that you mortals follow particular calendar. It is important therefore for me to share with you the calendar that exists within my world, for this and many stories to come. I have decided to break down the months in order of the year and even added the associated festivals celebrated throughout Baelia. I have limits to my patience; however, I have not added in every single festival that may be celebrated within Baelia. Be grateful I decided to help at all.

~Tixdarr, Lord of the Dead

Drak - Festival of Dragons *(Secretly Celebrated)*
   Bura - Festival of New Life
   Tiv - Festival of the Mother
   Anit - Festival of Water
   Byr - Festival of Fire
   Duele - Festival of Harvest
   Osi - Festival of Protection

Riari - Festival of Healing
Bene - Festival of Wind
Xita - Festival of War
Oxi - Festival of the Father
Tix - Festival of Death

religious hierarchy

TIXDARR

It's important, wayward mortal visiting our world, that you fully understand how our Pantheon functions. The Gods within the Pantheon each receive a temple, but only if the people of the land choose to honor them with one. Temples can be simple or complex. For our purposes, we will review the more complicated of our temple structures; I would hate for you to be confused. The more powerful Gods, such as my sister Tiva, have multiple temples throughout the continent. Be advised moving forward in our universe: this is not an exhaustive list of Gods worshipped in Baelia. That would take far too much of my precious time.

~Tixdarr, Lord of the Dead

TEMPLE POSITIONS

Oba: The head of the temple. One main Oba oversees many smaller temples; only the strongest of the Gods warrant multiple Obas. This position has only ever been held by a woman, chosen by the God in question.

Abbot/Abbess: The right hand to the Oba in the temple she resides in. In smaller temples, this individual will run the temple and report issues to the God's chosen Oba.

Acolyte: A member of Gods order. Serves the temple and spreads the word of the God they worship.

The Pantheon of Baelia

Gods:

    Goddess of Tiva ~ Fairy ~ Goddess of Motherhood

    God Oxius ~ Minotaur ~ God of Fatherhood

    God Tixdarr ~ Demon ~ God of the Dead and Afterlife

    God Burasil ~ unknown species ~ God of Animals and the Hunt

    God Benmes ~Winged ~ God of Air and Wind

    Goddess Deulla ~ Centaur ~ Goddess of the Earth and Harvest

    Goddess Byra ~ Dwarf ~ Goddess of Fire

    Goddess Anita ~ Merfolk ~ Goddess of Water

    God Xitar ~ unknown ~ God of Fighting and War

    God Osin ~ unknown ~ God of Protection

    Goddess Riarin ~ Elf ~ Goddess of Healing and Medicine

pronunciation guide

TIXDARR

The other Gods have suggested that you may want to know how to pronounce the various names presented in this story. So here you go, mortals-parse through these words and figure out how to enter my world completely.

~ Tixdarr, Lord of the Dead

People:

- Maledic - (Mal-e-dic)
- Aurelia - (a-Rey-li-a)
- Faziel - (Fæ-z-el)
- Balthor - (Bal-th-ar)
- Dulvak - (Dull-va-k)
- Estrez - (S-trez)
- Aewenna (Awe-win-a)
- Feginth - (Fe-g-in-th)
- Spréach - (Spree-ach)
- Lucian - (Loo-shin)
- Zadon - (Z-aid-on)
- Suzu - (Sue-zoo)

- Belvina - (Bell-vee-na)
- Ulfur -(Ul-ffur)
- Juro - (Jur-o)
- Kasria - (Kas-ree-a)
- Nastrud Lineare - (Nass-tr-ud Lyn-ear)
- Pinera Tenebris (Upper Mayor) - (Pin-ear Ten-br-is)
- Cryon Osdrak (Lower Mayor) - (Cry-on Os-drake)
- Jolvan - (Joel-van)
- Olrun - (Oll-run)
- Hura Dreuger - (Her-ah Drew-ger)
- Notus - (No-tus)
- Khal - (Call)
- Krooth - (Crew-th)
- Wulfric (Wool-fr-ic)
- Bashi - (Baa-shee)

Place:

- Baelia - (Bay-lee-a)
- Palion - (Pal-ee-on)
- Drakore – (Drr-a-k-ore)

Gods:

- Goddess of Tiva - (T-ee-va)
- God Oxius - (Ox-ee-us)
- God Tixdarr - (Tick-star)
- God Burasil - (Brr-a-sil)
- God Benmes - (Ben-mis)
- Goddess Deulla - (Do-el-a)
- Goddess Byra - (Bi-ra)
- Goddess Anita - (A-ni-ta)
- God Xitar - (Zi-tar)

- God Osin - (Aw-sin)
- Goddess Riarin - (Ree-are-in)
- God Culgan - (K-ul-g-an)

Months:

- Drak - (Dr-æ-k)
- Bura - (Brr-a)
- Tiv - (T-i-v)
- Anit (Æ-nit)
- Byr - (Bi-r)
- Duele - (Do-el)
- Osi - (O-see)
- Riari - (Ree-are-ee)
- Bene (Ben-a)
- Xita - (Zit-a)
- Oxi - (Ox)
- Tix - (Ticks)

contents

part one

LEGEND OF THE DRAGON

DRAGON HISTORY RECORDED BY MARGOTH, SEER OF BAELIA

Once upon a time, dragons roamed Baelia. Their one and only purpose was to ensure the planet ran smoothly and safely. Every species that found its way to Baelia was welcomed and cared for, so long as they cared for Baelia in return.

The issues began when humans settled in the center of Baelia, claiming prime farmland. It is believed that the humans brought their own ideas of religion, needing Gods to guide them in life and decisions. Yet the Gods they brought to Baelia could not compare to the magic of dragons.

It wasn't long before the hastily pieced-together Pantheon began to oppose the all-powerful dragons.

It started with one dragon disappearing south of the Meltem Islands. The world cried, but instead of demanding answers, they clung to the remaining dragons. The Pantheon grew more persistent.

More and more dragons vanished, one by one, until only one remained: The Dragon of Life, Feginth. The legend states she retreated from Baelia due to the heartbreak over her loss. She would return only when the people of Baelia were ready to care for their world, above all else, once more.

ONE

LUCIAN

DRAK - PALION - YEAR 7568

> *Soulbonds can be rejected by merely a thought in that direction. The person rejecting must be certain and fully aware of the consequences, but their bonded mate may not know of the rejection until it is too late.*
> ~*Temple of Tiva, Lost Records*

Ten years of pain and torment had passed, leaving him struggling to find the point in the madness. It was far easier to allow Zadon to run the kingdom while he merely showed his face for formal events. Instead, he spent his time trying desperately to remember the face of his beloved Kasria.

He would spend hours drawing bits of her that he could recall. Sometimes it was nothing but the shape of her nose, but on rare occasions, he would try to draw her entire face.

Someone had the servants bring him the freshest cuts of

roses every few days. The constant bombardment of her scent invaded every moment of every day, pulling him into visions of her deathbed, mixed with flashes of her sparkling eyes. It got harder with every day that passed to see her smile, and remembering her voice became an impossible.

Despondently, he lifted his head up from the sketch book where he was doodling her eyes again and again, clinging to the fear of forgetting them. A crash sounded from the hallway—something he determinedly ignored. Or tried to ignore, until the door to his study slammed open.

He observed Suzu, who always operated at an alarmingly fast pace, stride toward him with absolute purpose. She dipped into a hurried curtsy. "Sire. I need you to attend to the kingdom. Something big has happened."

Lucian's mind whirled, trying to interrupt the flow of words, needing silence. "I'm sorry? What was that, Suzu?"

She knelt at his feet, effectively hiding herself from view of the door. "Aurelia Berrid. Do you remember her?"

He sounded out her name, fragments of old conversations rising to the surface. "Kasria wanted to help her."

"Yes!"

"Where is she?"

"Zadon captured her. She's in the dungeon."

"He always said we would care for her. We would follow Kasria's plan."

"I know that's what he's said. Please try, for her. For us. We need help now. Zadon may not be doing what he claims."

Lucian met her eyes; they glistened with desperation. The monsters in his mind roared. Steps echoed in the hall. Suzu's eyes widened; she scrambled to a painting, pulling it aside to reveal a hole in the wall. "Hurry, Lucian. Find your way back to Kasria's path before it's too late."

two

AURELIA

Drak - Palion - Year 7568

The dank cold of the cell was trying to settle into her bones. She could feel it lying on her skin like a slimy blanket. She did her best to ignore it in favor of the many other new, yet oddly old, sensations vying for her attention within her mind.

The darkness that had become second nature to her still took up a large portion of her magical well, but now she could sense other styles of magic thrumming beneath her skin, begging to be used. She took a deep breath, sorting through the feelings until heat flooded her, battling the clammy dankness of the dungeon, keeping it at bay permanently.

A deep sigh of satisfaction escaped as her eyes fluttered open. Now that a semblance of comfort had been achieved, it was time to assess her newest predicament. Somehow, a demon had appeared in the upper reaches of Palion's court. Kygoss and his birdies hadn't uncovered that little tidbit during her training, or he had chosen to keep it secret. Perhaps this demon was similar to Balthor, cunning enough to have achieved the red hierarchy. That could explain how he attained his position in the court.

She stared around the cell, the dark grey stones turning green with slimy algae. A smell reminiscent of mold and dirt. High above, near the ceiling, there was a small window with iron bars across it far too high to offer any real hope of escape. Someone had decided the prisoners would benefit from a rickety bench. Across from the lonely bench sat a wall of bars, a door inset into them, a heavy chain keeping it shut. The bonus of an entire wall of bars meant she could see down the hallway, protecting her from the despair that came with the unknown.

She stared up at the ceiling, debating how to see outside. An idea struck when she glanced at the bench she laid on and then back at the window. It took a few minutes of grunting, but she got the bench positioned in just the right place. Once she had shoved it to the proper spot, she took a few minutes to study the hallway, to see if anyone would come to investigate. Silence met her, so she climbed atop the bench, reaching on her tiptoes.

She didn't expect much. The window was small and close to the ground level. She could make out boots, wheels, horse hooves, and in the far distance, mountains. She hopped back down to the ground. She could scream, but there was no guarantee the attention would be helpful.

Ultimately, she needed a way to escape this damn kingdom. Her goal was to head to the Meltem Islands hideout, perhaps grow a garden, avoiding all living creatures. If she did that, the days of pain and torture would finally be done, and perhaps she'd find her peace.

Visions of the scaly demons flashed through her mind, causing her blood to spike, fear coating her mouth. Her hair rustled—rising. Memories tumbled. Her hair continued to float, awkward due to the mats and dirt. *How was it moving?*

She whirled around, expecting to see someone holding it up, yet no one was there. Her shirt tugged. Panic rose. Maybe she had finally lost her mind.

Finally, broken.

A thrum took up in her blood. Her eyes snapped open as the wind picked up leaves that were moldering in the corner. The wind all but attacked her, swirling, invading her every pore.

It came back in a rush, causing Aurelia to giggle. New memories assaulting her mind. One's locked deep in her soul. Memories of experimenting with her inherent gift with the wind. Her first magic. And if this reaction meant anything, it missed her.

Aurelia took some deep breaths, centering herself, rolling through some of the basic air-magic exercises she could remember. Her fingers itched to experiment further. A clang on the bars of her cage had her tucking her hands behind her, a ready glare towards the newcomer.

A blonde man stood with his hands tucked into his pockets, observing her. The demon who had brought her stationed behind him. It clicked then who this blonde was. He didn't resemble the drawing Kygoss had once shown her. Instead, his face was hollow, eyes haunted, perhaps more than her own.

"The Palion Pup, in the flesh. What an honor." The words came out dry, "looking a little worse for wear, Lucian."

The blonde didn't even twitch, as if he couldn't hear her. The demon reacted instead, growling. "His name is Lucian Ronnet, and he is the King."

"Oh good! Then you no longer need me." She shrugged, examining her nails. "After all, this arrangement was only created to ensure the Pup inherited." She caught the demon tightening his fists and smirked.

Lucian shifted, glancing between them. "Zadon, care to explain why the Princess of Drakore is in the dungeon?"

Zadon flushed. "She was practically feral when I found her. Her powers are an unknown factor, and I didn't trust your safety."

Lucian raised an eyebrow and turned to her. She tilted her head back, mocking his curiosity.

"What is your power?"

"Vast." She grinned.

"I'm sure, seeing as you survived ten years in Dodsfell when many more deserving souls have perished in the mortal realm." He glanced at Zadon. "She can't look like that."

Zadon nodded. "We can have the ladies attend her."

"We could but can they handle her?"

"Can you?" She asked it with sugary sweetness falsely dripping from the words.

Lucian ignored her. "We need the appropriate motivation. Then perhaps she can be convinced to abide by the plan."

"Motivation. Great idea." She lifted her hands, digging into the well of air power growing within her since she arrived in the mortal realm. She flung the air at Zadon's chest, slamming him into the wall opposite her cage. "You see, there's one thing you haven't figured out. I have nothing you can use against me. As far as I know, I don't even have anything you want. So be a dear, use your mangy paw and let me go before I play with more power."

Zadon's eyes bulged, but she turned her glare on Lucian, waiting, hoping he made a decision before her fledgling grasp on her power broke.

Lucian grunted. "Point made. Put him down."

She merely loosened the hold enough for him to breathe, but didn't drop him. "It's time for some truth, Lucian. Or open the damn door."

Lucian crossed his arms and grunted. "Fine. You are still needed. I am King in name, not title. We are waiting until I can get a suitable bride tied to the power; to strengthen Palion. That's where you come in."

She nodded, unimpressed. "Palion is slow at problem-solving. Get a different princess. There's no true reason for me to help you."

"There is." Zadon squeaked.

She shoved her power harder against the demon. "Hush now, the adults are talking, not the pets."

"We have him."

Aurelia's brow furrowed. "Him? Him who? Really if it's so motivating I would expect that statement to have more weight."

Zadon gurgled his skin, going dusky. "Oh crap." She pulled back enough for him to breathe.

Lucian growled, his voice and demeanor going darker. "I have your soulbond, you feral waste of space. I thought you'd clue into that."

A chill went down her spine. *What soulbond?* "You don't have him. Wanna know how I know?" Lucian stepped to the bars, rattling them. "You just told me." She grinned confident they didn't have him. "Seems like one of us didn't grow up in the last ten years." She pulled her power from Zadon, her limbs feeling like jelly. "Off you go, find some nonexistent leverage." She managed a smirk.

She held herself together until they were gone. Collapsing on the rickety bench, emotions dragged her down the forbidden corridors of her mind. Silent sobs wracked her body as she rocked, waiting for the oblivion of sleep.

Palion was but another prison.

three

MALEDIC

Butterflies continued to swirl despite the several hours that had passed since Feginth had left the world. The multicolored rainbow of wings was enough to distract him from his new reality. His soulbond was back in Baelia, and now it was up to him to make their connection permanent. She had never learned about the bond before someone managed to steal her away.

He released a deep sigh as he scouted the large cavern, mentally marking the spots that would best hide Feginth's secrets from prying eyes. There were six in total, each weighing about the same as a sack of flour. He marveled at the colors and thoughts that bombarded him as he handled each one, each unique from the other. As if the creatures growing inside were communicating with him. Another surprise: each held an inner fire, warmth radiating from within, their shells softer than they appeared.

As he nestled the last one into its new home, a pang surged through his bond with Aurelia. He doubled over, breathing deeply. Theoretically, with enough concentration, he could channel her emotions and understand what she felt, made all the easier now that she was in the mortal realm. Relief came first, but it vanished quickly. What lingered was pain and sorrow. Sadness so deep, he feared he might drown in it himself. Delicate feet of butterflies alighting on his face grounded him again.

His mind felt clearer than it ever had when it came to *her*. Even though the bond had brought him nothing but pain for years, it was time to challenge that, to see if something more was possible. He needed to *see* her, to *show* her that she wasn't alone. If she wanted out of the bond, he would deal with that consequence. But if there was even a slight chance that she wanted him, as he needed her, he owed it to them both to try. He sent a thought of thanks to Feginth's spirit before hopping into the air, shifting quickly into his crow form, and swooping out of the cave.

T he journey was straight and true, his blood singing at the prospect of finally laying eyes on her. Perhaps that's what drove him to be rash. Regardless of the motivation, he found himself in the courtyard of the Palion palace, the tether connecting them growing tighter, and stronger. Despite the evidence to suggest her presence, he didn't see her anywhere. He circled twice, but all he witnessed were normal palace routines. Nothing to suggest otherwise.

He let out a frustrated caw, which unfortunately garnered unwanted attention. He risked one more circle of the court- yard, varying his elevation; unfortunately, an opportunistic archer opted to take aim, loosing an arrow straight at him. Mal's mind blanked. He rolled to the side, evening out his flight, mentally scrambling to figure out how to find her while keeping himself alive. Letting out another frustrated screech, he headed for the rows of trees bordering the palace grounds. He opted to hop around the trees until he ended up in one that gave him a great view of the palace. Conveniently, it was on the opposite side from where he entered the woods, hopefully dissuading followers. He roosted up high in the canopy, determined to wait for a sign of her.

He must have fallen asleep, because he jolted awake to a feeling of being watched. He startled, unused to waking in his crow body. He looked around and froze. Below his tree sat a large wolf, black as night with white splotches like stars across its fur. The creature was large, imposing, and unnervingly staring straight up at him. Two more sets of eyes glowed behind it, watching him as well. He couldn't make out much of them, but it was clear he had been found.

What now? He didn't want to leave without her. But how could he fight this?

A popping sound echoed, and where the black wolf had been, now stood a blonde warrior.

"I know who you are." Maledic shuffled two steps closer to the trunk of the tree. "Now, now, it wouldn't be wise to try to run. There are two trained archers with their sights on you right now. Do you happen to know who I am?"

Maledic debated. Of course, he knew this warrior was Lucian Ronnet, Prince of Palion, his commanding presence giving away his identity. It also helped that his own father had renderings of both Lucian and Harold hanging in the study, so no one would forget their likeness.

Mal nodded once, unclear what Lucian could actually know. "It took a lot less time than I thought for her soulbond to come looking. I should capture you right now so she knows I do indeed have the leverage, she doubts. It is what Zadon would want, and she has been rather rude; the idea of proving her wrong is tempting. However, I know from my own experiences that losing a soulbond is unthinkable, even if you are my enemy. Therefore, I will let you leave unharmed this once. I am unable to release her to you, but I can prevent your bond from cementing." Maledic watched as Lucian stared at the moon, bright and full. "Go, love someone else while you still have a chance to save your soul."

Mal ruffled his feathers, a deep sadness filling him for Lucian and for himself. His soul was already tied to hers, even if only partially. He needed her to choose as much as he needed air to breathe.

Lucian had begun walking away but stopped half in the shadow of a neighboring tree. "I shall leave a guard here for the night to ensure your safety and compliance. At first light, you fly, or you die."

Mal hunched down on the branch as a gray wolf took up residence on the ground beneath his tree. Once the last wolf left, another pop filled the air, the wolf becoming yet another warrior.

"Mister Crow. You won't believe me, but I have a vested interest in the Princess. I owe her a life debt. If you will allow it, I shall sneak you in to see her. Let her choose her own path."

Mal let out a soft caw, unbelieving of this random warrior; it had to be a trap.

The man toed the dirt uneasily. "My name is Baryn. It is my fault she ended up in Dodsfell. I trusted the wrong person. I have been waiting ten years to fix this. Please let me help you."

Anger raced through Mal's blood; he hopped down, shifting to his mortal form, uncaring of the risk. He pulled his dagger and held it at Baryn's throat. "You sent her to the land of the dead?"

Baryn didn't even flinch. Mal knew he could be overpowered, but fire filled his veins, and a whistling filled his ears.

Baryn met his gaze. "Yes. I was told that if I couldn't get her safely out, it was the safest place for her, to protect her from the coup. I didn't know of any other options."

"Who the fuck told you that?" Vaguely, he became aware —the blade he was holding was turning cherry red, the heat in his blood leaving through his hands.

Baryn's voice shook. "The damn demon. He was a trusted advisor to my brother and sister. I couldn't insult them by doubting him, so I chose to believe. We are all paying for that misplaced trust."

Mal huffed out a breath, forcing calm thoughts through his mind, the heat receding. "Brother?"

"Lucian was the soulbond to my sister. They were bonded in front of the Gods, and therefore, he will always be my brother."

Mal nodded once, pulling back. "The demon dies. No matter what she chooses in the end. I want him dead."

Baryn nodded once before grabbing a twig and settling down on the dirt. Mal knelt, ready to learn. The idea that he finally could do something to help filling him with a foreign sense of purpose.

four

LUCIAN

Drak - Palion - Year 7568

The sun was just breaking through the tree line as the council room filled with his court. Lucian swallowed his yawn. He didn't regret the mercy shown to her soulbond. For a time, he wished to be able to turn back the clock and not meet the decimator of his soul.

Giggling and gossiping filled the air with joy as everyone filed in. The door clicked shut behind Baryn as a hush fell. He smiled warmly, doing his best to stay present. All of these people were his family, and together they had kept the kingdom functioning, and together they would force the stubborn Drakore Princess to fall in line.

"Welcome, friends. The next stage of the plan has arrived. I am sure you are all aware by now that, two days past, Zadon caught Aurelia, Princess of Drakore, as she escaped Dodsfell's barrier. The Marriage Rite will take place tonight. The Rite of Inheritance will follow once we obtain King Harold's approval."

Suzu cleared her throat. "Will his Majesty feel well enough to join all of us at the Marriage Rite tonight?"

Lucian swallowed his growl of anger. His father's death was only known by three people: Zadon, himself, and whoever murdered him. The illusion of illness they had maintained for all these years was vital to stability.

"That is Zadon's task to determine. In fact, I have a task for everyone at this table. Each vital to ensure tonight goes smoothly." He glanced at all of them and was pleased to see that they all looked eager to aid him in the quest of stability through marriage. "Miss Belvina, I would appreciate it if you could dazzle up a gown for her. Suzu, we need the peasants to back her. They really wanted a queen before. If this is to be successful, they have to support her. Ulfur, you are, of course, in charge of making sure we can all reach the temple safely through the use of an armed escort. Highly visible, heavily armed, and safe." Lucian took a deep breath, his brain reeling at the idea that Kasria would be replaced by the rise of the moon.

"Baryn, my brother, can you ensure the wolves are on our side? She will be placed in the open Luna role as well. I can't handle an uprising over it right now. We all will need to keep unity in our hearts."

Baryn's face closed off, sadness deep and dark emanating from him. Lucian remained silent for a few minutes in honor of the loss of his other half, the rightful Luna of the Palion pack.

On an exhale, he asked, "Any questions?" He was met with nothing but silence as the sadness settled about them like a damp blanket. "Well then, off you go. There is a mountain to move today. Ladies, do be careful with her; she's a bit feral. Consider taking Valri with you; her demonic strength may come in handy. Zadon, stay behind for a moment."

Everyone filed out, the normal murmuring of conversation

and joking gone. The cloud of gloom hanging low. Zadon stood and took a seat closer to Lucian, steepling his hands, his expression blank.

"Talk me through how the fuck this is supposed to work." The growl from his dark side crawling through him.

Zadon cleared his throat. "We start with the marriage. Then we redouble…"

"Are you fucking serious? We've spent the last nine years searching for his murderer, and now suddenly they will just appear? You're either lying to me or you're delusional." Lucian slammed his hand on the table, standing. "She'll know, Zadon! She's not going to work with us! She has more fucking power in her pinky than I have in total without my inheritance of the Great Power."

His blood sang in anger. Zadon had been responsible for Harold and failed. Kasria's ghost frequently reminded him of Zadon's disrespect towards others in the inner court. It made Lucian wonder how Zadon had dared to treat Kasria.

Kasria had never directly complained, but that didn't mean much. He had made the choice to keep Zadon near him despite his current doubts, hoping that the demon could fix the oversight of his father's untimely death.

"Sire, once the marriage is consummated, the magic of that Rite will tie you with the Princess. You'll gain some access to her power. Access that will get stronger when you are both rightfully crowned." Lucian watched as Zadon rubbed at his temples in frustration.

"Right, and how exactly will we be crowned when the fucking King is already dead? He's supposed to be a key member of the ceremony!" Lucian stomped as he paced to the window, forcing deep breathes through his body desperate to snuff out the darkness that welled within. He stepped into the sunlight, letting the warmth seep into him as Kasria once had.

"Just leave, Zadon. Hunt for the power and leave me the fuck alone."

Lucian refused to look to see the face of the man who had been his best friend as he left the room, leaving him alone once again. Tears formed in his eyes as the warmth sank further into his skin. The rose smell that had clung to Kasria floated on the air, a haunting reminder that he was truly, undeniably alone. He sank to his knees, allowing the tears to finally fall.

five

AURELIA

DRAK - PALION - YEAR 7568

> *The Dodsfell crystal is a complex realm safeguard put in place by Tixdarr. A practical test to prove one's ability to handle immense amounts of power —or to succumb and fail. The crystal's original intention was to give power to the powerless demons, giving them ownership over new power without needing to petition Tixdarr. Mortals at the mercy of the crystal's power lose their souls, their own power completely muffled in the presence of a Gods power.*
>
> *~Temple of Tixdarr, Lost Records*

Sleep had been elusive at best; the bench was hard, the dungeon drafty. As the sun filtered through the small window above, broken up by various people going about their daily activities, her mind turned to her current situation. How long would Lucian keep her locked away? He didn't have any leverage. After yesterday they all knew as much. All he had shown her were his own problems and reasons why she needed to leave as fast as she could.

Feminine laughter and talking filled the hall, causing her to perk up. Women would be able to be manipulated, and through that, she could be free. She sat up on the bench, arms and ankles crossed, waiting. A redhead led the pack, lugging a large bucket of steaming water. Aurelia's mouth watered at the prospect of being clean. *What would she do for that privilege?*

Behind the redhead came a blonde juggling an armload of bags. It wasn't until the brunette bringing up the back got close enough that all hope snuffed out. "When did Palion get in bed with demons?"

The women stopped murmuring, all attention now focused on her.

"Hello to you too." The redhead fumbled at her belt, getting the key into the door.

Delight spiked in her at the prospect. The brunette dropped the few bags she carried, stepping forward quickly. "Suzu, that's not a smart idea just yet."

Suzu paused before the key actually entered the lock. Aurelia couldn't halt the growl. "Demons seriously need to fucking get out of my life."

All eyes turned back to her. Suzu sent a glare at the demon behind her, motioning the other two back. "I can handle this."

Aurelia began laughing. "Your Prince and his pet couldn't. What makes you so certain?"

Suzu opened the cage carefully, keeping the door just wide enough for her to slip inside. She kept the keys on the outside with the blonde. As Suzu stepped closer, she orchestrated a deep curtsy "My name is Suzu Zaral. I am an advisor within King Lucian's court."

Aurelia watched her carefully. "You're more than that, aren't you?" Suzu's eyes widened slightly. It was nominal and only happened for a second, yet Aurelia caught it. "Now what could it be?" Her mind stuttered as she let her magical aura loose in the room, coming in contact with a source of power rivaling even her own growing one. She switched tactics, suspicion of Suzu rising. "Why am I here, Suzu?"

Suzu glanced at the women in the hallway before meeting Aurelia's gaze. "Lucian has you here until the marriage tonight."

"I see." Aurelia stood taking a few steps closer. "He informed me he needs to marry someone to solidify a union to get a better grasp on the Power of the Land." She stepped into Suzu's personal space. "Yet, he doesn't have the right to worry about that anymore, now does he?"

The blonde gasped, causing Suzu to glance her way.

"Ah so you can't marry him because you are married to her. But that leads to the question of how did you manage to get the power that was destined for him?" Aurelia paced around the room. Suzu stood still as a frozen statue in the cell. "So the Palion Pup blackmails me with baseless threats hoping to force my hand. Yet, unwittingly sends me the mother load of destructive material straight to my cell." She hummed. "What do I do with this?"

Suzu jolted as if leaving a trance, a smile covering her face. "The Gods do work in mysterious ways. At the end of the day, I think you have to reevaluate who you see as the villain in the larger scheme."

Aurelia leaned a shoulder against the wall, an eyebrow raised. "Oh really, and who is the villain if not the court keeping me hostage and forcing me to wed?"

Much to Aurelia's surprise, the demon standing outside spoke first, stepping up to the bars. "Zadon of the Clan Dulvak."

It was said simply but rocked Aurelia's core. Images of

Estrez as she contorted in pain filled her mind. She sharpened her gaze on the demon. "I didn't catch your name."

"I didn't give it. You wouldn't know it. You would more than likely be familiar with my nickname, Shadow Dancer. Ring a bell?"

Aurelia's jaw hit the floor as she rolled through the instances she had heard of Shadow Dancer. This person had been targeting the Dulvak Clan for years. Her time at Balthor's compound had exposed her to as much. In fact, Balthor had promised Estrez that he would take care of the Shadow Dancer in exchange for her release.

Air whipped through the room. "You. Owe. Me. An. Explanation." Her voice was deadly calm, even as the wind swirled and a hint of dark fog began to seep from her.

"Oh no, that shouldn't be possible. Ladies, do not let the black fog touch you. Aurelia, you do deserve an explanation. My name is Valri and I am indeed a demon." Aurelia watched anger bubbling in her veins as Valri shifted. Her purple skin tinged slightly around the edges with red; it didn't scare her, but threw more memories hurtling through her mind.

"I belong to the now dismantled Jolvan Clan. The Dulvak's are why my clan fell. My mate and I lived on the edge of a village near the Dulvak compound. They were menaces, the lot of them, but more specifically Estrez's daughters. Those harpies thought they had a right to anything they desired because they were from a purple clan with aspirations to go red."

"You're purple," Aurelia growled, tracking Suzu out the corner of her eye as she edged away from the growing dark cloud.

"Yes, I am, and I never fell for their shit. I paid for my own naiveté. You see, my mate was kind. I've wondered since if he was a soul misplaced in a demon's body. He hated violence so deeply. Together, we wanted nothing more than to raise our family. No larger aspirations, but *her* daughters fell in love with my Olrun. They wanted what they couldn't have. When he told them no, they hatched a plan."

Dread filled Aurelia's veins at the possibilities. She sucked back the death magic, nausea rolling in her stomach. She needed to know how this story ended.

Valri took a steadying breath, holding the bars of the cage with a white-knuckle grip. "They lured me out of the house. Once I was gone, they killed Olrun and our littles." Valri's violet eyes met Aurelia's. "I vowed after I found their bodies, each engraved with the damn insignia of the Dulvak, that they would die. Each and every one."

Suzu broke the silence. "How did you get out of Dodsfell?"

Valri sighed heavily. "Some bastard stuck his nose in and got me removed. I got a note telling me where a hunting party of the Dulvak was expected. Right next to the barrier. When I got there, bigger, burlier purples ambushed me and dragged me to the gate. A hooded figure whispered to the gate, and I was shoved through. A bag came through soon after with a note telling me about the prodigal son of Estrez hiding in Palion. So while I have to figure out how to get back to kill the rest, I get to toy and torture her favorite until that puzzle is solved."

Aurelia cleared her throat. "You won't have many left to kill. I hunted them down. I am also personally responsible for the death of Estrez."

Valri dropped to her knees, sobbing openly. Dirt billowed up from her contact with the cell's hallway. "I don't know what to say. I worked so hard to get justice for them, and you managed it for me. I will live my life trying to find the best way to properly thank you."

Aurelia's mind swirled. Perhaps that was her way in; the weakness of this demon's personal life could create an opening for her, but it could also make one for someone else. It would take some thought.

The blonde sniffled. "Your Majesty—"

Aurelia grimaced, "No, no, that's not who I am, not truly."

"Aurelia," she spoke again. "We don't need to be enemies. Let us be friends. We lost the woman who would have gladly helped you, who loved Lucian. We suspect that Zadon had something to do with it, not that we can do anything about it. Let our need for justice unite us; while we can't free you, we could be allies."

She turned and eyed Suzu. "What leverage does he have, or thinks he has, on me?"

There was calculation in Suzu's gaze. "Technically, nothing. But..." Suzu glanced at the blonde. "He sent your soul-bond out of the kingdom last night."

Aurelia began laughing. "You've sealed your loyalty with such nonsense."

"Wait. No. I am serious. He showed up late in the day yesterday. A crow. Showed up right outside in the courtyard, cawing. The wolves tracked him down." Aurelia glanced at all their faces, earnestly nodding. "Our other soulbond was a part of that hunt. He witnessed Lucian send him away."

Aurelia rolled her eyes. "I don't have a bloody soulbond. I was sixteen and extremely sheltered prior to my expulsion."

Suzu walked closer with a look of sadness on her face. "I understand it's confusing. It could be possible that your partner had their side of it snap in place because they were old enough at the time. All I know for sure is it was a crow very determined to find something, more than likely you."

"You want me to stay to rid you of this Zadon person." All three women solemnly nodded. "You will help me do this?"

Again, they all nodded. "Even if I require you to rise against Lucian? If I want a blood oath?"

Her own oath mark throbbed on her back, the one her father required her to take, that bound her to care of the Drakore people. As her mind bucked the idea of staying, of helping—despite the possibility that it could aid her in returning to her home—the mark grew painful. Her knees threatened to buckle while Suzu and the blonde whispered hurriedly at the cage. "FINE! I'll do it. I'll help secure Palion. If you help me secure Drakore or whatever is left of it."

The three women all exchanged a glance before nodding. Their agreement seemed to settle the oath magic bound up in her wing mark on her back. The blonde opened the door, her movements tentative and slightly hesitant. "My name is Belvina Feo, and my magic revolves around appearance. If you will allow me, I would love to help you feel your best." Aurelia sighed defeat coursing through her.

"I'll do this, but I'll do this my way."

"Excellent." Suzu clapped her hands. "This isn't exactly the most pristine of quarters, but until you have a bit more power to your name, we shall make do."

Valri returned back to her mortal shell, aiding in arranging the garment bags to hang on the crossbars of the cage. Aurelia stood back as Suzu took decisive control.

"Once you have her cleaned and dolled up, meet me and Ulfur at the front hall. I will rush out to get the next stage prepared. We need to start your rule off on the correct foot, despite internal struggles we are fighting within the palace." Aurelia nodded once. "On my way out, I'll send more hot water down."

Aurelia couldn't stop the small smile; being clean would be nice. Belvina brought over the somehow still steaming bucket and gestured to the bench. "Lay down. We'll drape your hair into the water."

Aurelia complied. The process of de-matting took several bottles of sweet-smelling tonic and four bucket changes before

Belvina was able to comb through it all. "Milady, how would you like your hair styled for tonight's festivities."

"Honestly, I want it up, out of my way and not a liability." Belvina nodded, and after helping Aurelia sit up, she began the arduous task of taming the long locks. While she worked, she asked. "What do you want to wear to this ceremony? It's the first time the people of Palion will ever get to meet you."

"I've never liked dresses." Aurelia chuckled at the absurdity. "I drove my mother crazy. She insisted on these overly embroidered jackets over breeches and a tunic as a compromise." She laughed at the memory of that being her largest obstacle to life. "I suppose the Pup wants me in some ridiculous gown."

Belvina laughed, a hint of darkness to it. "He doesn't care; it's the demon who truly cares, and we are all on the same page with him."

Valri stepped into the light, a tray of food in her hands. "Let's do something edgy. Prove that you are going to be a unique Queen, not the same as Kasria. Wholly your own. It'll be good to remind the men, too."

Aurelia grinned. "Absolutely."

Once her hair was finished, Belvina pulled a clean bucket of water into the cell from where a servant had left it. She turned to Valri, "In the red bag is a sheet, washing clothes, and an old shirt of Ulfur's." She looked back at Aurelia, a small smile on her face, "This way, you can at least get your body cleaner."

Aurelia hummed at the luxury and the privacy. Belvina and Valri held the sheet up, enabling her to be hidden from any passerby. The kindness was a simple one, yet so far from her normal that she struggled to keep the tears inside.

It took longer than she intended, but was grateful that neither Valri nor Belvina complained. "Alright, I'm dressed. I do hope I'm not going to the temple in a shirt, though."

Belvina laughed. "Oh no. I have a far better idea. First, I need you to pick a color."

She headed to three different bags hanging up, and Aurelia followed. As Belvina unzipped the bags, distinct colors tumbled out of them: emerald green, midnight blue, and a striking silver, each heavily encrusted in gems and beads.

"Oh my." Aurelia was intimidated to even touch them, her hands rough from her time in Dodsfell. "Green wouldn't really fit the Rite; blue, I suppose would be okay." She stared between the blue and silver, her hand reached out involuntarily, caressing the silver fabric.

Belvina cleared her throat. "I think with your complexion and dark hair, you will absolutely glow in the silver."

Suzu cleared her throat. "I agree with Spar... I mean Belvina." an adorable blush colored both women's faces. "I came to drop these off."

She passed over a very familiar sword and dagger to Valri. "The silver will make these pop. See you soon!"

She disappeared down the hall before anyone could react. "How did she get my weapons back?"

"Honestly, knowing my wife, she probably stole them."

Aurelia laughed, the hope that had been wiped out upon their arrival sparking back to life. Life wouldn't be too terrible here; it wouldn't be perfect either, but she could survive this. "Let's do the silver."

Belvina nodded, a grin on her face, as she fully unwrapped a luxurious gown. Aurelia's face fell; she truly hated managing skirts. "Don't pay much attention to how it looks right now. I am going to customize it."

Valri cleared her throat. "I got you a few things I thought may be of use to help you be more comfortable."

Aurelia followed her down the row of bags to the last one, which was decidedly more lumpy than the bags holding the dresses. Valri cautiously unzipped it, revealing an assortment of face paints. Aurelia broke out into giggles, Valri joining her. "I know now that these aren't your thing, but I tried being prepared. I was given a necklace this morning by a refugee who had heard a rumor you were here."

She dug around until finally she started unloading the pots of paint onto the earthen floor. Aurelia marveled at the gunk women of the court coated themselves in just to attract the male gaze. *Utter nonsense.* Valri shoved a crown into Aurelia's stomach, leaving her balking at the sight. She caught it just before it fell, her gaze locked on it. The crown represented such a different life than what she had just survived. This crown was silver, all flowers and vines, no gems to be found. After a long pause, she tapped Valri on the shoulder and handed the crown back, bending so Valri could place the crown on her head.

Once it was situated, Valri turned back to the bag, digging once more. "Ah ha! Here it is. I think it's a piece from the Drakore court if the paintings I've seen are accurate."

Her blood ran cold at the idea, still unable to see the necklace. "Who was the refugee?"

"Oh, it was a man in the main hall. He was insistent I get this to you."

Valri held out a necklace that had Aurelia's hand trembling. The last time she saw it was on the neck of her mother. The dragon in flight delicately holding a rainbow gem, the symbol of the Drakore throne, had somehow made it to her even after ten years away. "Can you help me fasten it?" Her voice was thick as the necklace settled against her throat. The mantle of her heritage feeling heavy.

Six

SUZU

Drak - Palion - Year 7568

She watched Ulfur ordering the guards around, a thrill shooting down her spine. Ten years and he still got her blood pumping. She whistled long and low, catching his attention.

He strolled over to her, a smirk on his face. "When did you have a chance to change into that?" Suzu blushed a bit as she looked down. Her dress was a simple black gown designed to aid her in fading to the back and allowing Aurelia to shine. All the women would be wearing it, a sign of silent solidarity with their new Queen.

"This old thing? Sparkles made us matching outfits. Just wait till you see her." She shot him a cheeky wink.

"How is that going? Is everything working out with our new mistress Kitten?"

"Oh, she's gonna be fun. I even think today's little side quest will be perfect for our cause." She draped her arms around his neck, bathing in his grin.

"You call completely rerouting the journey to the temple a side quest, huh." He wrapped his arms around her waist. "You look delectable, Kitten." He bit her lower lip, teasing her until she opened up, welcoming his kiss.

She pulled away, a blush coloring her cheeks. "I've always loved a guy in uniform." She winked as she stepped back. Juro, Ulfur's second, cleared his throat, eyes latched on the palace doors.

Suzu turned, the smile growing to encompass her entire face. She dropped into the deepest curtsy she could, holding the pose until everyone clued in. The yard fell into shocked silence before the scraping of boots betrayed the unanimous movement. Suzu was the first to stand, her eyes glued to the trio of women making their way down the steps into the courtyard.

Aurelia led the group in the most daring outfit to ever grace a royal, causing Suzu's blood to light with excitement at the future. Belvina had used her amazing gift with fabrics to create a two-piece ensemble. The top was a jewel-encrusted sleeveless corset, leaving about an inch of skin tantalizingly in view above a high-slitted skirt. Suzu marveled at the ingenuity of the design. Under the skirt were leather leggings enabling free movement for the soon-to-be Queen, while the use of only one layer of silver silk ensured she couldn't get tripped by endless petticoats.

Peeking through the skirt's slit was the jeweled dagger strapped to Aurelia's thigh. Her sword holstered on her left side. Her bare shoulders and arms were a direct slap to royal customs, and Suzu loved it.

Aurelia glided down the steps, the picture of confidence, the only tell that she was even slightly nervous living in her shoulders and flitting gaze.

Suzu grinned. "Welcome, Your Highness. Let me introduce you to the people in charge of your safety on our way to the temple."

Aurelia hummed, lowering her voice for Suzu alone. "Is the Highness title necessary?"

Suzu hooked her arm in Aurelia's, leading her to Ulfur, swallowing a giggle. "Yes. Your Majesty, this is my other soul-bond, Ulfur."

She watched Aurelia process, "you are a polybond?"

"Yes, we are." Suzu glowed with pride. Palion truly had been blessed; Aewenna confirmed it when she fled Drakore. She had spent an entire day expounding the amazing things Tiva would do for polybond couples.

Ulfur bowed and took over the tour, showing Aurelia the carts and guards preparing to roll out. Belvina snaked an arm around her waist, resting her chin on Suzu's shoulder, both watching Aurelia and Ulfur walk around. "What have you got planned, my Chaos girl?"

Suzu laughed. "I don't know what you are referring to."

"Perhaps the stolen weapons dripping from the Queen. Or the four carts of goods that were definitely not mentioned this morning." Belvina kissed her neck, nipping at Suzu's earlobe.

"Hey, the weapons were returned to the rightful owner. Plus, the order was to make the public love her. Who doesn't love the hand that feeds them?" Suzu shot a smirk at her wife.

Belvina gasped, clearly the pieces of the past few months falling into place. "You didn't?"

"Didn't what?" Aurelia's strong voice intruded into their conversation.

Suzu swallowed, unsure how deep Aurelia would support this particular decision. "I most decidedly did not steal the food Zadon had arranged to be delivered to the peasants for the past few months. An initiative to ingratiate them to Lucian's rule. I would not wait for them to get so upset at Lucian, and subsequently Zadon, before releasing the food. It may have been the Gods own blessing that you came when you did. Now you will be the feeder of the poor. A sure-fire way for them to love you."

Aurelia's eyes went wide. "You mean I am walking and interacting with the peasantry today?"

Suzu blinked. *Wasn't she upset at the stealing? Had they forgotten to explain the plan for the day to her?* She stuttered. "Yes, Your Highness, we will be leaving momentarily to walk to the temple. It will take at least an hour."

Aurelia's face went even paler, causing Ulfur to step in behind her in case she fainted, a look of panic painting his features. Aurelia walked a few feet away, motioning for them to join her, arms crossed. "I can't possibly do that."

Suzu blanched, her gaze flitting to her family. Ulfur's lips thinned, a glare ready, while Belvina seemed to be the only one to stay present, merely nodding at Aurelia.

"Can I ask why, Your Highness?" Ulfur's voice gruffer than normal, undoubtedly due to the stress that their jobs may have just gotten harder to complete peacefully.

A flush crept over Aurelia's skin, tinting her too pale features a lovely pink. "These. Shoes!" She hissed, pointing down at the sky-high heels that donned her delicate feet. "There's absolutely no way."

Belvina stuffed her fist in her mouth to silence her laughter. "Your Highness." Aurelia rolled her eyes. Suzu giggled. "What shoes do you want?"

Shock rippled across Aurelia's face. "I... I want his." She pointed down at Ulfur's combat boots, satisfaction filling her expression.

Belvina nodded, continuing to swallow her laughter. She took Aurelia by the arm. "Let's go fix this."

Ulfur let out a laugh. "That's gonna go over well."

Suzu's smile hinted at malice. "Fuck them. Let's watch them squirm while she uproots the entire system."

F inally, they were off down Palace Hill, heading toward the less savory parts of town. The residents came out of their hovels in droves, lining the roadway. Suzu balked a bit, grateful that Ulfur had insisted on bringing the extra guards with them.

Aurelia, complete with her combat boots, led them down the lane. Suzu directed the women in taking the bags of food and distributing one per family. She also gave everyone but Aurelia a pouch of sweets for the children. Suzu grabbed two bags of food and went to Aurelia.

"Go! Mingle. Show them you are lovable and capable of caring for them. Your outfit hints that you can fight for them. Show them they should fight for you."

Aurelia nodded, taking one bag of food and heading straight to a family with three littles and one tired momma. Suzu stuck close just in case.

"Hello there! I'm Aurelia Berrid, I brought your family a gift." Suzu watched as Aurelia held the food out to the mother, a serpent shifter her skin an iridescent blue-green. The mother seemed caught in a daze, her eyes stuck on the Queen. The infant had the same idea lunging straight for Aurelia's arms. Suzu inhaled sharply, unsure how to help. Aurelia, moved catching the baby with ease.

"Aren't you a cutie?" The older children hid in their mother's skirts, peering up at Aurelia awe written on their faces.

Suzu dug in the pouch of candy and thrust a few pieces at Aurelia with a smile to the mother. The mother seemingly regained her bearings coming out of the trance. She nodded her thanks, a grateful smile on her face. "Children. What do you ssssay?"

The children grabbed the candy hurriedly and ran off down the lane zipping between people with the ease of practice. The mother sighed, taking the baby back. "Thank you, Your Highnesssss."

Aurelia smiled at her. "Please call me Aurelia. I am happy to help and meet my people—if they will have me." The serpent shifter smiled, balancing the food and baby with a nod of acknowledgement.

Suzu vibrated with excitement. Aurelia was the answer to all she wanted in a Queen. Someone who truly resonated with the people. Aurelia also seemed energized by it because she met with as many families as she could along the way. She offered kind words, crouched in the dirt to talk to the kids, and held babies. As they finished the first lane, making the turn to the last lane on their route before the temple yards, Suzu frowned. The air was filled with more noise than made sense. She glanced back to notice that the guards were forming a tighter perimeter.

The families that had interacted with Aurelia had sent a member to trail their caravan. Ulfur was by Suzu's side before she could process the need to find him.

"They want to escort their Queen. They are proud she has chosen them."

Suzu gaped, nodding slowly. She had never considered that the people would want Aurelia this badly. Speechless, she just turned back to Aurelia, intent on finishing the distribution.

***

The temple of Tiva, small and quaint in Palion, situated right on the cusp of the rougher side of the city's capital. It topped a small hill, which was enclosed with a wrought iron fence, enabling an illusion of safety for the more well-to-do patrons. Someone in the past had even gone to the trouble of planing an entire host of trees within said gate, to better block the sight of run-down buildings and hovels. As the merry parade made its way through the less than satisfactory side of town, the leaders could just make out two solitary figures standing at the top of the temple steps. Waiting, as they reached the end of the lane, it became apparent their entourage wasn't going to disappear. Aurelia came to stand next to Suzu, her words pitched low. "How much trouble will this cause?"

"Best guess? We are about to see how much self-control Zadon has." Suzu whispered back.

She had one more trick to pull out. Spring was just now beginning but it was clear that the ground would need a little encouragement for her plan. After all, every bride deserved flowers. She slipped between two of the carts and pressed her fingers into the dirt, digging into the Power of the Land. She sent a command: *give the true Queen the flowers she deserves.* Suzu stood quickly, joy and awe filling her just as it did every time the power followed her directions.

The people could be heard murmuring.

"Gods chosen."

"It's been blessed."

Then the words were drowned out by cheering and shouts. Flowers now led up to the temple steps, outlining Aurelia's path.

Aurelia turned a glare at Suzu, confirmation that Aurelia did indeed know of her secret. Suzu shrugged before organizing the order of everyone. Aurelia would lead with her three ladies, followed by one unit of guards led by Ulfur. The rest would chaperone the carts to the side of the temple until transport could be arranged. The citizens were a factor Suzu hadn't predicted. She would have to leave them to their own devices.

Suzu kept a few paces behind Aurelia, monitoring her every reaction. Aurelia gripped the pommel of her sword, her eyes back to scanning her environment, tension setting in. Her back held a large oath mark which grew ever tenser with each step that took them closer to the temple.

Zadon and Lucian waited on the steps, twin looks of disgust and confusion on their faces. Suzu watched as Aurelia visibly struggled to control her own facial expressions, attempting to place a look of happiness on her face despite her true feelings. Suzu made a mental note to help her practice that. *She will have to get better at masking in this court.*

Aurelia led them up the stairs, the wind picking up. Suzu held her breath hoping Lucian and Zadon behaved. "Hello, boys. What a fine day for a stroll."

Suzu choked on a laugh as Zadon went purple with indignation. Lucian, however, administered a bow fitting Aurelia's station. "Glad you chose the easy route."

Aurelia, the picture of femininity, as she tipped back her head laughing, bringing a hand up and placing it on Lucian's shoulder. It was then that it occurred to Suzu, Aurelia was playing a part to the people watching. Anyone out of earshot would see a woman in love, flirting with her soon to be husband. If they could hear the words, though, reality would hit them hard. "Perhaps I just picked the long route."

"Long route?" Zadon demanded, his voice harsh. Suzu noted he still had not bowed to Aurelia.

She didn't seem to have missed the slight. "I'm sorry, Suzu, did you hear someone speaking?"

Suzu failed at swallowing her own grin. "Your Highness perhaps you haven't been introduced yet. This is Zadon Dulvak and he is the one who spoke."

"Oh right. The Prince's pet." She scrunched her face adorably as she shot both men a glare. "I made it clear I don't speak to pets. I would hate to have to remind you what I do to misbehaving pets in front of our audience."

Suzu's curiosity soared. *What did she do?*

Lucian grunted. "You two will have to figure your shit out." Lucian took her hand and kissed her fingers, or at least pretended to. "What did you mean by the long route?"

She smiled prettily at him with half her face, her eyes stone cold. "It's where I get my revenge, in the cold distant future. Yet, it will still be just as satisfying as choking out your pet in the dungeon." Aurelia's eyes hinted at a ferocity that shocked even Suzu.

Lucian straightened as Zadon turned, stomping inside the temple. Lucian stepped closer to Aurelia, whispering, "You will learn to curb that blood thirsty nature of yours, or I will curb it for you. It will hurt worse than anything you've experienced yet."

Aurelia half turned, an act of coy femininity for the crowd, who ate up the display in front of them. "One thing you should know, Lucian." He halted his hand on the temple door. She took a few steps to stand next to him, her right side all the peasants could see. She reached up as if caressing the back of his shoulders, trailing her right hand down his arm. A vicious smile on her face. "I've died more times than you can imagine." Suzu moved to block the view from the crowd as she noticed the empty dagger sheath.

Aurelia brought the dagger between her and Lucian with her left hand, their own bodies hiding the crime from the Palion people. She touched it to his abdomen, pressing the sharp steel in. The sound of fabric slicing audible to Suzu. "Should I begin to catch you up to my death count, or shall we proceed with the sham of marriage for a power you don't actually control?"

Suzu cleared her throat. "Your Majesties, the audience. Perhaps we should step inside."

Aurelia deftly sheathed her dagger and looked at Lucian, still standing, his mouth slightly open from shock. She shrugged, shooting the people a warm smile and slight wave. "My point has been made."

Lucian snapped his mouth shut and slipped inside the temple without a backward glance to the peasants gathering in the woods around the temple. *What had they done, forcing her into this deal?*

SEVEN

MALEDIC

DRAK - PALION - YEAR 7568

Baryn had deposited him in the main hall with strict instructions to avoid both demons, but especially the lady. Baryn held some belief that, should Lucian continue to hold some strange pity over Maledic, Zadon would be harmless, but Valri was an unknown factor to most of those within the Palion Court.

Maledic saw her across the room, recognizing the clear description Baryn had given. Throwing caution to the wind, he moved quickly to corner her in the main room, desperation driving his actions.

"Excuse me, Miss? Are you Valri?"

She stared at him with a guarded expression. "Who sent you?"

"I am sorry to scare you. I am acquainted with Baryn, and he told me you may be able to help me." A total lie, but desperate times. He dug in his pocket, fingering his most prized possession.

Valri cocked her head and nodded once. "Alright. What do you need?"

"I heard a rumor that," he lowered his voice to a mere whisper. "Princess Aurelia was in the palace somewhere. You see, I stole something before I was evacuated from Drakore. Oh!" He hit his forehead, feigning forgetfulness. "I've been staying in the refugee camp praying she would return so I could give it to her."

Valri crossed her arms over her chest. "What did you steal?"

"Just this necklace." He pulled out the necklace Feginth had given him, the true relic of Drakore. He pressed it into Valri's reluctantly outstretched hand. He bowed slightly. "Thank you for even listening to me."

Valri gave him a half-smile, "Not a problem. I shall see she has it. I can't promise more than that."

Maledic nodded once, turning and melting into the crowd of peasants that mingled around, hoping to catch a glimpse of royalty. He bided his time, waiting for her to lead him the rest of the way. Unfortunately, as he tracked her movement, she made her way into a staircase heading down to the dungeon— his heart sank—not a place he could hope to infiltrate.

Baryn had been most helpful, though, and after assessing no one of importance lingered nearby, he casually made his way to the servant's stair, delivering the key phrase needed to the guard posted there. He headed up to the rooms Baryn had indicated would be given to her once her current trial was over. Casually, Mal shifted an arm, plucking a few feathers. He returned his arm to normal, wandering about the room, leaving the feathers in odd places, eager to leave his mark for her to find. If she were truly his Aurelia, she would know it was him.

The door opened abruptly, causing him to freeze in his tracks, breath locked in his chest. It came out in a rush as he recognized Baryn, disappointment flooding through his limbs. Baryn wasted no time, talking fast. "They are preparing to do a parade through the city ending at the temple. I have no way to get you to her before the Rite of Marriage, at least not in a situation where you two would be alone."

The truth poured from Baryn as Mal fought wave after wave of panic. He had gotten so close, only for her to be married off anyway. He stared at Baryn, his hurt laid bare and reflected back to him. "Understood. I will keep your involvement in my continued stay in the Kingdom to myself. Even if I get caught. I have to try one more time."

He went to her bedroom window, opening it just enough that he'd be able to wing into it. The ticking time bomb had him rushing from the room, ignoring the still stuttering Baryn. He set up a watch outside the stairwell Valri had disappeared down, waiting. His spot kept him in shadow between two large columns, yet allowed him to see her should she appear.

A redhead in a fancy black dress, carrying a sword and dagger, rushed past his hiding spot, intent on her destination heading towards his soulbond. The wait felt endless, the redhead coming and going without a sign of Aurelia's black locks. Then his connection with her felt like it was growing tight, shortening which could only be happening if she was drawing nearer to him.

His first impression of her was pure shock. She had changed so much in ten years, yet aging wasn't what had his stomach drop. Where once he had seen joy and mischief pouring out of her eyes, only an unfamiliar hardness remained. He watched as she got stiffer the closer she got to his hiding spot, disappointment flaring when she didn't meet his gaze, his identity still secreted between the columns.

She had once been a girl full of a stubborn tenacity, unwilling to bend to another's will, yet she was now being marched to a man she had just met. *An offering for what bene-fit? Where was her spunk and fire?*

He moved to catalogue her face, slinking behind the columns as carefully as he could. Her eyes the same blue that haunted him every cloudless day, yet now they held a foreign depth he needed to understand. Her cheeks were sunken, and her lips had clearly been chewed on. The stress of whatever she survived causing her to physically chew her own lips til they bled. Though one key feature stood out. She didn't wear even a brush of face paint. It struck an internal chord with him; she was going forth as her authentic self regardless of the conse-quences.

His eyes trailed down her body, taking in the entire outfit, and his heart stuttered in his chest. He clenched his fists, resisting the urge to stomp over and demand she wear a jacket. Then it clicked. She was complying with Palion in a pure Aurelia way, on her terms. Hope sparked beneath his skin. Perhaps she was still in there despite Feginth's warnings.

He waited until they left the Palace, giving them what felt like forever before exiting himself. He sighed at the empty courtyard, knowing they headed to the slums. He tucked his hands in his pockets, walking at a brisk pace following their tracks. No one took notice of him, a slightly too-pale and skinny male walking toward town. Luckily, he didn't have to look too hard to find her.

A mass of chaotic bodies followed her caravan, creatures in their shifted and mortal forms alike following her as if she was the air they breathed. It took some maneuvering, but he managed to get to the lead of the chaotic pack, his blood warming at the idea of seeing her once again. Maybe he could position himself ahead impersonating a family, forcing her to meet him.

But the timing wouldn't work. The pace her caravan kept up was grueling, far too quick for him to slip ahead, especially considering the massive amount of guards focused on preventing peasants from getting too close to her without her permission. As they reached the base of the Temple Yards, he had a minor flare of hope.

He found himself standing next to a huge and intimidating serpent as he debated how to cross the short distance between them despite the guards, when she turned, looking right at them while talking to the redhead lady. His breath clogged in his lungs, causing him to choke and cough as she turned away just as easily, facing the temple and the Palion Pup.

Disappointment flooded him; she had to have seen him. They had locked eyes. Yet she turned away. As his brain struggled to understand what happened, hope slammed into him. He could still feel his side of the bond. She hadn't rejected him; that would take a verbal announcement, which hadn't happened. If she were capable of speaking, she was capable of rejecting him, so there had to be a reason, and thus a chance. Once Aurelia and the women joined Lucian and Zadon, his window to speak to her had closed. Despite that reality, he couldn't take his eyes off of her. She smiled and laughed, causing irritation to spike, especially as she insisted on touching *him*.

His blood heated as she halted Lucian going into the temple. Those around Maledic cooed in joy, hoping she would kiss her Prince. Mal forced himself to focus on her eyes and the feelings coming through the bond. Her eyes had a cold gleam, and she was exuding cold fury through the bond. Whatever was said or done between the two ended quickly. As Aurelia gave the crowd a little wave, Mal opted to shift, ignoring the squeaks of shock.

He would never be okay with what was going to happen inside the temple, but he had to witness it, to see her exact reactions and hear, the exact words. There couldn't be room for rumors to tear them apart and force him to prematurely reject their bond. He arrowed his crow body through an upper window, shifting back to his mortal self once safely inside. It didn't take long to navigate the twisting halls and offices before he found a balcony view overlooking the main floor. It would give him unfettered access to a view of his soulbond uniting with another man.

His heart was in turmoil, stomach roiling, anger at the Gods brewing in his soul as he settled down to watch the ceremony below.

eight

AURELIA

DRAK - PALION - YEAR 7568

As she turned toward the door, she could have sworn she saw the familiar crow shape of Maledic. Her heart stopped, but she shook her head slightly, forcing herself onward. The Temple of Tiva in Palion was smaller than its Drakore equivalent, decorated in greens with the images of women dancing, couples being united, and motherhood engraved into the walls. Goddess Tiva's image frequently appeared above the mortals, overseeing all the activities.

The colors were soothing, but did little to comfort her racing heart. Maledic. Her best friend all those years ago. Could he be here? The Gods had to be toying with her. She could have sworn she saw her parents in the crowd of civilians following them to the temple. Cerial's blonde hair seemed to bounce ahead, yet with a quick shake of her head, Belvina's face replaced that of her sister.

Slowly, she rubbed her temple, reviewing what was left to the farce of the day. She had seen the Rite of Marriage before

47

as a child. It was simple; the complex aspects of royalty wouldn't come into play until they were crowned, the complexities coming with the addition of the Great Power. Today, she was just expected to walk down the aisle to her groom, pledging her love and loyalty.

Her stomach rolled at the thought of who it was taking that title, the man waiting for her at the end of the aisle. They would both be required to create a blood joining to publicly solidify their union—essentially confirming the promises as a blood oath. Her mind raced about how to do what was required while staying true to her objectives and herself.

Belvina and Suzu twittered around her, adjusting her hair, re-securing her crown, and straightening her skirt. Valri was a silent, ever-present shadow to her right, sword on her own hip.

Aurelia turned to Suzu, a question she hadn't thought to voice before this moment, filtering through the panic. "Who is overseeing the Rite? Isn't the Oba stationed in Drakore?"

Suzu glanced at the floor, "No. She fled. There is a lot to tell you when it comes to Drakore. We don't have the time right now." She grimaced, finally dragging her eyes up to meet Aurelia's. "I will help you with them. For now, though, you should know Aewenna is still Oba of Tiva, and she now resides here."

Aurelia sucked in a breath, her first interaction with a person of her past, unlike the ghostly images of her mind. She shook out her shoulders. "Alright. Let's get this finished."

Suzu walked first with Belvina on her arm to the twittering cheers of an audience. Aurelia gritted her teeth. "Valri. How many Gods' damned people are out there?"

Valri peeked around the corner. Her face paled. "It's full."

"Of course it is." She rolled her shoulders once more, cracking her neck in the process. "Let's see if we can make him regret that. They need to understand I'm not a doll to be moved around. I do only what I need to. No one controls me."

Valri eyed her, nodding along. "You've got this. Count to twenty, then follow."

Valri turned through the entry way that Suzu and Belvina had disappeared down. The crowd once again cheered and clapped. Aurelia leaned her back against the wall, her eyes fluttering shut, slamming a veil of black on her reality as she counted down to her destiny.

As her mind counted down, visions of those she left behind fluttered through the darkness. Her mother, statuesque, the embodiment of a queen. Her father, the soft side of parenting. Kygoss and Maie welcoming her as if tied by blood. Cerial, her bubbling personality caring for all who she loved. Faziel, the sister that could have been. Finally, Maledic —her one friend.

She mentally locked each treasured image away in her mind to look through once again when she was safe, safe from the lies she would have to live for the time being. There would be a time in the future when she figured out how Drakore fell and who had survived.

Her twenty seconds were up. She turned the corner, eyes focused on the end of the aisle and the familiar figure draped head to toe in green veils, obstructing even her face. Aurelia ignored the teeming benches full of strangers, judging and whispering as she walked past. The smaller temple made the walk quick, for which she was grateful. Lucian stood brooding in his designated spot, refusing to look directly at her.

She let out a breathy chuckle at the ridiculousness, low enough that only Aewenna and Lucian would hear. Their entourages were seated in the front rows, unable to hear any words between the three of them. At least until Aewenna clapped her hands, bringing up an intricately painted finger to her throat. She began to speak. It became clear that some sort of amplifying magic was at play, because even though she did not raise her voice, it echoed through the room.

"Lords and Ladies of Palion, welcome to this most auspicious day. The uniting of the ancient bloodlines of Drakore and Palion." She gestured to Lucian and then Aurelia, a cheer breaking out through the crowd. "This is merely part of an advantageous moment foretold ten long years ago, and many believed it would never be."

The cheers died down as everyone remembered the coup. Aurelia clenched her jaw, intent on keeping the memories of that day locked away. "This is but the beginning of a glorious union that will drive prosperity to this land." She turned toward Lucian. "As the Crown Prince of Palion you have a lot of responsibility thrust upon you. Are you prepared to take on the additional responsibility of a wife? To care for her? To defend her against your enemies along with your friends? To ensure she is happy?"

Aurelia watched him out of the corner of her eye, his face trying to squelch the indignation of the in-depth questions. He answered simply. "Yes."

Aewenna turned to Aurelia. "You have been gone for ten years, experiencing things only the Gods know." She paused, silence falling. "Yet you are standing by the promises made by those long gone, and for that Tiva is proud. Will you stand by Lucian as your husband, honoring and aiding in the running of the kingdom?"

Aurelia inhaled deeply. "I will honor the kingdom of Palion as I would have my home. I will allow Lucian to be my ruling partner."

Aewenna paused, Lucian's body stiff beside her, and Aurelia waited, her hands clasped loosely in front of her. The pause elongated, Aewenna looking between her and Lucian. When nothing else was said, she continued on after clearing her throat. "Tiva can see good coming from this union. Lucian, with your protective qualities, Aurelia need not live in fear any longer." It was Aurelia's turn to suppress an emotional response, a growl crawling up her throat. Fear died a long time ago.

"Aurelia, your immense magical potential will be needed to secure Baelia. You've conquered one of the six powers of our land in its entirety, though against your will. You will have the ability to gain just one more. She cautions you to choose carefully."

Aurelia filed that away for further dissection at a later time, feeling Lucian's eyes on her, unspoken questions boring into her mind. She ignored them, merely waiting Aewenna out, an eyebrow raised. As the silence lengthened, she rolled her eyes, using her right hand, she deftly unsheathed the dagger, affixing a look of shock to her face.

"Oh! Perhaps you forgot this." She proffered the weapon, her point clear. Aewenna ducked her head, Lucian grunted like a brute.

Aewenna took her proffered dagger and spoke for the room. "With this dagger, we shall slice through the barrier the outside world has brought down on you." She sliced through first Lucian's palm and then Aurelia's. "Together," She moved their palms toward one another until they clasped. "You become one."

Lucian tightened his grip on her hand as white-hot magic filled them. She breathed deep, not letting the tingling burn of power phase her. Instead, she met Lucian's green gaze, seeing a deep, radiating pain looking out at her. She refused to be moved by it, to be curious. His story wouldn't change the plans. All too soon the tingling pain rushed out of them, and they quickly unclasped their hands.

Aewenna nodded. "Just like that, the blood lines have been united. May your future children bless Baelia by continuing peace."

Aurelia bowed her head slightly as Lucian did. She turned to walk back down the aisle when Lucian's hand clasped around her wrist, yanking her around and into him. He trailed his hands up her arms to her chin. She schooled her shock; two could play the game. His hand cupped her chin as he dipped his mouth to hers. She grinned wickedly as her hand, hidden from the crowd by their bodies, clutched the dagger Aewenna had slipped back into it. She brought it up between them as he leaned closer, the tip angled in such a way that to seal the kiss he would bleed. Anger sparked in his eyes, but he changed his tactic, aiming for a chaste kiss on her cheek, which she returned a low chuckle for his ears alone.

A scream cut through the temple. Everyone's attention turned as one to the doors. She quickly sheathed the dagger, her eyes latching with Suzu's scared ones.

"Suzu, get all the women and children into the lower levels. The acolytes will assist. Valri, with me." Valri stood unsheathing her sword, easing back into her spot as Aurelia's silent shadow.

Lucian turned toward the men. "Ulfur and Juro, take what guards we have and go assess what is happening outside. Zadon, accompany the women and children to ensure they are safe."

Aurelia unsheathed her sword, standing in front of Zadon. "I don't fucking think so. The pet can go outside or stay with you, Lucian, but he steers clear of *my* ladies."

Lucian growled, glancing from her sword to the rapidly emptying pews. The acolytes indeed stepped in to help Suzu and Belvina get the citizens down below. She noted even the lords stepped below, apparently unwilling to help defend their Goddess' temple. She rolled her eyes at the thought.

"Fine," he ground out. "Zadon, outside."

Zadon slunk outside, a glare for her as he left the temple. When the door opened, a rush of battle noises came.

"WHO the fuck is attacking my Kingdom!?" roared Lucian, his voice echoing in the room.

A loud crash from up above drew Aurelia's attention to the ceiling.

"Baryn, you will stay with me." Aurelia's eyes latched onto the last man from Lucian's retinue, busy drawing his own sword. The world seemed to slow around her as she assessed the newcomer. He was oddly familiar; something about the way he held his sword tickled a memory. She didn't know him... did she?

She shook her head, determined to keep those thoughts to herself. She turned to Lucian. "Is there roof access here?"

"Yes," he growled.

"Where?" She asked, her own growl emerging. "That noise indicates we may be getting attacked from up above."

"The damn door is right there." He pointed at a door on the side of the room.

nine

AURELIA

DRAK - PALION - YEAR 7568

> *The wall between Dodsfell and Baelia is a magically reinforced barrier placed by the Gods to keep the demons away from the mortals. The day the wall went up, the seer of history envisioned the time it would also come down. The wall will fall when death is returned and mastered in the mortal realm of Baelia. Baelia will only have a chance at survival if the woman of raven hair, a wolf as dark as night and a demon red as flame come together to deny the evils at work.*
> *~Temple of Tixdarr, Lost Records*

Aurelia moved in that direction, scanning. She was pleased to see all acolytes, including Aewenna, had disappeared along with the civilians. Before she could get to the door handle, though, it flew open, air rushing out. She halted her forward motion, caution filling her. She could feel Valri slide into place on her left side. Lucian closed the distance between them before the enemy exited the doorway, bathed in deep shadows.

Aurelia twirled the sword, releasing her tension as she waited. It wasn't long before loud boots echoed down the steps, and the man who exited had her jaw dropping.

Darius Svenston.

Her foster brother, the man who followed her sister like a love sick fool. He was here, but larger; the anger that had haunted him as a child now matured into an emotional armor. He had wings, and she was left wondering what to say. After all, he was her foster brother. Her world view cracked as her mind tried to understand him, but it blew wide apart when a smaller figure stepped out from behind Darius' shadow.

"Faziel," she whispered the name, her sword falling a bit as she stood straighter trying to understand.

"Hello, Aurelia." She stepped around Darius, taking a few more steps closer to Aurelia.

"What..." Her eyes scanned Faziel, stopping at the crown on her head. It had been one of her mother's favorites. Darkness took root in her at the idea of how she got the crown. Aurelia brought her sword back up, locking her shock away for later.

Faziel smiled widely as if she could see the pieces Aurelia had put together. "Yes, Aurelia. It's hers." She caressed the crown. "Looks good on me. Better than your mother."

Aurelia gripped the handle of the sword tighter. She decided to let the comment slide in the hope they could get to the true reason for Drakore's presence.

"Why are you here?" Lucian barked, drawing their attention.

"Oh. We needed to face the rumors. After all, we have all missed the honored Drakore Princess."

Aurelia raised an eyebrow. "You've seen me."

Darius strode closer, stopping in front of Valri as if assessing her worthiness as an opponent. "We came to take you home, Aurelia."

Aurelia blinked, her mind raced to process the layers of that statement. She rested her sword tip down gently, giving the appearance of nonchalance.

"She is home," Lucian growled darkly.

Faziel turned her attention to Lucian, a look of sheer malice distorting her face. "Oh, the Pup of Palion, the Court of Strays, are you now adopting the Princess, or are you stealing her?"

Aurelia swallowed, her mouth finally moistening after all the shocks. "I was stolen ten years ago when my kingdom was taken. Lucian hasn't stolen me. He has provided me with a starting point to getting it back. Apparently it's you I will be removing from the thrones. Unless.." she paused, tapping her chin dramatically. "You want to hand them over right now. It would save me precious time."

Faziel started laughing as she shifted her wings out. Wings that resembled a cross between the scales of dragons and the leather of bats. She folded them against her back but held them at the ready, undoubtedly preparing for an arial attack.

An idea sparked, but she had to be sure. She needed to know what side Faziel was on. Lucian shifted from foot to foot, anxious to see them leave.

"Faz, do you not remember when we thought of each other as sisters?"

The laughter that fell was bitter, sounding brittle like crunching glass. "Which time? When you left for the Crowlands? When you were rescued? The time you promised we would be sisters of the heart, but it was me left in a puddle of piss! I was forced to marry!" Faziel clamped her mouth shut at the glower Darius shot her.

"I had no control over that, and you know it. I tried to get you out too."

Faziel spat at her, "Obviously you didn't try very hard. My life was ruined by your selfishness."

Aurelia stood up straight, bringing the sword to rest, the blade on her shoulder, Faziel's side clear. "What have you planned for me in Drakore?"

Darius sneered. "A proper welcome of course."

Aurelia nodded. Surprise filled her as Lucian began to talk quickly, desperate for her to hear him. "They are lying. They have been systematically killing the Drakorian people. We have been rescuing citizens ever since you've been gone. If you leave with them, he will kill you."

"Husband." She stressed the word, adding a sickly-sweet syrup to it. "How could I ever leave you?" She watched Faziel, intent on her retribution. "Our love runs deep, wolf boy." Faziel flung her wings open in anger at Aurelia's statements.

Aurelia risked a glance at Lucian, fully intent on her prize. Meeting his eyes, she winked. "You know that, though, don't you."

Lucian's mouth hung open a bit as she moved quickly. Throwing her body up, using her air magic to cushion her like steps. Once she had reached a few steps of height, she had adequate advantage on Faziel, allowing the momentum of the downward swing of her blade to slice cleanly through Faziel's wing.

Blood spurted fast, drenching Aurelia before her feet touched back down to the floor. Faziel's screaming ricocheted around the room, and everyone seemed to stall, staring at the twitching wing on the ground. Aurelia took a step back, holding her sword at the ready, curious as to how Darius would react.

Darius moved to Faziel, cursing, widely directing his words

to Aurelia. "Why couldn't you do what the hell you were asked to do?"

Aurelia smirked. "First, I would have to be asked. Since no one in this room has actually asked me to do a damn thing, perhaps a lesson is in order."

Faziel had sunk to the ground, curling around her injured side. It was apparent that the Great Power ran through her veins as the site of the injury was already knitting back together, sealing the stump.

Aurelia took her sword, stabbing at the wing she had removed, pulling some of the scaly bits off. Darius' face grew enraged, his eyes narrowing. Lucian moved quickly, stepping in front of him, aiming to pull Darius' wrath. "Stop making it worse, Aurelia, for Gods sake!"

Aurelia laughed. "Oh, Lucian. You need to rid yourself of fear; it's holding you back." She dug into her magic, shoving the wind around Darius and Faziel, moving them several inches.

Lucian shot her a glare as Darius howled in anger. Aurelia dropped her sword as she saw Darius reach to the sky. Excitement swarmed her, her own lightning calling to Darius'. He unleashed his, unable to concentrate it, so it flashed throughout the room, causing everyone but Aurelia to flinch and duck. Aurelia giggled, opening her arms wide as the lightning sprang toward her like a lost love coming home.

She turned her hardened gaze to Darius, pointing a finger. "Boom."

A strong, single-pointed bolt zipped from her finger toward him. Darius ground his teeth, absorbing the power into himself, the pain of the action clear on his face.

"You've learned some tricks, brother. I know you've missed me all these years, but you were not on this overly pretentious guest list. Now off you go the way you came, before you see me actually angry."

Valri chuckled, causing Aurelia to blink, having forgotten her shadow was there. "Gods forbid I see you angry, milady."

Aurelia shrugged, retrieving her sword. "It's a lesson everyone will learn with time."

She watched carefully as Darius knelt and scooped Faziel up. Her screams reaching new levels with the jostling. It left Aurelia with a sick joy. Lucian stalked behind them, Baryn at his side. It clicked then. One more revelation to slam into her. "Valri. Make sure our uninvited guests actually leave." Lucian grunted out the order.

Valri didn't move, looking instead to her. Aurelia took her time sheathing her sword and waiting. Once Lucian noted that Valri was not listening to him, Aurelia nodded her permission to the woman. Lucian rolled his eyes before walking toward the main door, heading out to the battlefield to assess the situation.

"I know you." She pointed her finger at Baryn before he could follow his master. Baryn halted, frozen by her words.

"Why do I know you, dog?"

"I saved you, only to curse you ten years ago."

She swallowed the bile that rose within her, the memories threatening to overwhelm. Instead, she walked up to Baryn, getting right into his personal space, discreetly palming her dagger. "Explain to me why I shouldn't take the life debt you owe me right now on the temple floor?" She held the dagger, her hand sure at his throat. "You know that last time we met, I didn't know how to use one of these. Time has passed, and I have learned a lot, including how to end men." She met Baryn's eyes, which looked achingly familiar. The emotions of the day and the coup mixing and filling her.

Baryn swallowed and spoke quietly. "I can be useful. I am a wolf and trusted in Lucian's circle. I can keep you informed of his moves, and I will prioritize your safety over my own."

"You will be my man in Palion until your life debt is

settled," she sliced her palm. "In exchange, I won't kill you here." She grabbed his hand, waiting for his words.

"I will." Relief was evident in his face. They shook hands, sealing the oath.

"Go before he comes looking for us. We will talk more about this and about that night." He nodded, heading outside.

She took a deep, shuddering breath. Aewenna stepped into the main room from the doorway of the lower levels. Her voice filled the room once more, echoing in the now empty temple. "It was foretold she would be released when Drakore was in peril. No one saw it happening like this." She stepped further into the room, the veil gone, revealing a wariness Aurelia didn't want to investigate.

Aurelia's hackles rose. "No. I don't want to hear any more riddles and nonsense. Tiva is either the cruelest mistress to exist or doesn't exist. I am not in a position to debate the details at the moment."

Aurelia opened the main doors, her breath stolen by the pandemonium facing her.

ten

AURELIA

DRAK - PALION - YEAR 7568

The scene outside was grotesque. Slain individuals littered the ground. Bird shifters lay partially shifted between mortal and true forms, blood pouring from the various wounds. Aurelia's mouth dried as she took in the murdered land shifters; almost none of the dead Palion people were warriors—instead, they were civilians. Slowly, she maneuvered through the dead, her eyes scanning the bodies, dodging the guards who roamed, looking for straggling air warriors. Her heart began to bleed as she came upon one particular body; a large serpent, clearly the father to the tiny serpent baby she had held earlier. He was partially shifted, blood oozing from an arrow to his neck and chest.

Her mind began to race as her eyes danced between all the bodies, the citizens whose greatest crime had been to support her claim to the Palion throne. Gradually, she turned, the magnanimity of the moment hitting home. Her breath came fast, too fast. Her heart pounding loud in her ears. She flexed her hands, doing her best to get a grip on her emotions and magic.

She caught movement out of the side of her eye. She moved on instinct, pulling her sword, turning as she brought it up, blocking Zadon's descending blade. As their blades clanged together, Lucian's barking order shouted across the field. "What the fuck, Zadon!?"

Aurelia waited, watching every slight twitch of Zadon's muscles. He let out a low growl, flitting his gaze to Lucian. It was enough of a distraction that she shifted her blade, shoving his aside and sliding her blade against his throat. Zadon immediately dropped his weapon, his hands going up in supplication. Lucian's heavy breathing sounded from her left, but she didn't remove her eyes from her prey.

"Zadon?" His voice going from anger to sounding broken, confused, adding fuel to the fire pounding in Aurelia's veins.

"Pet. This is where you beg for life." She sneered, her blade unwavering.

"Lucian. She caused this. She has ruined everything we've built!" Zadon's voice held a high-pitched whine that grated on Aurelia's ears, but the words settled.

Lucian grunted. "Aurelia, release him, and he will apologize for his show of temper."

Aurelia's jaw ticked, considering. "You know, Lucian, he is partly correct. I did inspire a group of innocents to come cheer for *our* rule. My presence brought Drakore here, where they slaughtered *our* people. So..." She stood tall, dragging her blade lightly across his neck, eliciting a string of blood to slide down. "You get to request that I hold death off one time. Is this that time?"

She turned her eyes to Lucian, her eyebrows raised delicately.

Lucian looked between them, his brow furrowed. "Yes."

She sheathed her sword with a sigh. "Fine. Where is Ulfur? We need to organize the transfer of all these bodies."

"No, Aurelia. Ulfur is already aiding the guards in loading the bodies. We will go by carriage to the palace. There is a reception already planned."

Aurelia's shoulders stiffened as she turned to Lucian. He had an arm around Zadon's shoulders, guiding him towards the waiting carriages. "Excuse me? Who is notifying the families?"

"The acolytes from Tixdarr's temple will, late tomorrow, I imagine."

A roaring began in her ears as she watched her new husband, the spineless man that he was, shove his demon best friend into a carriage. She opened her mouth to unleash a verbal storm when Suzu stepped up beside her, a hand on her arm. "I shall see that she gets to the palace, milord."

Lucian merely nodded once before clambering in behind Zadon. She turned to Suzu after the carriage disappeared behind its own dust cloud. "I am not going."

Suzu rolled her eyes. "Yes, yes, I know. Let's go find Ulfur."

Ulfur and Baryn were supervising the guards carefully piling the bodies into the carts that had once carried food to the same families now unknowingly facing destruction. Aurelia cleared her throat, gaining everyone's attention. "We are taking these people home. Then their families will be taken to the temple with the aid of the crown."

Everyone stared at her in disbelief.

"Your Majesty, death is not supposed to be handled except by the acolytes. We... we can't." Ulfur looked sadly at the bodies. "These men will have to take ritual baths at the temple just for loading them. If the citizens come into contact with them, they will also have to be cleaned."

Aurelia turned to Belvina, who stood on the edges of the

crowd, tears streaming down her face. "Belvina, please go request a few bolts of fabric from Aewenna."

She nodded, scampering off as the sun began its downward slide. Aurelia turned to Suzu. "You and Belvina will return to the palace with a squad of guards. I will go with Baryn and Valri to distribute the bodies with the other squadron. Once you get to the palace, send word to Kana and have her acolytes meet us in the slums. How many bodies are there?"

Ulfur looked down but answered quietly. "Twenty-six. The injured are in the temple being treated by Tiva's acolytes."

Belvina reappeared, two large bolts of undyed fabric juggled in her arms. "How many should I cut, Milady?"

"Just tuck the bolts in the cart. We will cut them for each individual shroud. Ladies, off you go distract Lucian as long as you can." They nodded as they climbed into the remaining carriage, both shooting furtive looks at Ulfur.

Ulfur looked between them and Aurelia, clearly torn. "Ulfur go protect your heart. I will be fine. I have Baryn and Valri. I also have some hidden tricks no one has seen yet."

He grimaced. "They are my everything. However, you are vital to the survival of the Kingdom. I can't choose myself over the greater good and keep my job title."

Aurelia rolled her eyes. "Ulfur." She twirled her hand in the air, pulling fire from within, forming a ball of it in her palm. "Here is another example of some of the magical ways I can protect myself. Neither you nor your girls can do the same. So go protect them."

Ulfur bowed low, a look of awe on his face. "Just don't forget we all need you."

Aurelia blushed, nodding her thanks to him.

I t didn't take long for the carts to be ready. She strode behind them, her face a mask of neutrality, unsure how this would go. Where once she had been surrounded by cheers and excitement, the road now filled with silent, solemn-faced women. Some gripped children, while others held onto one another.

They got past the first road to the junction. It had a lot of space available, so she called a halt. The women filling the road followed, creating a ring of people around the carts, more women and children coming from the other road.

Aurelia looked at their faces as their worlds cracked around them. She straightened her shoulders, grabbing the linen, and unfurling enough for the top body, that of a panther shifter. She detached it using her dagger and handed the fabric bolt to the guard standing next to her. The cut piece was laid out on the ground; all that was missing was the body. The guard took the bolt of fabric, stunned that she was doing any of the work herself.

She walked up to Baryn. "Time to prove yourself, wolf."

He nodded, following. She climbed up just enough to leverage the body out of the cart to Baryn, carefully cushioning the body with her own, exercising extreme care, having no concern as to the blood that transferred to her. Gasps erupted from the crowd as everyone turned their backs, unwilling to taint themselves with death. All but one little boy.

"Papa!! Papa?"

Aurelia closed her eyes, now stinging with tears, as she placed the body gently on the linen. She had enough time to catch the boy around the middle as his cries turned to screams of panic. His mother cut through the crowd, her eyes landing first on the boy and then finding her soulbond's body, bloody on the ground. She landed on her knees next to her man, hands shaking as she brushed his hair out of his face. The mother looked up at Aurelia, questions filling her gaze.

"He died protecting his kingdom; they all did. We will pay any death tithe, and your children will have a place at court when they are old enough. My sincerest apologies to you all."

The crowd murmured, a low roar. Aurelia moved to cut the next shroud, but the guard holding the fabric had already begun, a nod of acknowledgement to her. Soon, the rest of the guards took up jobs. Two were cutting shrouds while the remaining six paired off to bring the dead out, laying them on the shrouds so the families could claim the passed.

Valri walked around comforting the children as the mother's broke. Aurelia and Baryn continued to help where it worked, but eventually all she could do was watch the scene unfold. Her heart, which she thought had shattered enough for one lifetime, broke yet again.

Baryn cleared his throat as other neighbors unaffected by tragedy brought blankets and torches, the moon rising overhead. "Are you aware of who my sister was?"

Aurelia glanced at him, confusion filling her. "No." She turned back to the families as a tear slid unbidden down her cheek while the serpent family reunited. Valri took the older children far enough away that the mother was allowed to howl her distress to the sky.

"She was Lucian's soulbond, the destined Queen of this land."

Ire bubbled within her. "I see. Well, I don't need to hear how she was more loved or how she would have done this differently." More tears fell, and she brushed away the offense. Tears had to be better controlled moving forward.

"No. You misunderstand me, milady. My point is she was expected, and she would never have done this." He gestured at the reuniting families. "She was lovely and kind, but once she gained a foothold to the power one wields on the throne, she only used it to fortify herself and Lucian. She rarely left the palace." Baryn tugged on his overcoat, uncomfortable. "She brought out the best of Lucian, but not the Kingdom."

Aurelia pondered that, but Baryn continued. "These people have seen you at your core. You care for them, not yourself."

She blinked. "What do you mean?"

"You celebrated them before *your* day, you fought *for them,* and unlike other royal members, you're still here covered in the blood of our enemies, taking care of *your people.*"

Aurelia stood in stunned silence. "Perhaps it's proof I shouldn't bear the title. It's my fault our enemy was there."

The guards had finished unloading bodies, and the acolytes dressed in burgundy had started to arrive. Aurelia nodded in acceptance of the situation. Before she could turn to leave, though, the serpent mother approached. Her face was drawn, the toll of heartbreak evident. She stopped in front of Aurelia. "Aurelia. Do you know what they sssay when rulersss start their rulessss bathed in blood?"

Aurelia blinked, not expecting this "No, ma'am."

The woman reached up and touched Aurelia's face almost lovingly. Baryn growled, but Aurelia made no move to stop her. "They are the point on which the world turnss. When the time comesss, Aurelia Berrid the bessstower of death, we sssshall rissse with you."

"I shall have a program set up for your children."

The woman nodded. "We believe you. Now go continue the fight."

She turned after one more look, leading Baryn back to the palace.

Tiredness dragged on Aurelia's bones, yet as they entered the main hall, the noises of a party in full swing stole her attention. Baryn pointed to the stairs. "Your rooms are up on the residential wing. I can show you."

Aurelia debated. She should go get dressed, bathe the essence of death from her skin, but the fact that the court could host a party while the people mourned had her hackles rising. She tapped her boot. "Baryn, you can go ahead and head up. I have some unfinished business to attend to."

Baryn met her gaze. "If you are off to have this argument, I will come and be your back-up."

"Lead me in, Baryn. There's a party to shut down." Aurelia waved him ahead of her.

eleven

MALEDIC

Drak - Palion - Year 7568

The loud bellowing of Lucian's frustration caused Mal to jump from his spot on the balcony above. His mind still reeled from all that had been divulged during the ceremony. She hadn't agreed to anything excessive, instead opting to offer her own words to the Rite. It was never done that way; the Gods gave the words needed for each couple.

He shook his head as the sounds of footsteps on the upper level became clear; he needed to get to safety. Aurelia would be fine with as many protectors that she had around her. He had been too late to stake a claim for her, so now he must figure out what to do next.

He hustled to the nearest window, glancing out. Birds of all varieties arrowed toward the ground, shifting when close enough to battle the creatures standing there. Mal debated what to do. The land shifters could take aim at him, if any were armed with long-range weapons, and it wasn't out of the realm of possibility that some of the air shifters would know who he was in his shifted form. Groaning, he took a chance shifting and arrowing as fast as his wings would take him, not to the trees surrounding the temple but instead to the hovels beyond. He could see peasants attempting to get the innocent off the streets. He cowered on the roof, remaining in his crow form, trying his best to not get misidentified as an enemy.

His mind raced at the prospects of a full-scale attack from Drakore. This would rock the neutral feelings the two kingdoms maintained. He waited, peering down; the flying warriors had stopped. Then he saw something that had his blood chilling. The large form of none other than Darius flying from the temple roof, carrying something off. From below, the sounds of a carriage pulled his attention once more. He watched it trundle away and decided it would be better to meet her at the palace instead of meeting up with her out in the open.

He flew back, the city eerily quiet at least until he got to the palace. There it was loud and clearly preparing for a party. He landed in the back, shifting, and then subtly blending into the crowd. Shortly after Mal found a spot where he faded from notice, the carriage pulled up. He watched from the edges of the crowd as a very tense Lucian and a man resembling the demon Baryn warned him about came through the front door.

They headed up the staircase whispering tensely, not even acknowledging the group of cheering courtiers in front of them. Mal was left confused. Where was Aurelia if she had not come with Lucian? Had she been injured? Surely he wouldn't have left his wife to bleed out somewhere.

Not long after their arrival, the crowd of courtiers were ushered into a large ballroom, lavishly decorated. Greenery hung from the ceiling, the massive candelabras decorated with flowers entwining the candles, and large dark curtains covered the walls, making it all feel rather intimate.

He took up a spot against the back wall farthest from the windows. It gave him a good overview of the room while enabling him to hide behind others if needed. Lucian and Zadon entered dressed in fresh court finery to applause and cheering. Mal watched as Lucian preened, a forced happiness pouring out of him.

Mal's jaw ticked as Lucian slung an arm around a random blonde female. He just married Aurelia; he had no right to drape himself on someone else. The insult was clear. A new round of fanfare erupted as the redhead who had helped Aurelia so much walked in with two others who undoubtedly were her soulbonds. They bowed to Lucian, and after a tense, quiet discussion, plenty of space was placed between them all.

The whispers began close to Lucian and Zadon. Maledic watched them float on the air, almost as a crow rode on a breeze. He listened intently as the rush of words reached the partygoers near him.

"The Queen refused to come. More interested in associating with the unclean peasants than her own people."

"I heard she refused the wording at the ceremony."

"She brought Drakore to our door."

"You all forget she's not even really our Queen. Merely his wife, and clearly not one that's missed."

Mal glanced back to Lucian, where another scantily clad woman was whispering in his ear. A group of musicians began to drown out the wave of rumors. Maledic paced, unsure what was happening or where Aurelia could be hiding. Would Lucian have locked her away?

A few hours went by at a mind-numbing pace before he began to sense her getting closer. Her connection, as faint as it was, felt farther away, undoubtedly due to her marriage. Her emotions were still highly volatile and loud in his mind.

The double doors swung open violently. Baryn stepped aside and bowed low, allowing Aurelia to step in ahead of him.

Mal's mouth dried as he took in her appearance. Her once immaculate silver-jeweled top now blackened and browning with an immense amount of blood. The copper smell filled the air. The blood had trailed down her body, leaving a clear mark.

The room fell silent. Mal clenched his hands, wanting to rush to her, but was forced to stay put. Aurelia strode slowly through the parted crowd, surveying the room. He moved behind her, always sure to keep a few people between them. She made it to Lucian, and Maledic couldn't help the smirk as she circled around her new husband and the girl currently draped over him. He noted the look of wrath exuding from Zadon directed at Aurelia.

"Has my husband forgotten his vows already?" She tsked loudly. "Is this behavior supposed to ensure I am happy?" She chuckled darkly. "One must choose their words carefully when making an oath mark, you know. Does it burn yet?"

Lucian growled darkly, but Aurelia seemingly ignored him. "This room is supposed to have windows." She tapped her boot, surveying the walls. "Ah. Yes. I bet these nasty curtains hide the city you're all supposed to love." She walked over and grabbed the heavy fabric.

Mal could feel her magic fill the air, her beloved use of wind aiding her in pulling the curtains down. Once it was down, the room gasped at what was now visible below the Palace. In the middle of the city, a substantial glow of light flickered.

"Yes. Exactly what I thought. You *CAN* see the fallout of this afternoon from here. To those interested that glow represents..."

Mal took a sharp breath of air, moving to get to her but knowing he'd be far too late. Luckily, Baryn moved as well, physically stopping Zadon, barring him from reaching Aurelia.

She began to laugh. "Oh Lucian. Your pet has broken free of his leash again. Never worry; he won't stop me." She turned to the crowd of people as if teaching a lesson. "The glow is Palion's people, out there processing their dead."

Lucian rushed her, getting right in her face, blocking Mal's view of her. He could hear, though, as Lucian ordered. "Out. Now."

twelve

LUCIAN

DRAK - PALION - YEAR 7568

The party had been amazing until Aurelia actually deigned to show up. She just had to pull all the attention and then expose the terrible reality he had tried to hide from the money bags in the court. Then there was Zadon's issue with her. The entire carriage ride to the palace, he had vented about the stupidity that came with women, but particularly about this woman. She would be the end of Palion. She would destroy all that they had built since Kasria's death. Lucian eventually tuned him no longer listening, knowing that in the end, Zadon had always had the best intentions for him. Yet, he had started them on this track. Zadon had been at the heart of the marriage idea. Watching Zadon almost attack the banshee didn't help anything, including his mindset.

"Out. Now." His voice thankfully didn't shake or crack despite the confusion and anger that filled his entire being.

Aurelia cocked an eyebrow. "Do you happen to have me confused with your pet? I don't take orders."

Lucian's mind stuttered, trying to keep the monsters at bay. He gripped her upper arm with enough strength to bruise, turning her toward the windows, which were actually glass doors leading to a terrace. He let out a sharp yelp as her skin grew impossibly hot, forcing him to relinquish his hold. "I also don't allow anyone to manhandle me."

His mind whirled. She had air and fire? That combination never happened. Suzu stepped from the crowd, Ulfur and Belvina visible behind her.

"Sire, milady. Perhaps this could all be solved by a refreshing moment outside and out of earshot." She opened the terrace door and waited, eyes downcast.

He caught Zadon stepping around Baryn out onto the terrace, clearly trying to taunt the headstrong girl to follow him. Instead, she chuckled. "He has no idea what's to come. But one day, that arrogant smirk will get wiped away."

Lucian rubbed his temples, a migraine building. "Aurelia, please step outside with us to discuss this continued problem."

She smirked, causing his irritation to soar. "That wasn't too hard, was it?" She stepped lightly around him to the terrace, pointedly ignoring Zadon.

Baryn fell into step behind her, but Lucian gripped his shoulder. "Where are you going, brother?"

Baryn's eyes hit the ground, but he spoke clearly. "I am her sworn sword until Valri returns."

Lucian felt like he had been walloped in the stomach. "You... you betrayed me?"

"No. I am doing what we both know Kas wanted. I am seeing the lost Princess safely to the Drakore throne. Seeing as Zadon and I are to blame for her disappearance, I shall see her through this, Sire." He bowed before jerking out of Lucian's hold and placing himself between Zadon and his wayward bride.

Lucian turned to the still-too-quiet ballroom. "Music,

dancing. The party shall continue!" There was a scramble to comply; he nodded, satisfied that someone still obeyed him. No one on the damn balcony did.

A whisper floated through his mind, dark and foreboding *—An example of your authority will do wonders.* His wolf whined, but he couldn't keep looking so weak. His father's snide comments filled his head and drowned out his wolf's protests. He headed out onto the balcony, debating how to move forward.

He surveyed the city, his heart twinging at the idea that people were dealing with their own loss of soulbonds. He could never witness that again without being brought right back to the abyss of madness Zadon had pulled him from.

He tightened his grip on the railing before looking at Aurelia. "What power have you mastered?"

She blinked, crossing her arms. Her eyes shuttering. "That's not knowledge that belongs to you."

He nodded, expecting nothing less. "This is why Zadon's spot is secure. He has let me in. We have no secrets, and his advice for the running of the kingdom is invaluable. You are an unproven entity who doesn't give information when asked." Lucian stepped closer to Zadon, showing his alliance. "As such, for your time here, you are expected to treat members of my court with respect. Including saying his name when speaking. Weapons will remain sheathed from you both, and we leave here under a truce."

He could feel the air picking up, pulling at all their clothes. He glanced at Aurelia, but she outwardly appeared calm and collected. He watched as Baryn turned toward her and noticed the oath mark just under his ear, a dragon wing, small but clearly showing his promise to her. *When had that even occurred?*

The dark voice sounded in his mind once more. *She's a disease turning those around you away from your authority.*

Make an example that everyone can reflect on. He gritted his teeth, doing his best to ignore the voice.

Aurelia cleared her throat. "If I am not a member of this court, what am I?" Her voice was calm, detached even.

He sighed deeply. "You are as my departed soulbond wished: a guest. All while my kingdom works to reunite you with yours."

Aurelia walked to the balcony's edge, the wind whipping harder. It pulled at his jacket and his hair had completely lost its styling. "Then why marry me? One would assume she wouldn't have wanted that."

His breath kicked up a bit. "I need a partner to tie to the Great Power for the betterment of Palion. You are a powerful-blooded princess, the perfect solution. It wouldn't have been an issue had she lived."

Aurelia nodded once. "So what do you want, Lucian?"

"I want to rule Palion."

The wind kicked up severely, whipping around the palace edge, roaring. She raised her voice to be heard. "You already do that. What role am I to take in this future?"

Zadon stepped up beside him. His voice grew in volume to be heard over the wind. "You are supposed to quietly follow directions until we can give you Drakore to play with."

Lucian smiled and nodded. Zadon always had the best way to explain things. The smile melted off his face at the look on Aurelia's. "I haven't had the opportunity to tell you what all happened to me in Dodsfell." Sparks flew from her fingertips. "I may never. But I will tell you that the Duvlak will never have a hand in my life again."

She raised her hand, black tendrils whipping out and fastening around Zadon, dragging him up to the window and securing him by his wrists and ankles. Lucian gaped. Zadon had gone deathly pale.

He turned back to Aurelia, a look of sick pleasure shining

back at him. Indignation crested through him along with panic. "You told me you would spare him!"

"You told the Gods a lot of things today. One of us was lying. Lets see who, shall we?"

Zadon started gasping, but she hadn't moved. Lucian glanced between the two of them, trying to understand how she was attacking him. "What are you doing?"

She shrugged indifferently, "It's surprising where in the body air goes. Did you know air was the first element I ever played with? It loves to come when I call."

The monsters in his mind cried out, desperate for him to do something to save his friend. The image of the wing flashed in his mind the split second before he moved. He grabbed Baryn by the throat, tightening as he half walked, half dragged the male to the balcony edge. It satisfied part of his mind to exact his revenge on her loyal subject. There was no space in this world for him to exact this kind of revenge on her, no matter how deeply he wanted to; a substitute would have to work.

Aurelia gasped, her attention torn from Zadon enough that he began to cough, though he was still fastened to the window. Lucian focused his attention on the traitor in his grasp. "You just had to give her an oath, didn't you, brother?" He couldn't help sneering the endearment so clearly betrayed.

His mind filled with a memory, shoved down the pack bond and into him. He saw a child-sized version of Aurelia scrambling out of a darkened palace corridor, terror evident on her face. Screams and the sounds of fighting clearly came through the memory. It shifted to show the same young Aurelia being shoved by Baryn through a small gap in the tall wall marking the boundary between Drakore and Dodsfell. She whimpered, and he heard whispered reassurances from Baryn that he would find her and help her. The memories sped up, and it was the gate of Dodsfell standing open and broken as always, near the Temple of Tixdarr. Baryn's hand pushed at the magic that prevented mortals from entering the realm beyond. Baryn screamed his anger into the air as he hit the magic again and again.

"Lucian," her voice broke through the memories, finally holding caution and perhaps something approaching fear. "Let him go. All he's ever done is follow orders. He's a no one." The wind whipped, and the sparks that were shining off her hands morphed into lightning striking haphazardly in the grounds beyond the balcony, much closer than he was comfortable with. The cracking snap of the bolts caused the hair on his body to stand tall.

"Step closer, Aurelia. See what happens then." He gripped Baryn's throat harder, causing Baryn to whimper, scrambling at Lucian's hands, desperate to free himself. "Free Zadon." He gritted out the order, needing her to listen, to finally obey.

"You won't kill your pack, Lucian. He sent me to Dods-fell. You can't blame him for the guilt he carries. The wish he has to help me. I am alone on foreign soil!"

Lucian growled. "He was pack. He was my brother. My last connection to her." Tears built up inside of him at the prospect that she would be wiped off the land completely.

"Then don't do this. Leave him be."

Lucian grunted. "He has an oath to you, forever tainted. He is no longer pack."

A high-pitched squeal left Baryn, the pack echoing through the pack bond. "He stood in the way of Zadon, my right-hand man. He stayed with you to do Gods know what after the ceremony. He has signed his fate."

An idea struck. "Perhaps you can take this moment to show your loyalty to those who follow you. After all, you seem overly confident in your own skills."

He pulled Baryn closer, as if to embrace him, whispering

to him alone. "It didn't have to be this way. Tell your sister to wait for me."

Baryn whimpered as Lucian shoved with all the might of his Alpha strength. Baryn's arms and legs immediately pinwheeled, searching for something to save him. Lucian met Aurelia's shocked gaze, crossing his now shaking arms as his mind began to take hold of the finality that came with his action.

Faintly, down the disintegrating pack bond, he heard Baryn's wolf. "Protect her."

thirteen

AURELIA

DRAK - PALION - YEAR 7568

> *It is said in the land of the Fae, death is treated as just another journey. The deceased is placed in traveling gear with enough gold and silver for any destination. Then they are wrapped in linen of their favorite color, carefully including their illustrious wings. Their most treasured family will take the deceased to the shoreline, walking the shrouded body into the deepest water before the unknown magic of death drags it under.*
>
> *~Ancient Death Rites, Margoth's Journal*

All air from Aurelia's lungs seemed to have disappeared as Baryn's body went pinwheeling over the edge. She fought for breath and for a way to save him. Digging deep, while keeping the tethers on Zadon, grasping at all the air magic she could to try and create a cloud for him to land on.

Yet whether it was due to her time in the realm of the dead, her use of magic against Zadon, or just an over-exuberant use of the power, the magic seemed to cause Baryn's body to fall harder.

She could hear screaming echoing from everywhere. She threw herself to the ledge to see what her heart already knew. His body lay below them, twisted, his head at an unnatural angle.

She whirled on Zadon, ignoring Lucian entirely. It was now abundantly clear how to make him feel anything. "I said quite clearly a Duvlak won't have a hand in my future ever again. There's one painfully clear way to make that a reality."

She touched the dark power that writhed within her, taking over the holes left by her mortal magic. This power of death could end him right then, and by the look on his face, he knew. Just like with his scaly mother, he would suffer for a while before she gave him the sweet release death would provide.

She tightened the restraint around one of his wrists, his face flushing, a sweat breaking out. "Oh, is the pet going to actually swallow his screams? How interesting. Come on, be a good boy. Just open that twisted little mouth and voice the anguish."

"Aurelia, what the fuck?"

She merely raised a hand, halting Lucian's speech as more black escaped her palms, falling to the ground heavy like a fog. Zadon's eyes widened, true fear showing as the fog encircled Aurelia, making it impossible for anyone to reach her without touching it.

"Don't," Zadon panted, looking desperately at Lucian, who was moving toward her. "Don't. Touch. Fog. Death." He groaned, but groaning didn't satisfy her blood rage.

"Now, now, pet. That wasn't a scream. I need your

scream." She tightened the magic again, causing it to sink into his skin, blood beginning to flow down the window's glass.

Zadon's eyes latched onto hers. "How?"

She smirked. "Give in and perhaps, if you play the part adequately, you can earn the answer."

She squeezed the power until it reached some resistance—bone, perhaps. The blood flowed thicker. The faces beyond the window all showed various expressions of anguish. Zadon lifted his head, looking over her shoulder once more, a look of panic on his face before he finally opened his mouth, releasing a guttural scream.

Her smirk grew. He played the victim well.

"Good job, pet." She spoke louder, ensuring Lucian and the shocked Suzu could hear her over the screaming. "The fog will kill what it touches, painfully. The power the Gods know I have mastered is that of Death. They feared it, hiding it away in Dodsfell, because no mortal being walks there. Death magic is rather clingy. It seeks the living. As they said, I had no choice." She slid her gaze to Lucian's. "Watch where you step."

She turned back to Zadon and finished the process, severing his right hand completely. It flopped to the terrace floor with a wet smack. Zadon's screams reached new levels of agony. Satisfied, she pulled the fog back within her, her head beginning to swim. Power had limits, and the world required balance. Lucian was seething, but clearly unsure what to do as his best friend lay cradling a stump.

She looked at him, disgust rolling through her. "For the record, I am not happy. How is the oath mark feeling now, Lucian?"

She watched him pant, trying to control his emotions. "Go away, Aurelia."

She bowed dramatically. "As you command."

As she turned to stare into the ballroom, her blood ran

cold, freezing her in place. Maledic stood there in the front, staring back at her. Her mouth dried, and her limbs felt heavy.

Suzu must have noticed her demeanor change because she was there, grabbing her and pulling her through the door and out of the ballroom. Aurelia tried to keep his face in her line of sight, but as she blinked he disappeared into the crowd. The realization that he might actually be here or could be here shuddered through her. They were heading to an unmarked door on the main level when she found her voice.

"Where?"

"Hush. We have to get Baryn."

"He's—" she choked on the words. "He's dead, Suzu."

"We have to get him safely to the temple. A last act of kindness. You owe him this."

Aurelia swallowed her rebuttal. She did owe him. Perhaps she could give him something back. She could take life so easily; there had to be a chance she could give it back. They entered the unmarked door and walked down a cold, barren hallway, probably a servants' corridor.

Suzu whispered, "This will put us outside under the balcony. Be careful what you say. Sound carries, and I don't know how far gone Lucian is right now."

Gone? What could that mean? Aurelia held her tongue, gathering her remaining powers in preparation for her last shot at saving Baryn. They exited a door, and dread filled her. She shoved any lingering thoughts about Maledic aside and stepped onto the darkened grass.

His body lay in a strip of moonlight, face down, his neck at an odd angle. Her heart broke. This man may have led her to Dodsfell, but he had also protected her at her most vulnerable. He chose her over his own Alpha. All because he believed she would be better for the Kingdom.

She sank to her knees at the crown of his head. Clearing her throat, she pointed. Suzu mumbled under her breath, but complied, helping to turn his cooling body. Using the utmost care, Aurelia straightened his neck, sinking her fingers into his soft hair. She closed her eyes and threw herself into her death magic.

It was different from the elemental magic she dabbled with. It was almost tangible, taking shapes that she visualized. She visualized a blanket, stretching it to lay on top of Baryn's body. Releasing her hold on it once it was clear it would cover him.

She envisioned Baryn walking around. She envisioned the man who saved her, channeling the essence of who she had gotten to know. She expected the magic to sink into him to animate his form once more. Yet the magic stayed hovering over him. It appeared as if there was a barrier preventing the magic from sinking in. Her eyes grew hot, her head pounding to a beat unique to itself.

"No." She whispered.

She pushed the magic again, placing her hands on it, trying to muscle it onto his skin. Upon contact, however, the magic sank back into her skin. She shoved at his shoulders, her mind refusing to accept that while she may be able to grant death and in whichever way she wanted, she couldn't restore what had been taken. Her tears fell like rain on his face as her head fell to her chest.

Suzu's hand tentatively gripped her shoulder. "They need to take him."

She looked back. Ulfur stood, and next to him was a large man, a board resting against the palace walls. The men were solemn-faced.

The crown on her head began to weigh heavy. Baryn's beliefs echoing in her mind. She reached up, pulling hard, desperate to get it off, to free herself. She hissed as hair came loose, as the crown began to separate from her braid. Suzu batted her hands away, hovering over Aurelia's crouched form, unfastening the crown for her.

Aurelia nodded to the men, who both came silently, loading Baryn's body onto the board. They hoisted him up between them. Aurelia stood up as well, bending slightly so her lips brushed his ear, whispering. "Your soul is probably still right here, waiting for permission to leave. I'm sorry, Baryn. You deserved more, know you are forgiven. Choose the Void, Baryn. Don't stay in Dodsfell, not for anyone."

She took a deep breath, straightening and meeting the eyes of the men. She placed the crown on his chest. "For his tithe." She let herself look at him once more before heading back into the palace.

Suzu fell into step behind her gently, directing her to the quarters she had been assigned. Aurelia's mind was reeling. In the course of one day, she had charmed a populace, seen the start of a potential war, married the man seemingly destined to be her enemy, and became directly responsible for a man's death. Add on top of all of that, Maledic was mysteriously in the palace. She rested her forehead on the wooden door to her room, closing her eyes and attempting to center herself.

"Do you need company?" Suzu asked kindly.

"How do you live with him?" The weariness came through despite her best efforts.

"He's misguided, but at one time he was harmless. I truly think he could be again."

"Or are you blind to your own reality?" Aurelia grimaced, forcing her exhausted body upright. The extensive use of magic was going to have dire consequences. "I'm sorry, that was rather rude. I just don't know how to move forward with him while he has a demon-shaped growth." There was a long pause, causing Aurelia to shift her eyes to Suzu's face.

She looked pained, but then blurted. "Minus a hand."

Suzu giggled wildly. "Sorry, I know that's inappropriate but I'm tired."

Aurelia broke out laughing, exhaustion getting the best of her as well. "Damn right, minus a hand. Perhaps that is the answer, just carve the growth off. I will think it over. Go to your mates and get some sleep, Suzu. We shall plan more tomorrow."

Aurelia watched her smile shyly before wandering down the hall of doors. She sighed heavily, letting herself into the room. It took about ten seconds before the hair on her arms started to rise. *Seriously?*

On the mantle right at eye level next to the door, a very familiar feather sat on the shelf. She picked it up, sniffing it, and knew who it had belonged to, as Maledic's familiar scent of parchment and fresh pine washed through her nose. *He really was here.*

Against all the instincts, she turned her back to the room, surveying the mantle shelf. She casually unhooked her sword, sheath and all, placing it on the shelf next to the incriminating feather. Using a small sleight of hand, she unhooked the dagger sheath and palmed the blade, her body blocking the movement from the room. She let the sheath fall onto the shelf and then stared down at the blade, cursing that she didn't have sleeves.

"If you were wearing more substantial clothing, you would be able to hide that blade. As it stands right now, you look rather foolish, Spréach." His voice was laced with anger. She felt the anger beating on her back where his eyes drilled into her.

She casually flipped the blade in her hand, giving up the pretense of hiding it. She kept her body stubbornly facing away from him. "What are you doing here, Maledic?"

fourteen

MALEDIC

Drak - Palion - Year 7568

Her words lay heavy on the air. *What was he doing here?* He shook his head, desperate for those blue eyes to meet his just one more time. "I'm here for you, just like we talked about all those years ago." He watched as the tension in her shoulders loosened.

"That was a different time. The girl who made that promise died repeatedly. She needed different things. She would have been a different Queen. As it stands, I don't need your advice now." Her shoulders slumped, the incessant knife flipping stopped.

"Turn around, Aurelia."

He half expected her to argue with him, to show more of the fire he had witnessed on the balcony. Instead, she simply obeyed. As she did turn, her shoulders resumed their impossible stiffness. Her sky-blue eyes met his; the sound of a lock sliding closed sounded in his head. Her eyes didn't flicker though, their gaze deadened.

"Aurelia."

She jolted a bit, nodding once before walking farther into the room.

"Aurelia!"

She waved a dismissive hand over her shoulder.

Ire swamped him. "What are you doing?"

She rummaged in the wardrobe, finding a nightgown and tossing it to the bed. "I'm going to bed. After I finally clean off Faziel's blood, the death of Palion citizens, and Baryn."

Maledic took a calm breath. "We have to talk about this." He tugged on his hair. Before, he had known just how to push her, but now? Even with the bond in place and his access to her internal emotions, he couldn't figure out what to do.

She leaned back on the wardrobe, balancing on one foot as she unlaced her boots. The silence dragged on for a few precious moments, only the thump of her boots landing on the floor one at a time. Just as he was going to beg, she began to speak.

"What should we talk about, Maledic? How we are destined to forever be apart? About how I am stuck married to a man who actively hates me? How you have been here long enough that this could have been stopped?" She paused her rant, unfastening the skirt contraption, leaving her in just the top and form-fitting pants.

"Or perhaps let's talk about how you knew we were soul-bonded, or at least suspected, before. Yet you didn't come for me! How you got to live your life while I fought for mine." She shoved past him and headed, to the bathing chamber.

He followed, a glutton for punishment, unable to stay away. He leaned against the doorway, his eyes fixed on the tiled floor. His heart hurt, and it was impossible to tell if it was due to his emotions or hers.

"We aren't destined to be apart." He actively ignored her loud scoff. "We are destined to have to fight for our connection." His mind stuttered as he realized that she was shucking off her remaining clothes. A quick glance showed him the scarred wreckage of her back, the oath mark from her father; the visage of wings once whole, now broken and scraggly with scars. He cleared his throat, closing his eyes, forcing his brain to continue.

"Lucian may hate you, but if you surround yourself with people who love and respect you, that won't matter. I did try to get to you before you wed him. Baryn. Baryn helped get me into the palace. I couldn't get close enough, and it was made clear that if I was caught, I would be removed. One way or another."

He glanced down at her. He couldn't see anything important, just the curve of her shoulder. Her hair floating in the water around her. Her eyes were red-rimmed but still lacked the warmth and life he remembered.

"Towel."

It was said simply and quietly. Yet it rocked Mal's core. An ask for help. He reached into the cupboard and grabbed one, holding it outstretched to her. His eyes held hers, not straying elsewhere. Not until she invited him to. Once she had stepped out of the pool and into the towel, he wrapped it securely around her.

"Thanks." It was muttered, but it sparked the most dangerous emotion. Hope.

He stayed still, allowing her a few minutes to get dressed before following. He grabbed the wooden comb before entering the room once more, handing it to her as she sat on the bed. He took a seat in the chair, studying her, trying to find the right way to tell his side.

"When we met all those years ago, I was suspicious. Before you, I was a person who never made friends with strangers. When the Manor had visitors, I would hide. Then you appeared and I had an insatiable need to be near you. We all suspected, but we couldn't tell you, it's forbidden. You must make your choice in regards to us all on your own."

He shifted in his seat, crossing his ankle over his knee. Mal closed his eyes, dreading the next part. "The night everything ... changed. I woke to your fear. I mistakenly sought out my mother, thinking she would know what to do. Instead she drugged me to keep me in Slana. Once I surfaced from the drug-laced stupor, you were already in Dodsfell." He let the gravity of that fall heavy between them. He watched for a moment as she braided her hair into one long strand.

"I didn't just live my life without you. I was forced to stay in Slana. I was offered up as meat to Faziel, and I felt every-thing you ever endured. Sometimes I could even see you. You were never alone."

He watched as Aurelia crawled under the covers. His heart stopped when she pulled back the blanket on the opposite side, an unspoken invitation. He toed off his shoes and climbed into the bed, careful to not touch her. Not yet.

She placed her hand in the middle between them, staring at it, careful to not meet his gaze. He placed his hand next to hers, still not initiating contact. He could see from even the small amount of skin on her hand and lower arm that there was puckering of scars marring its entirety.

His breath caught in his chest as her fingers delicately traced over his hand. Everywhere her fingers touched, sparks lit off under his skin. He slowly exhaled, his fingers twitching involuntarily.

"We can't act on this bond, and it will be impossible to do what has to be done here if you stay. You have to leave, Maledic." Her voice was filled with an unspoken emotion, leaving pain radiating in his chest.

"What has to be done, Spréach?"

"Doesn't matter. You'll be safer somewhere else."

He traced his way up Aurelia's arm to her elbow before going back to her hand. "I won't leave you."

"I could force you. I could end this right here and now." He caught her gaze.

"I still wouldn't leave, Aurelia. I'd just be the broken shadow behind you." He danced his fingers up to her shoulder, venturing up to her neck and face.

His heart raced. If she rejected their bond, he would struggle to survive. He saw a flicker in her eyes, the barest glimmer of life coming back.

Leaping into the unknown, he whispered. "Go to sleep, we can talk more later. After all, you promised me an advisor role."

She cocked an eyebrow, a smirk playing on her mouth. "We shall see, Maledic Corvus."

It didn't take long before Aurelia fell asleep. Once she was out, he reluctantly rolled off the bed, staring back at her in awe.

She was back.

She hadn't denied their bond.

Now he needed to check on his eggs. Then they could continue building their relationship into something more. He scribbled a note, leaving it on her nightstand before shifting and flying from the room.

fifteen

SUZU

Drak - Palion - Year 7568

She made her way to her room, shaking her head. Had she really made a joke about Zadon losing his hand? Shame mingled with satisfaction as she opened the door, only to be ambushed by the sweet-smelling arms of Belvina. "Hello Sparkles."

"Where have you been? Why did you go on that balcony?" Each question was followed with a sniffle.

Ulfur cleared his throat. "She had no choice, Beauty. You know that. If they had entertained that argument in the ballroom, innocents would have died. She had to get them out on their own."

Belvina retracted her arms on a huff. "I know, but it doesn't mean I have to like that it always falls on her to fix the problems."

Suzu chuckled, moving further into the room and closing the door. She touched the well of power boiling inside of her. Slowly, vines filled the gaps between the stones; the windows and the doors became covered with growing things. "We desperately need to talk."

Belvina groaned but sat on the couch, patting the place next to her. Suzu toed off her heels and wandered over to Ulfur, giving his hand a quick squeeze before falling onto the couch next to Belvina. "We have to decide whose side we will end up on, because after tonight there will most decidedly be sides."

Ulfur sat on the end of the couch, scooping her feet into his lap, kneading them with his thumb. "I am stuck, Kitten. He's the interim king, as rude as it sounds, she's naught but his wife. To keep my position, I have to follow him."

Belvina hummed, doubt heavy in the noise. "Tell her what the men said."

Suzu met Ulfur's brown gaze. "What men? When?"

Ulfur leaned his head back, the weight of the day forcing his eyes closed as he continued the slow, delicious torture on her feet. "When we took Baryn, we stopped by the Barracks to notify his other comrades. Give them a chance to say goodbye. The wolves knew, of course, that it was Lucian who killed him." He cleared his throat of the emotion she could hear building in his voice. "They connected with my wolf and saw it."

He paused, wiping his eyes. "They also saw Aurelia try to save him twice."

Suzu nodded, thinking it over. "Zadon won't believe that we are all happily mated and on two completely different teams."

"She has the civilians—at least the poor ones—and the wolves are leaning in her direction despite him being the Alpha. The only ones she has effectively alienated are the rich courtiers. Though once she learns of the kingdom's money situation, I am sure she will find a way to pull them into her sphere of influence." Suzu ticked off the facts.

"There's one more thing you need to know," Ulfur muttered.

"What?"

"She has a soulbond, who I am betting was working with Baryn to stay in the kingdom."

Suzu pulled her feet from his lap abruptly. "You can't be serious." The pieces clicked in her mind. "He was in the ballroom. She saw him."

"That only adds more problems, doesn't it?" Belvina whispered.

"Depends on what he wants in the end."

She stood and began to pace. "We are going to have to separate for a while."

Belvina shot to her feet, protests on her lips, but Suzu watched Ulfur, who stayed seated. *He knows I'm right.* The thought bolstered her and made her heart sink simultaneously. "I have to back her, Belvina. She has no one on her side now besides perhaps Valri. I won't let Zadon kill another woman for opposing him. I am going to give her my oath, as such, I will have to distance myself from those who support Lucian."

Tears began to stream silently from Belvina. She stomped her bare foot. "No! We are a family. You should stay neutral."

Suzu grabbed her hands and stared hard into her eyes. "My love. I hold the Power of the Land within me. I do not have the privilege to stay neutral. I need to be ready if she needs this power. Zadon can not have it."

Belvina hiccuped, looking between Ulfur and her. "We can't be separated. I won't allow it."

Ulfur stood slowly, his face impossible to read. "We need a wolf supportive of Lucian, at least in name, so he does not suspect the pack. Otherwise, we risk him killing more of them. I will be unable to take her oath, Beauty. You need to go with Suzu. Be the pack representative with her. I will shield your oath from Lucian. If you stay with Aurelia and

Suzu, you will be safer. Two major powers of Baelia are better."

He walked toward Belvina, stroking her face, kissing her forehead. Suzu leaned her head on his shoulder. "Zadon is going to insist on an oath. His paranoia will skyrocket, especially after we come out in favor of Aurelia."

He stroked up her spine. "I know, Kitten."

She stiffened. "Ulfur Hanklin, you have to keep yourself safe. Do not say an oath you can't keep. Once we do away with the demon, you will return to us."

She could feel him closing up emotionally, placing their connection in the safest corner of his mind. She nodded, understanding why he was doing it, even as her heart broke for all of them.

"I will stay as safe as I can. You need to protect Beauty."

Belvina grabbed his face, pulling him into a searing kiss. When it broke, she demanded, "Why does this feel like we won't be the same after this? We will. We'll see each other all the time and no one can poison a soulbond."

Ulfur nuzzled against Belvina's neck, trying to reassure her. "They can't poison me, no, but the time apart will hurt and be confusing. I will have to hide our bond. You won't be able to feel me like you can now." He turned to Suzu, tracing her face with a delicate touch. "I shall leave missives and reports in your favorite book, coded like we used to when we were children." Suzu smiled sadly.

She stepped as close as she could get to him, soaking in what she could. "Let us enjoy tonight. Tomorrow it all changes yet again." She pulled the vines back as Ulfur led them all to the safety of their bed chamber.

sixteen

LUCIAN

Drak - Palion - Year 7568

Zadon groaned against the window, cradling his still-bleeding stump. Lucian's mind was curiously blank, as if all that had happened had wiped it clean. He took things in small bursts; the cold air, the oozing blood, the smell of copper, the darkened grounds beneath them. He had no idea what to do next. The woman who was supposed to secure his throne would instead cause him to lose it. He was startled from his thoughts by the raspy voice of his friend. "Lucian?"

"Yes, Zadon. I'm here."

"She took my hand."

"That she did. Don't ask what the plan is now, because I don't know." He couldn't even muster the sound of anger.

A thunk on the glass had Lucian glancing at Zadon. Zadon's head had fallen back, hitting the window. "I have a plan."

Lucian's eyebrows crept into his hair. "If you're going to suggest taking her hand, I am going to have to say no."

Zadon let out a bitter laugh, the pain evident. "I know. I wasn't going to say, but if you ever change your mind, I can use a knife just as easily with my left. No, I plan to take some of her power. Level the playing field."

Lucian looked down, grimacing at the stains Zadon's blood had left on his pants, the dampened cloth sticking to his legs. A glance through the window showed that someone had shut down the reception. Probably for the best. His wolf had disappeared from his mind, a loss that cut so deeply he couldn't look too closely or risk falling deeply to the depths of madness.

Zadon slowly gained his feet. "There's a crystal I've been collecting. It will work wonders to teach her a lesson."

Lucian crossed his arms. "Rocks are somehow supposed to tip the scales?"

Zadon rubbed his throat with his left hand. "Yes. They're prominent in Dodsfell, growing throughout much like your ever-present weeds in spring. During those years of waiting for the banshee, I noticed they were growing on this side of the barrier. It took some time to figure out how to remove them around the magical wards, but I managed. These rocks can dampen, or in severe cases remove powers, but we won't get that lucky."

Lucian mulled it over. Rocks weren't that bad, and if they were caught, he could blame a random servant. "Alright. I'm willing to do that, but if we get caught, this was neither of our ideas."

Zadon shot him a manic grin, cuddling his arm close to his chest as he peeled himself up off the ground. Lucian followed him out, skirting around the straggling partygoers. They avoided the hall that held Lucian and Aurelia's rooms. Instead, going to Zadon's room, which was located on the floor below. Lucian had only ever been inside of it a handful of times. It was dark and dingy but immaculately organized.

In the bottom drawer of Zadon's desk was a small mound of quartz-like crystals clear, and jagged but Lucian could feel the effect of the rocks immediately upon entering the room. His small amount of fire elemental power was unreachable. The monsters surged, seemingly more powerful in the presence of the crystals.

His skin crawled at the idea of touching them. He looked at Zadon, shock filling him, "These are powerful. How did I not feel these in the palace? Why did you gather them? We didn't know she'd be a monster."

Zadon shrugged, his face pain stricken. "I kept them in a lined drawer, just in case. I didn't have a plan, Lucian. I just figured it would come in handy one day. Be sure to wrap them, don't touch them to your skin."

Lucian nodded, pulling on the gloves he found on the desktop. He tried his best to smother the tickle of suspicion beginning in his mind. He shoved it back, though, as he took the crystals and pocketed them. "Zadon, you should head to the medics wing. They can give you some tonics and bind the stump properly."

Zadon groaned, his skin looking flushed and sweaty. "I will. Just make sure the stones don't come in contact with her directly. Skin contact for either of you could lead to some random and nasty results. Just slide them in the corners of her room."

Lucian nodded decisively. "Simple."

He watched Zadon sway a little, internally debating if he should take him to the medics' wing himself. Instead, Lucian led him into the hall and watched carefully as the swaying Zadon made his way towards the medics' wing. Once he was out of sight, Lucian headed to Aurelia's room. The sooner these stones were deposited and out of his immediate vicinity, the better.

He fished a key out of his pocket, but was pleasantly

surprised to see she had not locked her door. The room was dark, but clear signs of her presence were visible: her weaponry on the mantle, the boots next to the wardrobe, and her clothes strewn haphazardly on the ground.

He placed a rock inside the fireplace, half-buried in the ash. His magic immediately felt better for not having it pressed so close. His skin crawled at the idea of what direct contact may do. He gently eased the door of the wardrobe open, thanking the Gods for well oiled hinges.

He wandered into the bathing chamber, dropping one into the tub. The water making it appear just like the bottom of the small pool. Then he placed one in the cupboard of towels. He had two more, aiming to place them under her bed and on her nightstand. When she woke up, she may see it, but there was no way she'd find them all. He surveyed her curled in on herself, reaching out to the other side of the bed. Her hair braided neatly. The bedspread was rumpled across the entire bed, the spare pillow indented. *Odd.*

She looked so innocent. Pure. Yet he wouldn't be fooled; once she opened her mouth, it'd be more violence and vitriol. His wolf appeared on the corner of his mind, as if the release of the rocks were clearing the way for his shifter powers to return. The wolf whined, wanting to inexplicably protect this woman, but he couldn't—not after all she'd done to undermine him.

He placed the crystal on the nightstand, his gloved hand fiddling with the last crystal, planning on tossing it under the bed itself. His eye caught on a scrap of paper, a quick scrawl across it.

Thank you for your openness, Spréach. We will find our way. I will return with the sun to stand by your side. ~Mal

Lucian's blood ran cold. The soulbond hadn't left. He had warned the bird to leave or die, yet somehow, he not only stayed, but he reconnected with Aurelia. Panic surged within him. *How could he keep her under control if she didn't need him, instead relying on her soulbond?* Anger burned the panic away, she had a soulbond, but his had died. No. She was always at the center of the injustices and would pay. He looked down at the crystal, then walked around the bed close to her outstretched hand. Her palm was up, fingers slightly curled, and he slipped the crystal onto her unprotected skin.

He held his breath, curious as to what would happen. Zadon had been so vague. The monsters in his mind cheered as her eyes flew open, showing only the whites, pain twisting on her face. Her body seized and a scream fled from her. Her eyes slammed shut, her body shuddering. Lucian crept from the room, cruel satisfaction filling him. For once, the monsters sat silently, sated on her pain, in the back of his mind.

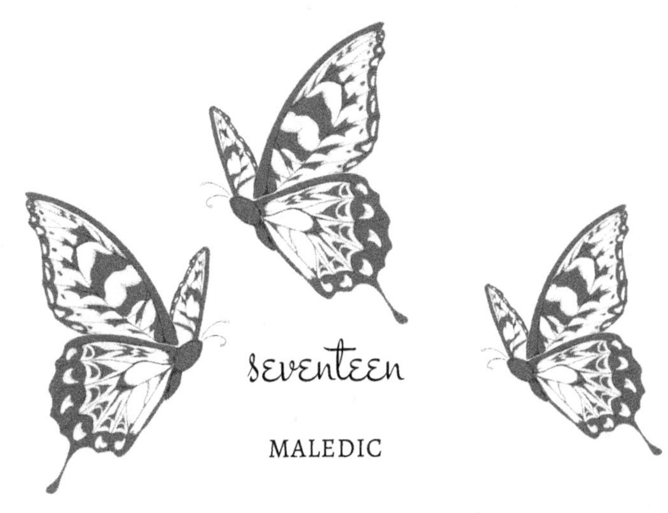

seventeen

MALEDIC

Bura - Slana - Year 7568

Mermaids live in the deepest depths of the water, believing that to be the way to salvation. When a mermaid dies their family does the rarest act of all: the closest member choosing to surface with the body. The member choosing to accompany the deceased will stay in the sunlight as the body slowly dissolves into sea foam. The sea foam will cling to that family member as a last goodbye before leaving with the waves to see a new side of the world.

~Ancient Death Rites, Margoth's Journal

He winged his way into the cave, an unusual lightness filling him. Perhaps he should stop and check on his family before returning; it may be a while before he would get to see them again. His joy lent to a feeling of forgiveness, which would come in handy when talking to his parents. It was time to set their relationship to rights now that he lived in Palion.

He toured the egg-hiding holes, each spot carefully covered with sand, various butterflies resting on top. He marveled that Feginth's soul still stayed watching the eggs; two entire weeks had passed, and yet so many remained. He carefully shooed them away, brushing the sand from his charges. As the sand fell away, a blue shell of swirly inlaid pattern appeared, throbbing to an unseen beat. More sand loosened, exposing an orange shell, emitting a happy glow. He replaced the sand with a small pat of satisfaction, the butterflies settling back on top. He didn't know if it was right, but it felt like the correct thing to do for each.

In the next hiding hole, there was a light grey egg and a green one. The grey egg gave him a bit of concern; its lack of color in comparison to its siblings stirred his inner worry. He laid a hand upon its shell, and relief seeped into his bones as he felt the heat and gentle thrum from within. He reburied them, ensuring sand covered every small bit of the grey egg. A butterfly promptly landed over it, as if Feginth herself was reassuring him that he had done what was proper.

The last stop revealed the most curious eggs—a bright yellow one and a black one. He felt oddly drawn to these eggs but he expected them to be the same size as all the rest. Yet the black egg was larger, at least double in volume.

He cocked his head, considering. The yellow egg rested on top, so he easily pulled it off lugging it to another safe sandy alcove, reburying it in warm sand. He returned to the black egg, tapping his foot, considering where to place the obviously growing creature. As he leaned into the craggy hole, trying to get a good grip, a sudden, intense pain ricocheted through his chest. He released the egg standing up quickly, so quickly that he caught his arm on one of the sharper crags. He barely noticed the sting or the hot drips as they fell down his arms. His left hand pulsated with pain. He glared down, confused, an odd-shaped burn appearing. The pain seared in his chest again. *Aurelia.*

What happened? What could have happened? He had just left her safe in her bed.

He glanced at the egg, his mind torn. Moving as fast as he could, he hoisted the egg out, aiming for an open alcove that wouldn't hinder its growth. Nestling it in without concern for his bleeding arm, he buried it in the sand. Silently, he sent an apology to the memory of Feginth as the remaining butterflies swarmed the eggs in their new homes.

He shifted, aiming straight for her window, flying as fast as his small wings could take him. The few hours separating them flew quickly; dawn barely beginning to break as he reached her sill. She lay just where he left her, except something felt odd. He could barely shift to his mortal shell. He pulled the sheets back, desperation filling him as he tried to rouse her, more than willing to raise her anger.

Yet she didn't even flinch. His hand throbbed again, causing him to look at hers. Her left hand was clenched into a fist. *Odd.*

He leaned over her and began to peel her fingers open, revealing a smokey quartz crystal. His instinct told him not to touch it. He shook it out of her hand onto the sheet. As soon as the crystal left her skin, Aurelia's body sighed, relaxing into a more natural sleep.

Maledic left and grabbed a washcloth, wrapping the crystal in it. He placed the wrapped crystal onto her nightstand and then gripped her shoulder once more. "Aurelia. Wake up."

She didn't move. Didn't twitch. He could see her chest moving up and down so she lived, but remained unresponsive. He looked at the rock; something bad had happened with it. Yet what?

He combed through her room, following the sense of uneasiness. He found more rocks, every time using a wash cloth to pick them up, protecting his own skin. The pile on her nightstand led to one conclusion: after he left, someone had come and made sure she felt the suppression of her magic. He pulled a chair to the foot of her bed and grabbed Aurelia's sword from the mantle.

The next time someone made a move on her, they would go through him. Meanwhile, he would brainstorm; there had to be something specific he could do to fix her situation.

BURA - PALION - YEAR 7568

Suzu stretched as dawn rays broke through her curtains. Sadness crested in her as she realized the bed was empty. Groaning, she pulled herself up. No matter what she truly wanted, the day wouldn't wait for her. Aurelia needed to create a long-term plan, which would mean they had a lot of work to do.

Once she was dressed, she wandered into the living area, unsurprised to see Belvina hand-sewing on their couch. "Ulfur's moved into the bunk house," Her tone dark and pained.

Suzu nodded once. "Let's just see what Aurelia has planned."

Belvina stood, straightening her already perfect clothes. Suzu went to her intending to give her a reassuring embrace, but Belvina side stepped her. Suzu stopped short, pain lancing through her. "Alright then."

When they reached Aurelia's room, Suzu could sense that something was massively wrong. Her head was screaming, her power clawing its way out. The wooden door groaned, desperate to grow limbs and leaves, remembering its past life as a tree.

"Belvina. Something's wrong." Suzu took a few halting steps, desperately reaching toward the door.

"I will not stand here like a helpless maiden, Suzu. Shove that idea right out of your mind. After last night, I'm done with people making decisions for me." Belvina shoved in next to her, a glare shot her way for good measure.

"Sparkles." Suzu's senses went on high alert. "Go. Get. Valri." She muttered through gritted teeth.

"Absolutely not."

Suzu dug deep into her power, which was getting harder to do once she got the door open. They both caught sight of the armed man at the foot of Aurelia's bed. The man merely glared at them, his hand on the hilt, waiting.

Suzu tried to send vines to wrap around the man's ankles, but her power didn't answer her. "Belvina, we need that demon right now. Go and stop arguing." Out of the corner of her eye, Belvina stomped her foot, before turning and exiting the room at a run.

Suzu focused all of her attention on the stranger, twisting her neck to see if there was any blood coming from the bed. "While she gets our friend, wanna explain exactly what you've done to my Queen?" Suzu asked, trying to stay calm.

The man glared at her. "How about you tell me? You are awfully familiar with her to be able to just enter her chambers. Perhaps it's you who should be questioned. After all, when I left here last night, she was fine, and now she's not."

Suzu's mind blanked. "I last saw her outside that door." It occurred to her now where she'd seen this man. "You're the person that distracted her in the ballroom, which means you're her soulbond."

The man didn't make any indication that Suzu was correct; instead just sat there waiting. Suzu changed tactics. "What is wrong with her?"

The man cocked an eyebrow. "She will not wake up."

"Right." Given how her powers were acting, she suspected it was more than that. Luckily, Valri and Belvina crashed through the door before she could give more thought to it. "Valri," She inclined her head towards the demon, "is Aurelia's sworn sword. I think she is a great candidate to examine the Queen, since you don't seem to want anyone else."

Valri cocked her head, examining the man intently. "I know you."

"Yes."

"He's her soulbond, Valri."

"That may be. I have also met him before. He is the one who gave me her necklace—the one from Drakore."

Suzu contemplated that. "I wish you had spoken up then, Mr. Stranger. Yet we can't go backward. Will you let Valri look at her?"

The man stood, sword in hand, giving a small nod to them. Suzu held her breath, waiting to hear what could possibly have gone wrong. Valri walked with care, despite her hastily donned breeches and untucked shirt. Suzu watched as her slender fingers felt along Aurelia's chin. "She lives, but," Valri cocked her head before leaning down and inhaling deeply, "her soul." Valri's head whipped around quickly.

"What is it, Valri?" Suzu watched as Valri's jaw tightened.

"Her soul's been banished."

Silence blanketed the room. Valri moved first, carefully poking at the pile of rocks on the nightstand, covered by a wash cloth.

"Oh shit."

"What?" The man gruffly asked.

"Those rocks grow only in Dodsfell. They are power dampeners, but if they touched her skin, it would have pushed her soul out. It would have pushed it to Dodsfell."

Suzu swore under her breath. "We need to guard her until we can get her back. Zadon was undeniably behind this. How do we dispose of those stones?"

"That is the start of the problem. We can't get rid of them because we will need them to restore her soul. We need a lead-lined box where we can store the crystals. It will dampen the effect on our magic. Then at least we can protect her body while we figure out how to get her soul."

Belvina stepped up beside Suzu. "I shall research the ways to reunite her soul."

Suzu squeezed her hand. "I will find concrete evidence on who did this."

Valri looked to the man. "I will need a day or two to try and find a way back into Dodsfell. You will need to stay and guard her."

"They will have to go through me to get to her from now on. I won't be leaving her side again." He settled back into his seat.

Suzu's heart leapt at this. "We will make sure that won't happen. We will also make sure you are taken care of, Mr. Stranger. If you are hers, then you are also ours."

"Don't bother to make promises you can't keep, Red." He motioned for them all to leave the room the way they had come, his eyes oddly haunted.

nineteen

LUCIAN

Bura - Palion - Year 7568

Lucian had fallen into a deep, dreamless sleep, the first since Kasria had died. The sound of pounding footsteps woke him. Someone was running in the hallway. *Perhaps Aurelia was panicking over not being able to use her power.* The thrill that thought gave him sent the creatures haunting his mind into a frenzy.

He leveraged himself up and rang the inner bell. He managed to get ready just in time for the servants to knock on his door. "I need Ulfur and Zadon to meet me in the council room, now."

The servant bowed and ran off. He followed slowly behind, going out of his way to ensure he passed in front of Aurelia's room. He noticed fairly quickly that her door was cracked, just enough that he could make out the familiar head of Suzu.

His blood ran cold. The constant presence of Suzu had been a staple of his childhood and his father's court. She had been around so much that, there had been a rumor before the alliance with Drakore, that she would be married off to him. Once that clearly wasn't going to happen, she just became an accepted fixture. Then, when Kasria had been around, Suzu had agreed to be a part of his court. He had witnessed her own mating for Gods sake. Now she dared attend to Aurelia instead of him. That type of betrayal couldn't go unanswered.

He walked with a purpose, intent on seeing Ulfur answer for his wife's indiscretion. After all, the behavior of one mate reflected them all. Pleasure swamped him as he saw both men waiting for him when he arrived at the conference room. He strode at the head of the table and sat, leaning back indolently.

"Welcome to the start of my rule, gentleman. It's time to solidify the crown, which also means securing allegiances."

Ulfur shifted slightly, his face a mask of sadness and determination. "Ulfur, you look sick. Whatever could be wrong? This is a time for celebration!"

"It's nothing, Your Grace." Ulfur bowed slightly, attempting to place a look of interest on his face.

"I see. Something interesting caught my eye on the way here, any idea what that could be?"

Ulfur sighed heavily. "I can guess, Sire." He shifted from foot to foot. "Suzu, Belvina, and I had a falling out. You undoubtedly witnessed them with Aurelia. She had to choose Aurelia or you, Sire, but my choice was made. I will stay on your side, Sire. Even though my mates have chosen Aurelia."

"Interesting. It will come as no surprise to you that I need an oath of loyalty. I have never heard of mates being so diametrically opposed, the mating bond being something so powerful as to override other feelings." Lucian tapped the table, motioning Ulfur forward.

Ulfur walked around the table to take a knee as he reached Lucian's chair. Withdrawing his knife, he sliced up his palm. Lucian leaned closer, intent on the show of submission. "I, Ulfur Hanklin, swear to be loyal to Lucian Ronnet as my liege lord." Ulfur's eyes remained glued to the ground as he held the knife up hilt-first.

Lucian took the handle of the proffered knife, slicing through his own palm. "I, Lucian Ronnet, accept your oath of fealty to me." He grasped Ulfur's bleeding hand tighter, a smirk unfurling on his face. "You shall swear fealty to Zadon as well as swear to report any treasonous behavior you come across, no matter who is behind the treason."

Ulfur paled as their blood intermixed. "I so swear."

Zadon interjected. "Say the words, dog."

A flash of anger lit Ulfur's face before he repeated Lucian's wording exactly. Zadon's oath didn't take as long, since Lucian only required the vague wording of loyalty to Lucian; specifics weren't needed for his best friend.

"Ulfur, you are going to stay in charge of the warriors as well as run the guards in the palace. I don't want to have a formal spy master, but Zadon, perhaps you can keep your ear out since you've lost your hand." He waved at Zadon's newly wrapped stump with a shrug. Zadon nodded, a spark of interest lighting his eyes. "Next, we need to schedule the coronation."

Ulfur nodded. "Shall I notify Aurelia of this?"

"No. She shall not be crowned." Lucian scrutinized Ulfur's reaction, still not trusting the man, but Ulfur didn't even flinch, only nodded. A burn seared across his abs. His hands flew to the spot, concern filtering through the monsters. As swiftly as it burned, the spot stopped hurting. "We should hold a council meeting to confirm their loyalty and solidify the plans for the ceremony."

Zadon nodded once. "I shall send a message out to the upper and lower mayors. Do you know which aristocrat was appointed to their seat?"

Lucian tapped his chin thoughtfully. "No, I don't, but we

shall send a personal invite to Nastrud Lineare. He's always supported my plans."

Zadon nodded. "I shall send it to him. Are we setting the meeting for today or tomorrow?"

"Tomorrow."

Ulfur cleared his throat. "I suppose I shall fulfill the wolf seat?"

Lucian nodded, humming. "Yes. However, we won't keep the Luna seat, after all, we don't have one, nor will we appoint one." He expected Ulfur to push but he didn't—just nodded, accepting the information.

L ucian strode into the council room, knowing he had timed it perfectly. Everyone else was seated and forced to rise to greet him. "Hello, gentlemen. Welcome to my first official council meeting. Our only real point of conversation today is my impending coronation."

There was a long pause filled with everyone glancing nervously around at each other. Nastrud Lineare cleared his throat. "My lord... we need to figure out how to control that wife of yours first."

Anger spiked. "She won't be an issue."

The Mayor of Upper Palion, Pinera Tenebris, smiled awkwardly. "Excellent, Sire. When will your father be available to do the power transfer?"

Lucian's jaw ticked, his teeth grinding. "He is unable to do the transfer."

Silence thickened. Lucian cleared his throat, deciding to throw caution to the wind. "My father was brutally murdered years ago, and the Power of the Land was stolen. I chose to stay silent as I conducted a private investigation. For now, we will refuse to let the criminal win. So it is on us to craft a coronation without that aspect."

The Council all stared at him, mouths agape.

The lower Mayor, Cryon Osdrak, shook his head. "No—no, we can't do this without the power. The Gods will punish Palion even more than has already begun after your wedding."

Lucian watched the nod flood the room, leaving only Ulfur and Zadon, unmoving. The monsters reared their head, insulted at the refusal of his plans. His wolf shuddered in the corner of his mind. His voice deepened. "What would you suggest then, Cryon? The investigation has long since run cold. No sign, no divine intervention, no one has come forth to claim the throne."

He glared daggers around the table before adding. "To announce the missing powers would be tantamount to throwing our kingdom to Darius. We have all seen how he treats Drakore. Are you prepared to have that happen here? A small lie to the public, claiming it happened in private, protects us all. If you'd prefer, we can replace you so you are more comfortable."

Cryon exchanged another round of looks before shaking his head. "No, Sire. We will make it work."

"Excellent."

The rest of the meeting went through without a hitch, even as the required oaths were detailed. The ceremony was officially planned for three weeks in the future. He dismissed everyone, satisfied that he would forge his path despite the setbacks.

twenty

BALTHOR

BURA - PALION - YEAR 7568

There was a pronounced shift in the air, a heaviness never once felt in the Realm of the Dead. Balthor had lived around five centuries, and never in that time had he witnessed weather of any type occur within the overcast grayness of Dodsfell's existence.

A sudden thundering noise filled the air. Balthor stood from his desk, his steps quickening as he made his way outside. The noise built, becoming almost tangible. Static grew, causing his arm hair to rise. *What in the world?* He spun slowly, trying to find where the noise and electricity were coming from. No matter where he looked, he didn't see an explanation to the phenomenon.

A voice swam through the air—faint and tenuous—scattered through the breeze swirling around him. "Balthor? Balthor, save me!"

His blood filled his ears, pounding so hard he could no longer hear her. That voice belonged to one he hadn't spoken to since 7564, four years prior. He had left her believing that the Dulvak clan had matured as they had claimed. In return, he had released The Shadow Assassin. He had known of their failure and opted to wait for Aurelia to grow. She had to choose to set the world on fire. It had taken a few choice words to Estrez's heir, but eventually the correct moves were put in play, resulting in her release. How could he hear her now?

Suddenly, lightning began to strike. Balthor's mouth grew dry; something had gone terribly wrong. He didn't know what to do or where to go, an odd feeling for one his age. Her voice grew louder as if she stood next to him. "Balthor, how am I here?"

Balthor whipped around, shock ricocheting through him as a vapor cloud vaguely resembling the girl he had mentored clung together. Another lightning bolt hit the ground, the crackling snap causing her form to break apart.

"Wait!" He shouted into the air.

She rematerialized again. "What happened to me?" Her voice grew stronger. "I need to go back. I can't leave Maledic."

Balthor grunted. "Aurelia. What happened?"

"I was asleep. There was a pain in my hand." Her eyes darted down to where her hand should have been, but smoke was all that rested there now. "I woke up, but I didn't—couldn't—see anything. My body just reacted."

Gods strike him. He knew what had happened. Someone had used a Dodsfell crystal on her. How had they even gotten the crystals, let alone known how to use them? His mind scrambled. "Alright. It's alright. I will fix this."

He could feel her glare even if he couldn't see it. "Will you? You left me last time."

"I will explain. I swear I will. For now, hold still. I am going to trap your soul so I can return you to your body." He only hoped her body was still there for her soul to return to and not declared dead.

He could hear her sniffle. He saw two of the crystal clusters near him and moved quickly. Breaking off one large crystal spear, he turned to her. "This will feel uncomfortable, but it's the only way."

A sigh escaped. "Just do it."

He stabbed the vaporous apparition in its chest, holding the crystal tightly as it shuddered and jumped in his grip. He had long ago mastered the magic of the crystals. It had taken two centuries of study with a twisted mistress, but he had done the work needed to no longer fear the jutting rocks that littered his world. Aurelia screamed long and loud as her soul was sucked into the crystal. He shuddered, his own mind remembering his own screams that had echoed into the vast gray of Dodsfell all those years ago.

Once she was safely ensconced, he tucked it into his pocket. His mind ran over the next step. Swiftly, he entered his villa, throwing the necessities into a bag. When a cloak was secured around his shoulders, he blinked himself to the large and imposing gate near Tixdarr's temple.

The next part would be tricky; evading or manipulating the Gods always was. He unsheathed his dagger, slicing his palm and placing it against the hot magic. In a whisper, he muttered, "With this blood, I vow to use my powers in the name of Tixdarr."

There was a long pause, as if Tixdarr debated the legitimacy of the blood vow. Then the magic groaned, opening a hole that Balthor was only just able to squeeze through. As his feet landed on mortal soil, he forced his demon skin inward, compressing it into the much smaller body of his mortal shell, a process he hadn't done in at least three centuries. This wouldn't be fun; time in Baelia rarely was, but he would endure it for the betterment of one of the few creatures he'd ever called friend.

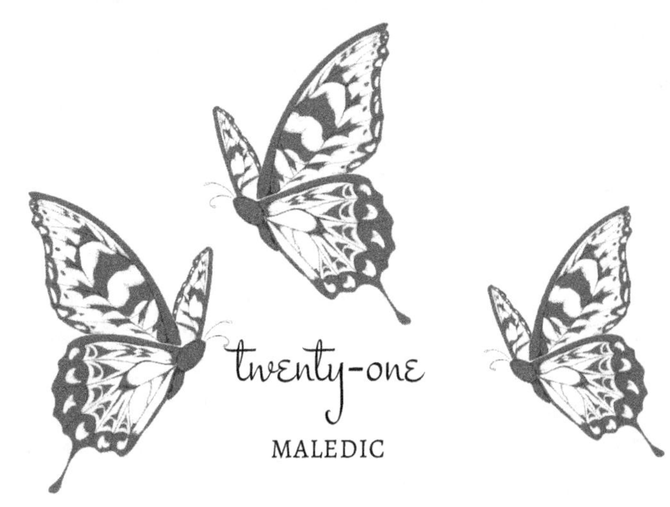

twenty-one

MALEDIC

Bura - Palion - Year 7568

He covered the night shift, refusing to give up his guard post to the woman who was called her sworn sword. The demon woman haunted Aurelia's chambers regardless, meditating, attempting to gain divine permission to enter Dodsfell.

The door opened of its own accord, leaving Mal convinced that he had entered a twisted dreamscape. Either that, or his lack of sleep had started giving him hallucinations. Nothing came through the door. A glance at Valri showed her still unmoving on the sofa. As the door clicked shut, the sound of the lock sliding home echoed through the room. Valri shot to her feet.

"Show yourself." Her voice was loud and demanding, snapping him out of his stupor.

He straightened in his seat. "Who?"

"We are no longer alone, Crow Man."

Mal huffed; he understood that much. He strode over to

Aurelia's side of the bed, standing with her sword at the ready. His body going tense as a deep chuckle bounced off the walls.

"How interesting that somehow you ended up in her service. I wonder how that happened."

There still wasn't a body to accompany the voice. Mal growled, his hand tightening on the hilt as Valri methodically strode through the space. His stomach rolled as his eyes darted around the room. Valri stalked forward, a woman on a mission.

The deep voice seemed to turn its attention on him. "I assume you must be Maledic. It is a pleasure to meet you. I knew her other half would be a strong, formidable male. I am happy to be proven correct."

Maledic growled. "I haven't met you. You need to show yourself to meet anyone."

Mal watched as Valri's eyes lit with glee. She grunted as she thrust the dagger into mid air, where nothing seemed to be there. Yet blood dripped, and the air rippled. A large man appeared with Valri's dagger buried in his side, a dark stain blooming across his shirt. "That was rather rude." The man appeared affronted, insulted even, though the lack of concern on the blade was disturbing.

"It was rude to appear in the Queen's rooms without express permission. Yet you felt entitled to such privilege and chose to conceal your identity." Valri then brought the dagger to her mouth and licked the blood from it. "And you're a demon!" It was an accusation that had Maledic stiffening.

"Is she the Queen? I was fairly certain that the coronation hadn't happened. Also, you don't need to state the obvious; you could just ask." He withdrew another one of those damn crystals that would haunt Maledic's nightmares for years to come.

Valri sucked in a deep breath. "How are you holding that

without gloves? How did you get here? How did you cross the barrier so quickly?"

"So many questions, so little time. What is most important—bringing her back or answering your questions?" The male rolled the crystal between his fingers.

Valri growled, poking at him with the dagger. "Name and clan. Then you can fix what's broken."

A smirk unfurled on the man's face. "You'll regret wanting to know this. Names have power, as you should know, Shadow Assassin."

Valri balked at that, but Mal didn't miss the glance she threw his way. "Name now."

"Balthor of the Ixdar Clan." A smirk on his face.

Valri's mouth dropped open, but she didn't comment as Mal expected; instead demanding. "Fix her."

Balthor winked before striding toward the bed. Maledic stayed where he was, sword out and ready. Balthor stopped in front of him bowing shortly. "Maledic, I can reunite you with your soulbond, but it will require you to stand over by the door. Ensure that no one interrupts us."

Mal huffed out a long breath. He brought up the sword, inwardly amazed it didn't shake with his nerves, pointing it at the man's throat. "She dies. You die."

Balthor nodded. "This won't kill her, but it won't be pleasant. Go guard the room, my friend."

Mal shook his head. "No. I stay with her. Valri has the door."

"Actually, I do." The damn annoying red-head had just closed the door behind herself and her wife.

"It's a bloody party now," Balthor muttered before looking back at Mal. "Alright. Sword down. Then climb up onto the bed. You're going to cradle her body and force her to maintain contact with the crystals."

Maledic hesitated long enough to see Valri nodding

encouragingly before climbing onto the bed. He gently maneuvered Aurelia so her back lay on his chest, her head under his chin. From this angle, he could see the red head putting her hands on the main door, vines pouring out to cover the door and walls. "Now no one will interrupt."

Balthor grunted a laugh. "The web gets more tangled."

He watched as Balthor brought up the crystal filled with a smoky black substance. He used the long stone to poke around the pile of rocks on the nightstand until he found the smoky match, a small one with the same substance swirling inside of it. Balthor met his gaze once more. "Don't touch them yourself. Only she will be able to. Unless..." The demon's voice trailed off. "Let me see your hands."

Maledic raised his hands, palms out. Balthor hummed low before moving fast—too fast for Maledic to track. A small stone landed in his hand. A sharp exhale left Valri's mouth, but Mal struggled to follow what happened. The stone was stinging but not painful. Yet Valri had launched knife after knife at Balthor, who had summoned some sort of invisible shield deflecting them, hunching a bit as the metal made contact with his magic.

"See, female. He's fine. Stop trying to poke me!"

Valri roared. "Poke you? I am going to kill you! You don't use crystals on anyone, let alone mortals."

Balthor grinned meeting Mal's confused gaze. "Ah, now female. You haven't been trained on the use of the crystal magic." He plucked the stone from Mal's still stunned palm.

"They dampen power, a process that should be eased into. This pile suggests she was doused in it. When it comes to touching the crystal, it is also something to be eased into, though we can all guess she was forced." Balthor opened Aurelia's hand, placing the smaller smoky stone into it, motioning Maledic to cover her hands with his. "Their bonding must be deep, because he has the burn. Therefore, he can wield the power as well." Balthor placed the larger crystal in Aurelia's other hand, nodding at Maledic to cover it. "Now Maledic needs to call her home."

Mal's mind blanked. *Call her home?* He could feel all eyes on him, but he nuzzled into her neck, whispering. "Aurelia, you need to come home now. You can't leave me with all these demons. Come home, my sassy Spréach."

Silence thickened, time ticking by. Then Aurelia's body began to twitch. A moan long and painful, emerged from her mouth. Her legs began to scissor, her body fighting to be released. Mal looked at Balthor, his eyes bulging, unsure what to do next.

Balthor nodded encouragingly. "Keep her hands closed on the crystals. She's returning to us."

Mal nodded, but as her body got more violent, he struggled to keep her hands closed. The red-head strode forward, dismissing the head shake of Balthor.

"Sparkles, grab her ankle."

Both women leaned over, holding her flailing limbs, making it easier for him to keep her hand closed. "Mr. Stranger, it's about time we introduced ourselves. I am Suzu and she's—"

"Perfectly capable of introducing herself." The quiet blonde bit out while glaring at Suzu. "I'm Belvina."

It took an eternity that boiled down to a few hours before Aurelia started to calm, and with that, Mal's heart rate started to come down. Aurelia curled into him, turning her body, forcing the women to let her go. Balthor cleared his throat.

"Reli, my dear. Have you returned to us?"

Mal glanced down at her, relief flooded him as first one and then both bright blue eyes locked onto him, before she turned to look at Balthor. "You look terrible as a mortal, B."

Balthor began to laugh. "Ever direct. Glad to see that hasn't changed."

Mal plucked the crystals up and put them on the night-stand. He caught the eye roll but froze as she nuzzled back into his chest. Her order was muffled, "Get rid of those, B."

Suzu cleared her throat, "Your Highness. I'm glad you've returned, but perhaps we should keep some in a safe space. If I had to guess, those who did this aren't proficient in that magic and could perhaps have a weakness to it."

Mal watched the gazes volley around each other. Balthor's grin widened. "Reli, you have found the most interesting friends. Perhaps this time in Baelia will be entertaining after all."

"We move in the morning. Suzu, Belvina, we need our own suite of rooms. Make it so." Aurelia was still issuing the order into his neck, and he did his best not to preen. His mind calmed the longer she stayed on him.

Suzu tapped her booted feet on the floor awkwardly. "We need to do oaths. You should know Ulfur vowed to Lucian. He's attempting to be a double agent."

Aurelia didn't even flinch at the idea of betrayal, but Mal beat her to speak. "Anyone in this room who betrays us will die for it."

He could feel her smile against his skin. "We will do formal vows in our new base of operations. Balthor and Valri are the only guards we have for now, so work together."

"Yes, work together. Not slice your new partner to ribbons." Balthor griped. Valri groaned.

"Everyone out. Guard duty can happen outside this room." Aurelia demanded. "I need actual sleep."

Mal caressed her back soothingly. "Sleep, Spréach. I won't let anyone near you until you're ready."

He felt her ease into sleep and felt whole for the first time in his adult life. She was safe. She was here. Together, they would battle for her crown.

twenty-two

AURELIA

Bura - Palion - Year 7568

The Dwarves live in the mountains, their ambitions to mine out precious metals and create a kingdom within the hulk of the land. When death finds them, their people hold a grand ceremony. It matters not what the person's class or place within the social strata. They all get wrapped in gold-embellished cloth, gemstones of all varieties tucked into their braids. Then the body is paraded through the tunnels to great fanfare until they reach the center of the mountain. The spot where lava lives and the forges function. The deceased would be gently eased into the lava, to give back to the mountain that gives so much to them.

~Ancient Death Rites, Margoth's Journal

She had allowed herself the one moment of weakness—sleeping safely wrapped in Maledic's arms. When the sun came, so did her strength, along with the resolution that Maledic must be kept safe from the evils within the Palion court. She pulled herself up without looking at him, choosing instead to mentally arm up. She used her time bathing and dressing to assess if anything was different since her souls hijacking. She was grateful that she was saved from any awkward interactions with Maledic by the appearance of Suzu.

"Your Highness." She bowed low. "I have worked with Rusk, the housekeeper, and the Southern Tower is completely unoccupied. There are three levels of bedchambers, and on the main level there's a huge ballroom and what used to be a library." Aurelia couldn't help but smile at the efficiency as she braided her still, damp hair.

"We need to get a hold of Lucian and Zadon to acquire my own household guards."

Suzu blinked, and Maledic glowered. "Do you trust anyone he gives you?" Suzu asked bluntly.

Aurelia laughed a bit. "Of course not, Suzu. But I will take note and meet with them alongside Balthor. Balthor will be able to tell who is trainable, and once we get around ten or so, we'll hold an oath-taking."

They both nodded. "While Balthor and I are busy, will you work with Belvina and Rusk to get us all moved over to the Southern Tower? I want the guards housed in the guardhouse, but all of the inner circle will have residences. Plus, perhaps Belvina can create an insignia for us, something people can rally around."

Suzu clapped. "Absolutely."

She left, exuding an air of excitement. Maledic stepped forward as if to embrace her but she stepped around him, arming up. "You need to go, Mal."

"Go? Go where?"

"Go home."

"I am home. I've waited ten years to find my home." He stood still, as if knowing that if he got too close, she would explode.

"You are now at risk. They will know you exist, and I can't do what I need to if I am constantly worried about you." She knew her words were harsh, but it was time to face their reality.

Balthor chose that moment to enter, a smirk on his face. "Reli, stop shoving your male away. I can taste the heartache from the hallway. You have to trust the Gods paired you well, and this man will care for you as well as himself."

Aurelia turned a glare on Balthor. "B. Did I ask you for your help?"

"Nope." The p annoyingly popping. "But males must stick together."

Maledic had his arms crossed over his chest. "I am going with you, Spréach. I will show you that I am worthy of you."

"It doesn't matter. Have the two of you forgotten I married Lucian? It doesn't matter how well matched we are." She stomped her foot before she realized how childish it looked.

"I have never asked for more than my advisor role, Spréach. Yet, you're shoving me away." She growled a bit, turning to the door.

"On your own head be it." She stomped down the hall, rolling her shoulders.

Balthor cleared his throat. "The Prince is in the Northern Council room."

Aurelia nodded, leading the men toward the inevitable explosion. She didn't bother knocking, striding in confidence in every step, throwing the double doors open, a smirk plastered to her face. Lucian and Zadon's look of complete shock thrilled her. "Hello, husband. Husband's pet."

Zadon growled, taking a menacing step forward. "How are you here?"

Balthor strode to the front, flashing a wide grin. "That is because of me, young Dulvak. It was quite a surprise to find my friend's soul wandering the other realm. It was only right to bring her home."

Zadon blinked. "Who are you?"

Balthor glanced back at her, an eyebrow raised. She nodded, a thrill racing through her. She knew that demons relied heavily on hierarchy, and Zadon was about to realize just how much power Balthor had. It took a mere moment for Balthor to take on his demon form, his red body vibrating with his immense power. Aurelia grinned as Zadon and Lucian took a step back.

"Husband, I am here because it's apparent I need personal guards. My parents aren't around to provide the full retinue that was my due as your bride; therefore, it falls to you to protect me—a duty you apparently need reminding of, seeing that my first night here someone tried to kill me."

Lucian cleared his throat. "It is within your right, as my wife, to have guards. Zadon can provide you with the names of two or three. You also need to understand that you can't just have independent control here, Aurelia." His condescending tone sank beneath her skin, causing an incessant itch to erupt. "You can't have just anyone in your entourage." He gestured dramatically at the still demon-sized Balthor, then pointed accusingly at Maledic.

Maledic moved to storm forward, but Aurelia held up a hand. In her palm, she called fire, nodding once when her hand was successfully coated in a warm, pleasant flame. "Did you know in Dodsfell, all mortal magic is stripped from you? It has been a fascinating feeling having the elemental magic I was destined to have intermingle with the death magic that grew fond of me there." Everyone's eyes were on her, so she dramatically tossed the fireball at the fireplace. "Sometimes control is questionable. It's such a blessing to have things that I can control. Balthor is my Captain of the Guards, and Maledic is my advisor." She turned, ready to leave, locking eyes with Maledic, seeing pride shining back at her. "Oh, and as Queen-to-be, I will have ten guards."

The sound of steel leaving a sheath had her turning back around, her whole body on high alert. Balthor, who had shifted back to his mortal self, had drawn his sword. "I can see the Dulvak personality did not get dampened by his time in the mortal realms."

Aurelia scanned the room, trying to understand what had happened. Lucian stared at the empty air, a dazed, confused expression on his face. A quick glance showed her Zadon had disappeared. She spoke quickly, fear gripping her insides, "Mal, shift now. Fly."

The pop from behind her told her he had listened. She whirled, her back to Balthor's as she pulled her sword.

"Perhaps we would have been more productive just going to the bunkhouse." Balthor's voice laced heavily with sarcasm.

"Duly noted. Can you sense him?" She knew one of Balthor's many powers revolved around sensing demons.

"You know, it hadn't occurred to me to try. Thank you so much for the suggestion, Reli. Without you, we would be lost."

She snorted a laugh, and Maledic issued a shrill whistle. Zadon must have a way to evade even Balthor's detection. Lucian remained muttering in the corner. An idea clicked in her mind. "Oh pet," She called loudly, knowing that due to the closed doors, he remained in the room. "Last time you crossed me, I took a hand. What shall I take next?"

"You took his hand? I wish I had seen that." Balthor's voice was laced with love.

Lucian cleared his throat. "We had an agreement. We would all work together."

She traded places with Balthor, now staring into Lucian's half-crazed eyes. "He tried to kill me!"

Lucian threw his hands up. "You took his hand!"

Coldness swept through her. "So a hand is worth my life?" She swept her sword up, holding it at his throat. "What is your life worth?" She saw an eagerness flicker through his gaze, but it was gone so fast she was half convinced she had imagined it. She pulled her sword back with a shake of her head. "My issue is with the pet, not you. Someday your eyes will open. Until then, understand that I will have my own court. I know there will be no Inheritance Rite, but we need to do a public coronation. For you, as well as, for me. I shall stand with you united, wearing Palion regalia, but the pet will be seated next to the crowd. Balthor will ensure it."

Balthor led her out of the room, Mal swooping out alongside them, leaving Lucian and his invisible pet to their own devices.

twenty-three

LUCIAN

After long weeks of tiptoeing around Aurelia and her paranoia, Lucian was pleased that coronation day was finally here. The palace just wasn't the same ever since the crystal incident, which made little sense to him since she'd only been inconvenienced for a day or two. Overly sensitive females.

The day dawned overcast, with the promise of sun and heat later—perfect to claim the throne that haunted him. Zadon had even promised that Aurelia would be busy in another section of the kingdom, representing his throne on such an auspicious day, just like a good wife should.

He dressed simply, knowing that Belvina had created an elaborately jeweled overcoat in butter yellow, a strip of dove gray around the edges. She claimed it signified him overcoming the dark and wearing the colors of Palion. Whatever the symbolism, the added embroideries and jewels made it into a woven masterpiece. It made sense that the rest of his attire would be basic.

He had even gone to the trouble of commissioning a crown to match Belvina's genius. Today brought him more joy than any other since the moment he lost his other half.

His pleasure grew as he realized the temple was full to bursting with people of all walks of life. A singular throne was placed where the altar had previously sat. He waited at the door for Oba Aewenna to give him the signal to walk toward his destiny. The only part of the scene in front of him that didn't line up was Zadon. He was already seated closest to the throne, but his body was angled off to the side. Something in the wings distracted his attention.

It made Lucian's mind crawl a bit. After all, Zadon had worked just as hard as Lucian had. Zadon should reap the joy as well. An acolyte in light green robes cleared her throat, causing Lucian to jump slightly. He returned his gaze to Oba Aewenna and realized he had missed his cue. His face flushed, but he straightened the jacket and strode forward, ready for his reward.

twenty-four

SUZU

Tiv - Palion - Year 7568

"Stop fidgeting!" She straightened the voluminous skirt once more.

"I. Hate. Dresses." Aurelia stomped her booted foot, her curled hair flipping over her shoulder.

She wore an intricate dress in dove gray, covered with delicate butter-yellow embroidery, jewels flirting with thread over the delicate gems across the entire bodice and down the skirt, the glimmering almost like tears.

Belvina worked tirelessly to make the coronation gown an exact mirror to Lucian's own outfit. When standing next to one another, they would match quite well.

"This was your idea, Aurelia," Suzu reminded her with a mock glare. She watched as Aurelia rolled her eyes before straightening her shoulders, determination taking root.

Belvina jogged—as best as someone could while wearing spiked heels. "He's in position! You need to go. NOW! Valri is signaling the orchestra to introduce you."

"Let's go. I would hate to miss the show." Aurelia followed Belvina, a mask of pure, innocent joy on her face.

Suzu marveled at Aurelia's ability to throw on a completely false mask. She hurried along the wings of the church to the front row, sliding down to sit opposite Zadon. Lucian glanced at her, his eyebrows furrowed in confusion. She sent a smile and mouthed *sorry* before sitting contritely.

The musicians struck up once more, causing Lucian to spin around, shock fully present on his face. She swallowed her smile as she turned to look at the doors. There, Aurelia stood in all her glory.

A gasp and then a small cheer started near her and soon rippled through the room. While everyone watched Aurelia, Suzu watched Lucian. It took almost too long for him to school his features, which rolled through confusion and then hatred. By the time Aurelia made it to his side, he had donned a neutral facial expression.

Suzu struggled to stifle her grin as Oba Aewenna stepped forward. Her magic amplified her voice as she approached the royal pair. "Your Highnesses, what an honor it is to bestow the treasured posts of King and Queen."

Lucian leaned closer to Aewenna, muttering quickly as Aurelia beamed. Aurelia's voice rose, drowning out Lucian's obvious anger and frustration.

"It is such an honor to be welcomed to this kingdom as its Queen, especially after such immense personal tragedy."

Lucian shot a broken glare at her before he stiffened and stood back a bit. Aewenna shook her head subtly at Lucian, drawing a ceremonial knife from her belt. Lucian's cold voice rang out, interrupting her movements and drawing Aurelia's attention.

"I thought you had a task elsewhere, wife." His growl was loud enough to penetrate the first few rows of spectators. Suzu could feel them all lean in, intent on the drama unfolding.

"I did find it rather odd you tasked me so far away on the day we get our crowns. You know the one thing I was told to help you obtain." She shrugged, flipping her curled tresses off her shoulder and shooting the crowd a warm smile. "Thus, I assumed it was an oversight. I know there have been communication issues between you and your associate." She reached out a hand imploringly. "I came to help, just like you told me when we reconnected. Remember? When I was brought back to Palion?"

Suzu could hear the mischievous glint in her tone while Lucian was beginning to turn purple, his skin mottling.

"Lucian. Dear husband. You must remember to breathe." Aurelia crossed the short distance, her hands clasping around his arm, in what looked like a caress. Aewenna muttered back to an acolyte, who left at a dead run. She also approached the purpling man.

"Sire?"

Lucian let out a strangled breath, coughing and stumbling as he yanked away from Aurelia. "No. This is mine. You will have Drakore."

"Now, now, husband," She ground out his title. "You agreed, on pain of an oath, to keep me happy. You also implied I would be crowned here as well. How does the oath feel, knowing how greatly distressed I am?" Her face fell into a pitiful pout.

The acolyte returned with a med witch, standing to the side, ready to aid if needed. Lucian's hand went involuntarily to his side, gripping as if he had a painful stitch from running.

The crowd inside the temple went deathly silent, unsure what to do now that both proposed leaders fought so openly against each other.

Aurelia stood looking demure and gorgeous while Lucian visibly fumed, his anger potent. Oba Aewenna stepped forward once more, placing herself between them both, the dagger having been sheathed amongst the arguing.

"Goddess Tiva can recognize the stress of this moment and implores you both to search within yourself for what will make you happy. Princess Aurelia, what will placate you the most?"

"I will have my thrones."

Oba Aewenna swallowed once, nodding. "What will you sacrifice to Prince Lucian for that privilege?"

Aurelia chuckled darkly, bringing her hand up to cover her mouth, fully selling her innocent act. Suzu's awe grew. Aurelia leaned over and whispered words for Oba Aewenna alone. Whatever was said was enough for her eyes to widen and her caramel skin to pale.

She nodded and turned to Lucian. "What do you want, Prince Lucian?"

"I want my inheritance!"

"Excellent. All of this can be obtained if we continue forward. If you would both stand here, please."

Oba Aewenna gestured imperiously. Aurelia settled in exactly where she was directed, her back showing the elaborate oath wings to the crowd. Suzu watched Lucian's face as he struggled to accept his new reality. His steps were slow, and she didn't miss the glare Lucian sent to Zadon.

Oba Aewenna, however, captured the crowd's attention, her voice amplifying magic, letting her words roll to all corners of the temple.

"Ladies and Gentlemen of Palion, Goddess Tiva and I welcome you to this auspicious event. It's the first crowning of a Queen since our beloved Larial. Prince Lucian has waited for a long time to find a partner in rule, and it's quite fortuitous that it happens to be the long lost Aurelia Berrid, Princess of Drakore."

Oba Aewenna turned her attention to Lucian. "Everyone

in this glorious room knows Prince Lucian. Goddess Tiva knows how long you have waited and all that you have endured to get it. I am proud that we have finally reached the day we could proclaim you, King Lucian."

The crown was lowered first to Lucian's head, and his face glowed with joy. The crowd stormed to its feet, the room deafening with the cheers and whoops of excitement.

Oba Aewenna lowered herself to the ground in a bow as her second in command, an acolyte, lowered a crown to Aurelia's brow. Suzu watched with bated breath, knowing this would be a moment not to miss.

As the metal circlet settled onto her head, a sharp shrill tone filled the air. Silence fell as everyone slammed their hands over their ears, searching for the sound. The ground began to shake, and Suzu grabbed the pew, her eyes glued to the scene unfolding.

Aurelia's face had grown tense, almost pained, while Lucian spun, trying to find the threat. The whine grew in intensity, causing the glass of the windows to shatter. Shards rained down, glinting in the sunlight. The shaking swelled. Aurelia doubled over, a scream tearing from her throat, hands clutching at her stomach. A crow landed next to her, quickly shifting into her soulbond, Maledic. He crouched in pain, his focus remaining solely on her.

Lucian rushed them, demanding answers, but no one seemed to have any. Maledic put himself between Lucian and Aurelia. Her scream tapered off to a whine, her wide eyes found Suzu. Suzu clearly made out the word being mouthed to her. "Run"

As Suzu's brain registered the word, it became clear it was too late. Aurelia flung her arms wide, a scream escaping swiftly, right before her body was replaced in a blink by a large and very angry dragon-shaped creature.

"Oh Gods." Suzu turned to the people nearest her. "Run! Get out! MOVE NOW!!"

She turned back to the front just as Aurelia's shifted form swallowed a screaming acolyte.

Maledic shifted back into a crow, circling her head, trying to lead her up to a high window and out into the night, fully risking himself. Lucian had also shifted into his Alpha Wolf, taking charge of the screaming attendees.

Suzu ignored the chaos, staring at the creature Aurelia transformed into. It was a dragon shape, but what should have been glorious scales was instead a vaporous skeleton, the skin hanging as if decaying. The wing membranes were transparent and torn. Jagged scars and evidence of holes having been ripped into her echoed across her skin. Suzu's heart broke at the visual representation of the pain Aurelia must have endured.

Her concentration was broken by a large red-demon barreling toward the throne. "AURELIA!"

twenty-five

AURELIA

Tiv - Palion - Year 7568

Pain ricocheted through her head. Her mind refusing to stop pulling her into the dark recesses, the places locked away. It replayed scenes in the dungeon with Estrez and her beloved knife. She lunged to the side as if dodging the blade.

She threw her head back, screaming—though it sounded wrong, more like a rumbling roar and not her mortal one. Her vision was red-tinged and a different scream drew her attention. She wasn't able to control herself; she just needed to stop the screaming. Her giant head swooped, her jaw swallowing the sound.

A black streak flew across her vision, cawing loudly. Emotions filled her, and her brain couldn't—or wouldn't—come back online. Instead, her body moved on instinct, following the little speck upwards, needing the tasty snack. Just as her body left the ground, a bellow drew her head back to the main chamber. "Aurelia!"

Her head swayed as it tried to focus on the large red mass

barreling towards them. The black spot flew around her head again, trying to pull her upwards.

"Maledic stop! We need her to realize what's happening. Her mind, body, and soul are in transition. She has to choose to live, to be mortal."

A pop drew her eyes downward.

"What do you mean? As soon as we get her calm, she'll shift back. It's her first shift, Balthor. This is normal."

"Does that look normal, Crow Man? Her soul is being torn apart by the death magic. The magic is finally taking its price, her shifted form."

"That makes no sense, Balthor!"

"Her shifted form is a Gods—damned Wraith Dragon. Dodsfell has affected her more than any of us realized."

She roared, not recognizing the creatures in front of her. She turned from them intent on the sound of screaming that had begun once more near her. She scooped up the source of the noise, taking pleasure in the squelching silence.

Her attention was once more redirected, this time as vines wrapped around her form, forcing her body to the ground. She roared again, thrashing as memories of chains and dark dungeons filled her mind. A feeling of power swelled under her skin.

Balthor roared, "Everyone, brace for impact or get out. She's likely to bring the building down!"

She wanted freedom, silence—peace. All she ever got was pain, forced into a life she didn't even want. The power swelled, but she didn't know how to release it; all that happened was the building once more shook.

A woman's voice broke through. "Maledic, slice your palm and place it on her snout. She's turning fully into a wraith. You have to remind her of your connection, or you will lose her forever."

Aurelia snapped her jaws, daring anyone to touch her. The

vines tightened around her body; her wings tried flapping, but to no avail. She couldn't see much directly in front of her, but she could smell the pine as a man approached, and the coppery scent of blood filled her nostrils. She flicked out her tongue. The air smelled so good; perhaps she could just eat the annoying mortal.

She felt tingling heat as he placed his bloodied hand on her nose. But nothing else happened; she still stayed lashed to the ground, her annoyance growing.

"It's not working! Get Lucian, he ties her to this plane as well."

The women gasped, and Aurelia could feel a slackening in the vines. Her mind raced at the possibilities. As the mortals scrambled, Aurelia pushed her muscles out, doing her best to be as large as possible, creating much needed space.

"Who is making these vines?" A new gruff voice joined the crowd. He smelled of lemon and rose.

"Just slice your palm and join Maledic. The rest will be sorted later." The red mass forced the gruff male to her head. She snapped at him. The scent of fear wafting off him tasting better with each passing moment.

She tested her plan, focusing her attention on her tail. She moved it up and down and was pleased to note some space. She used all her strength and thrust her tail toward the sky.

The vines snapped, and Aurelia felt joy intermixed with sharp pain. The effect was instantaneous. The women shrieked, and the red mass bellowed. "Touch her! Bring back our girl before she loses her soul for good."

Lucian grumbled, but his palm landed next to Maledic's.

The sensation of falling from a great height filled her, fear lodging in her throat. She opened her mouth and let out all the feelings built within her—the pain, the terror, the anger. Her body felt odd, like it was being stretched then squeezed, forced into a particular shape. Her eyes felt hot, the pressure building.

She closed her eyes as water began leaking out of them. She didn't register the hands leaving her, but she did feel arms encircling her. She blinked away the tears, her eyes clearing as Maledic's scent filled her nose.

"What... What happened?" She tried to step back, but Mal's arms tightened.

"You shifted."

She shook her head. "I don't have a shifted form."

"You do now. You told me a long time ago you would get your form when you were crowned."

She shuddered. Warmth began to creep into her face as she looked beyond Mal's shoulder and saw an array of fear—filled citizens.

She whispered into his chest, "What have I done?"

Balthor stepped in, blocking the other faces. "You did what your instincts told you—and you showed us a lot more."

"Yeah. That I am an unhinged monster."

Mal's body stiffened as he shook his head, his hands stroking up her back.

"You showed us that you died there. Your shifted form is a dead dragon—a dragon that has become a wraith. Your soul isn't fully alive anymore, Reli. You will have to learn what that means. Now we know why the death magic likes you so much. Your soul is dead, or mostly, while your essence remains alive. The perfect toy for its chaotic energy."

Aurelia couldn't stop the tears that flowed. Her sniffling muffled into Maledic's chest. Lucian's voice came out clearly, the notes of smugness evident. "Well, I may have been resistant to your crowning, but it went far better than I thought possible. Now the Palion people see the monster I've seen all along."

Balthor growled menacingly. "You may be the King now,

but if you continue to insult my Queen and friend, I will end you."

Lucian scoffed as he left, heading out of the temple. Maledic leaned down, whispering. "You are not a monster. At the end of the day, what you believe is all that matters."

She wrapped her arms around him, taking just a second of peace while he offered it. Slowly, she nodded.

"Let's go home. Away from all the prying eyes." Maledic's words made sense, but she had to walk through the crowd of cowering Palion citizens. Balthor leaned over Maledic's shoulder.

"Head up. You're a Queen now; their thoughts won't matter in the long run. You have bigger problems. So deep breath, square your shoulders, and don your mask, Queen Aurelia."

Maledic stiffened as if to protest, but Aurelia knew he was right. She withdrew her arms and stood tall, her face sliding into the courtly expression of earlier.

Belvina stepped forward, pulling out a kerchief and dabbing at Aurelia's mouth, cleaning the remnants of whoever she had eaten. Belvina straightened her dress and nodded, stepping out of the way.

Aurelia smiled and avoided the look of anguish still on Maledic's face. Instead, she walked forward, mentally noting each person who rushed out of her way. Time would tell.

part two

DRAGON BONDS

THE DRAKORE TIE

As dragons dwindled and the mortals realized the Gods true intent. A committee was created. That committee consisted of powerful shifters who attempted to solidify the future of magic. Feginth, the Dragon of Life, volunteered to be tied to the reigning family in Drakore. The hope being that the shifter family tied to the sky would be the best option to keep her and the future of the species safe.

twenty-six

DARIUS

DRAK - DRAKORE - YEAR 7568

> *Panthers are some of the most secluded creatures.*
> *Their death ritual is a closely guarded secret, but*
> *what is important to note is that it is done per*
> *family unit. Lone panthers are rare, as they are*
> *always welcomed back into their original family*
> *unit.*
>
> *~Ancient Death Rites, Margoth's Journal*

As soon as he was able, he dropped Faziel in a whimpering heap on the forest floor. They were just outside of Drakore, and her pitiful whimpers were making his ears bleed.

Her oddly faithful guard, Notus, bent over her crumpled form, easily maneuvering her into a makeshift swing. Darius glared. "Did I say she was supposed to be picked up?"

Notus stiffened, gently lowering her back into the dirt, his face a neutral mask, though Darius didn't miss the tightening fists nor the way Faziel clung to him. Khal, the other guard, stood at attention waiting. Notus joined Khal, doing his best not to look at Faziel.

"We need to get her to the physicians. I want Khal to touch her, and only Khal. Though you both shall carry the sling so that I no longer have to listen to her nonsense."

Notus straightened up his chin, jutting out. "I can carry her easily enough, leaving Khal to aid you in notifying the palace of how the battle went."

Darius took two strides forward, putting himself nose to nose with the bastard. "I did not ask your opinion, scum. If you know what's good for you, you will do your best to disappear from my attention."

Notus clenched his hands and stepped back. Darius glared at him and then motioned to Khal to situate his sniveling wife. Once she was settled—moaning all the way—they took off into the sky, flying straight to the palace.

***

Darius landed with a grunt. "Notus, get Gerard and Kygoss, then meet me in my office. Khal, take the bitch to the healing wing."

They left, and Darius ground his heels as he stomped toward his office. He threw his body into his chair, anger and shock flowing through him.

She was alive.

Her eyes brought the memories of Cerial slamming into his mind. Their eyes had always been the same. Although the eyes he had looked into in the temple had been hardened—a side Cerial's had never achieved—perhaps the world would have hardened her as well.

He had always been fond of Aurelia for Cerial's sake, and the part of him who could remember needed to know what had put that look there. His thoughts were brought to a screeching halt as the door opened and his assistant and spy master came into the room.

They both stood waiting, knowing well that, should they move without permission, they could expect to be put into his pit. Fear was all that kept him on the throne, and his inner self quaked at that. He had never, in a million years, wanted to be feared like his father. Yet the Gods put him in the position.

"Aurelia is alive." He watched for reactions, but neither moved. "The tips Kygoss provided brought us the truth. For that, Old Bird, you have earned a bit of breathing room despite your constant nagging over the Bitch. We were, however, too late to stop the wedding. My powers could sense the Power of the Land, but not from either of them. Something foreign came from her, and the Pup has the same pitiful levels of power as before."

Kygoss rubbed his chin. "So they married but didn't complete the Rite? Was Harold there?"

Darius swallowed back his demand for silence, his mind instead thinking over the audience. "No. He wasn't there—but the power was I am sure of it. The Power of the Sky sang in my veins in a way that has never happened before."

Kygoss nodded, opening his mouth to comment, but paled as his eyes fell back to the ground. Gerard stepped up and cleared his throat. "So Harold has to be dead, right?"

"Yes." Darius hit the desk in frustration. His long-term goals now twisted out of his reach.

Kygoss, still staring at the floor, cleared his throat. "What happened to Queen Faziel?"

Darius growled, hating the Bitch to the depths of his soul. A part of him knew why Kygoss had done what he did, but he still blamed the Old Bird for being chained to the manipulative witch. "What does she say about the incident?"

He knew that the spy had gone to her first. Kygoss had an

unexplainable attachment to the girl. He watched as Gerard sidled left, putting space between the two. "She claims Aurelia did it, but that girl couldn't hurt a fly. She was kind."

Darius could feel his nails cutting into his palms. "For once, Faziel speaks the truth. Aurelia sliced her wing off rather than try and talk. She has become quite formidable in her time away."

Kygoss took a few steps back, as if physically pushed. "Oh."

"Now go make sure the Bitch heals. I have to make new plans." Darius waved them out as he strode to his window, contemplating how to pull off the next step as smoothly as possible.

twenty-seven

DARIUS

DRAK - DRAKORE - YEAR 7568

He watched the sunrise, his entire night spent staring into the darkness, trying to figure out how to get Aurelia alone. He had to talk to her, even if ropes and gags were involved. For Cerial, he had to talk to her. As the sun peeked over the trees in the distance, a knock came at the door. He grunted, his patience with words and people nearing its end. He turned toward the door to see a timid medic twisting his robes in his hands.

"Sire. Uh. I've been sent because—well—because Her Majesty isn't recovering as expected. You are needed."

Darius' mind blanked. If she died, his way forward would be less rocky; however, his kingdom would be in shambles, making it less desirable in the end. He rubbed his temples, his heart aching, needing to ask Cerial what he should do. "Take me to her."

The medic nodded, leading him toward the infirmary. The head physician met them at the threshold, but it didn't distract Darius from seeing Notus clutching Faziel's hands and kissing her brow.

That. Bitch.

The physician pulled Darius into his office. "Sire. What administered the injury?"

"A sword." He was nonplussed; there had been zero indication her sword was special.

"I see. Apparently, magic coats the blade in such a way that it prevents the wound from healing. Her saving grace in all of this is that she is tied to the Great Power, which is keeping her from bleeding out. However, I can't address her pain unless we can remove the magical barrier that is currently in the wound."

"So she will get even whinier. Is there a potion that will help?" He pulled his hair, needing Cerial; she would have known the answer.

The physician paused, weighing his words. "She would have to consent."

"She will." Darius walked over to the room where his wife lay, the bloody, gauze-covered stump beginning to perfume the air. Her face now held the pinched look of constant pain, her hair oily and unkempt. It sent satisfaction unfurling into his soul. Seeing Notus draped over her like a love sick fool hardened his resolve. He wasn't an idiot; she had found her soulbond. Yet, if she thought she would get to keep hers when he had been forced to give his up, she was mistaken.

"Notus, I gave you orders that would put you away from here. Why, pray tell, have you ignored my direction?" Darius' darkness begged to play, the despair always lurking in his mind, ready to shield his softer side from the world.

Notus tried to stand, but Faziel tightened her grip, her eyes narrowed defiantly on Darius. Darius merely smirked darkly, throwing the challenge back at her. "You won't win this, no matter how much you squirm and whine. You may as well save his life by letting go; otherwise, he can die in your arms. Choice is yours."

Tears filled her eyes, but the hard, calculating glint hadn't left. Slowly, she pulled her hands off him, her body spasming with sobs. Notus stood staring at Darius, his face a mask. "You, guard, are now assigned to the dungeons. There will no longer be a reason for you to be near my wife." He ground out the last word, glaring into the harpies eyes as she ground her own teeth. Notus dropped a bow before exiting quickly.

"Now, wife, you will take whatever medicine the physician requires, or I will force it down your throat." The physician brought a dark green vial forward, the smell like rotten eggs.

"This, Your Highness, will hopefully expel the foreign magic from the stump and thus speed healing."

She gagged as the smell reached her nose. "No. Please. Darius, don't make me."

He merely crossed his arms and glared. She tossed her head a few times, tears pouring from her eyes. Darius allowed the nonsense to continue for a few minutes before he growled, "Enough." He stalked towards the bed, capturing her bloody stump in one hand. She screamed as he pushed on the wound. "Open your damn mouth."

She complied, but not without a glare designed to kill. The physician stepped in, dripping the viscous liquid down her throat without meeting anyone's gaze. Once the vial of stinking liquid was empty, Darius released the stump. Her blood staining his already deeply marked skin, without a backward glance, he strode to the dungeons, needing to balance his mind. He had to stay level to approach the Aurelia situation calmly, as Cerial would have wanted. After all, Aurelia was her favorite person.

twenty-eight

DARIUS

Drak - Drakore - Year 7568

Darius walked right into Kygoss, his mind occupied with how to overcome the many obstacles to get Aurelia alone.

"Sire?"

"Old Bird, yes. I need you to call a council meeting immediately."

Kygoss blinked twice before bowing and running off. Darius continued on his way to the deepest dungeon. Once there, he took note of Notus standing at attention, his face full of anger. Darius walked the cages, his magic touching each inhabitant as he chose the next victim for the pile. He had figured out the Arena was the best way for him to reign in his despair and madness over Cerial; he aimed to use it in the only way she would have approved of. Criminals were the obvious choice, but those quickly grew scarce, so he resorted to terminally ill or injured. His magic could feel the vitality of each soul it touched, and he only chose the sickest. As the years had passed, he had done his best to increase his ability to go longer between punishments. Barring triggering episodes such as meeting Aurelia again, he managed to go two weeks between trips to the Arena.

An elderly eagle shifter huddled in the corner, his breath quivering in his chest.

Darius pointed. "This one."

Notus and another guard strode over, grabbing the man roughly and manhandling him into the Arena by shoving between his shoulder blades.

Darius slipped in before the door shut and the guards locked them in together. The man glared at him defiantly, choosing not to shift. Darius smirked. "It goes quicker the other way, you know."

The man's eyes widened and his throat bobbled. The prisoner crossed his arms over his chest in silent refusal. Darius chuckled while unstrapping two daggers, launching one at the prisoner's feet. Disappointment flared as the man continued to refuse to fight, choosing to just stand there, arms crossed.

Darius strode forward, stabbing into the man's bicep, eliciting a groan of pain. Growling, he sliced down, opening the arm. "You know you won't survive much longer. The sickness has taken hold in your chest. You should go into the Void as a warrior. Fight for your place, just like all the rest."

The older eagle shifter glared, stooping to pry the spare dagger out of the wooden planks with his good arm. Pleasure spiked through Darius at the idea that he wouldn't have to fully slaughter an immobile man. The elderly man lowered himself begrudgingly into a fighting stance. Darius grinned, following his opponent into a guard stance. The battle was indeed worthy of the male's place in the Void. He got to fully exercise the madness that his disgusting wife brought out in him. When the man's energy began to flag, Darius made the death swift taking his knife and slicing deep across the man's throat, life flowing from him.

Darius straightened, prying the knife from the man's loosened fingers. He tucked the blades into their sheaths before leveraging the man's corpse into his arms. He carried the body out of the dungeon through the darkened tunnel to a large pit that he had commissioned years ago. He tossed the body in, nodding to the guard whose sole job was to ensure that no one stole the bodies for Dodsfell internment.

H e entered the council room, his emotions finally nearing calm. That calm was threatened by the near-empty room. Kygoss sat at his spot, his wife Maie, sitting next to him, representing the crows. The bumbling fool in charge of the sparrows was also seated. He scanned and saw that there was a member of the Flightless clan seated, but no one else.

"Where is everyone?"

Kygoss stood. "Gerard is off to figure it out, but the notices were sent."

Wulfric, the Flightless Clan Leader tapped the table. "We have to consider that they are preparing to join Aurelia, which will lead us right into a civil war."

Darius turned abruptly, punching the wall next to him. "For fuck's sake. Can you not give me a chance to fix this before the whole bloody kingdom comes apart at the seams!"

Maie cleared her throat. "How would you fix it?"

"I would tell you, Great Lady, but your husband would likely die trying to aid me in my quest." He stalked to his seat. "Send out the guards and bring me the leaders of the missing clans. They will answer for their insolence."

Kygoss stood, a short bow to him, and kissed Maie's temple before he left the room. Darius growled at the remaining council members. "I want you all to plan—including the others who are not here—to welcome your rightful Queen. I know she is what everyone wants, and whether you believe me or not, I want her as well."

Maie cleared her throat. "I shall make sure the kingdom welcomes her once we have her safely home."

Darius nodded once, not trusting his words as he stood and walked to the door, needing a break from people.

twenty-nine

DARIUS

DRAK - DRAKORE/VOID - YEAR 7568

Sleep overtook him fast, the stress of the past two days pulling him under. Yet the dreams that normally haunted him, those with his beautiful blonde love, morphed. Darkness obscuring everything. He could feel his heart beat increasing, anxiety pulling at him. He couldn't handle the nightmares right now, not on top of it all.

A sinister, skin-crawling chuckle emerged from the impenetrable dark. "Don't want to see her die again tonight? Pity. She died so well."

A snap echoed in his mind and then light flooded in, making him recoil. In his mind's eye sat an unimposing man. Something about the man had Darius on edge, but he couldn't tell what.

The man gestured and a couch appeared in the overly white space. "Do you miss her?"

"Who?" Darius didn't know why he was compelled to speak, but he couldn't stop the words from leaving his mouth.

"Cerial Berrid, of course. You spend enough time thinking about her."

Darius lowered himself into the couch and asked, his mouth going dry at the implications. "Who are you? How do you know what I am thinking about?"

"Ah. That is a rather long story. But I am a man with means. Perhaps I can work out a way to make your dreams come true."

The hair rose on Darius' arms, triggering two warring thoughts. *How could that happen in a dream? This couldn't be simply any man.* "She's dead. What you are implying is impossible."

"My dear son. Nothing is truly impossible. That is not the right way to go about thinking. Try again." The man crossed his ankle over his knee, waiting patiently.

Darius rubbed his temple; no matter how he went about it, he came to the same conclusion. "It is impossible. There is no other possibility."

"Stubborn one. Alright. What do you need most in life right now?"

Darius spoke on instinct. "I need to get Aurelia to talk to me."

"Interesting. So your biggest request is not to be reunited with your soulbond?"

Nausea swept through him at even the idea. "She's dead. I won't tolerate you throwing around such an impossibility—even in a dream."

"Oh, that is the rub. You think this is merely a dream to be forgotten upon the rising sun. Lets fix that, then we can discuss business."

The man lifted his hand, and a searing pain—enough to wake anyone—lanced through his head. Darius gripped his temples, groaning loudly, his breath coming out in pants. "Make. It. Stop."

"Do you still think this is a dream?"

The pain intensified, eliciting a scream. Darius managed to shake his head once, his vision starting to fade. "No."

Suddenly, the pain ceased.

"Now that we have settled that, let's begin again. What do you want most?"

Darius panted, his brain struggling to process the simple question. "I want Cerial. I've only ever wanted Cerial."

"That's what I thought. Now what will you pay to make that happen?"

Darius didn't hesitate. Any price would be well worth it. "Anything."

"I want Aurelia."

The blood drained from Darius' face as dread descended. "I can't."

"You just claimed you would pay anything."

"If I give you her sister, she will never forgive me." Tears pricked at his eyes at the thought of her distress.

"Interesting. Mortals and your ethical qualms. Alright, instead of Aurelia, I shall take something from you—but I won't tell you what it is. No one can claim I am unreasonable; I do know how to bargain."

Darius' throat felt constricted as he stared at the man. "Who are you?"

"Someone capable of releasing your great love to you. That's all that matters, after all, isn't it?" After an elongated pause, the man sighed heavily, merely snapping his fingers.

Cerial, in all her glory, stood before him, a large smile on her face. She opened her mouth, her eyes beginning to spill over, but no sound emerged. Darius stood, closing the distance, but as he tried to touch her, to reassure her, his hand went right through her. Cerial turned a hateful gaze to the stranger.

"I won't release her voice or essence to you until I know

your decision. What will it be, Darius Svenston, son of Rayner, soulbonded to Cerial Berrid? Will you give me whatever I want from you? Or shall I release her?"

Darius couldn't tear his eyes from his true love. "Yes. You can have whatever you want from me."

"I really must be rusty in the ways of mortals. A helpful hint to you, my lad: take what she treasures most, and then she will do what you want. I mean, look at you." The man strode over, standing behind Cerial. "Darius, look at me."

Darius forced his eyes up, meeting the glowing yellow eyes. *Glowing yellow eyes? When had that happened?*

The man began to grow, expanding to nearly nine feet tall, his skin becoming pebbled and vibrant red. He didn't have time to scream, Darius' mind stuttering over the horns and wings. Faster than his eyes could track, the taloned fingered hand shot through the ghost vision of Cerial and into him. The pain searing hot into his chest, causing him to black out.

* * *

The world came into blurry focus as sleep released him. Something on his chest ached like fire. He blinked, his hands involuntarily touching his chest, only to cause a hiss of pain, his fingers came away sticky with what looked suspiciously like blood.

He leveraged himself up, heading to the bathing chamber, only to stand staring in shock at his body. His tunic had a gaping hole, and his chest had a crescent-shaped scar, jagged and raw, still dripping blood. His stomach rumbled. He forced his feet to move, an inner need demanding he bathe himself of the blood to release the dregs of the awful, half remembered dream.

As he crossed back into his bed chamber, a knock sounded on his door. "What?" He growled, his throat oddly hoarse.

"Sire?"

"Enter, for Gods sake." He rubbed his blood-stained fingers over his throat and grimaced. He needed to pull himself together.

Notus entered, confusion and apprehension on his face. "Sire, are you alright?"

Darius' hunger rose, as if Notus carried a platter of steaming meats, only he didn't. "What do you mean, Notus?"

"You've been missing for three days. We haven't been able to reach this room, as if there was some sort of magical barrier. Kygoss has been running the Kingdom with Faziel—I mean, the Queen's help. I started to hear screaming an hour ago, but I couldn't get through until just now."

A pounding filled Darius' head, rhythmically.

...ba boom ba boom ba boom...

Something niggled his brain. He knew that pounding sound. Notus came closer, clearing his throat. "Sire?"

"What?" Gritted Darius.

...ba boom ba boom ba boom...

"I asked if you would like something sent up from the kitchens... or if you needed the Arena."

The sound grew louder the closer Notus got to Darius. A tantalizing scent emerging from Notus' very pores. Darius couldn't stop his feet; a need much greater than he had ever experienced before filling his core. Notus stilled, fear coating his smell with a tang of salt. His hands came around the man's throat.

"What... Are... You?" Choked Notus.

...ba boom ba boom ba boom...

"I can't stop myself. I have to." Darius opened his mouth, fangs elongating as the hunger peaked. Acting completely on instinct, Darius sank his fangs into Notus' neck, drawing on the blood that gushed free. He fed violently, not worrying about the state he could be leaving Notus in at the end. When the hunger finally eased, Notus' head barely clung to his neck. The once strong-column now a mess of minced meat and his body drained of the vital life blood.

A sickening, familiar voice echoed loudly into Darius' mind. "Very well done. This little adjustment to the mortal condition will prove to be quite entertaining. Your spy knows who to capture to gain the girl's attention."

Darius threw Notus' corpse off him, staring in horror at what he had done. He had killed his first truly innocent man. Putting him on the same level as his father.

"No." He shook his head, stumbling back to the bathing chamber, only to scream at the bloody face that peered back at him from the mirror. He punched the reflective surface, determined to destroy the man staring back at him. Punch after punch, leaving him sobbing in a room surrounded by splintered glass.

thirty

DARIUS

TIV - DRAKORE - YEAR 7568

> *The Alpha leads the wolf pack on their mourning journey, focusing on what the deceased person did for the pack. Due to their mind-link capabilities and the vastness of their numbers, ceremonies tend to happen at the end of each day for those who were lost. The bodies of those lost are attended by their families, wrapped in fine linen, and placed upon a pyre after the Alpha has made his statements.*
> *~Ancient Death Rites, Margoth's Journal*

It had taken a few weeks to come to terms with his new blood craving. Once the panic and pain had receded, he relived the words imparted by the monster responsible for the gift. He sent a servant to bring Kygoss to his office. The door opening revealed Kygoss entering rather cautiously, careful to stand at attention.

"Old Bird." Darius inclined his head, indicating that

Kygoss was free to take a seat. He inwardly smiled as the old man refused, standing. "Who is it that Aurelia treasures the most?"

Kygoss' eyebrows went up, clearly confused by this line of questioning. "What do you mean, Sire?"

Darius sat back in his chair, staring at the ceiling. "I need to talk to Aurelia. The one time I tried to talk to her, Faziel lost her wing, and Lucian has appeared to crawl under her skin, getting closer to her than I thought possible—essentially blocking me."

Kygoss nodded, audibly swallowing. "I see."

"You don't, though; otherwise, you would tell me who the person is. I have a theory. Would you like to hear it?" He didn't wait for an answer; after all, he didn't really need one. "I had this weird nightmare, in it, I was told you hold the answer to my dilemma. I also think talking to Aurelia is standing in the way of the promise that was made. Tell me, Old Bird, who is Aurelia's secret soulbond?" He met Kygoss' eyes and knew he had plucked the right thread by the shock that stared at him. "How did the sheltered princess meet him, I wonder?"

Kygoss' mouth fell open as if his brain had truly begun malfunctioning. "I can't tell you."

"You can—or the darling Maie can. I shall send guards to pick her up if I have to. Though if we go down that road, I can't promise her safety." Darius straightened, looking Kygoss in the eye. "I know you don't trust me. No one does. Whether you believe me or not, I don't want any harm to come to her."

Kygoss groaned, rubbing at his head, desperation leaking from his every movement. "Can you say the same of her soulbond? Or is he destined for the pit?"

So that's the concern. Then it dawned on him. "If you can get him here without the need of guards, I can promise no pain will be administered by me."

Blood drained from Kygoss' face. "Alright. Don't tell Maie this is happening."

"Your wife—you can handle it your way. However, I want Aurelia's soulbond in my chambers by sundown tomorrow."

Kygoss bowed, but not fast enough to hide the glimmer of tears.

thirty-one

MALEDIC

TIV - PALION - YEAR 7568

Life had taken on an unfortunate rhythm since the coronation. Aurelia had distanced herself as completely as she could without actively removing him from the palace or rejecting their bond. The nights of her sleeping in his arms felt like a distant daydream. Yet he stubbornly remained. At least he felt more complete being in her presence than he had in all the years without her.

It was a relief to get a letter directly from his father.

Son, come to Drakore. Meet in my study. I need to speak to you urgently. ~K.C.

He went to Balthor, who was busy monitoring the volunteer guards. Ever since the coronation ceremony, they had more than the ten guards they needed. Almost the entire bunkhouse agreed to her oath of loyalty, all in the name of Baryn. She now loaned wolves to Lucian and Ulfur when their manning was low. It rankled them, which he knew thrilled her to her core.

"Balthor, do you have a minute?"

"For the male of my only friend, of course. Valri, my love," Maledic swallowed the laugh as Valri fixed a look of pure hatred onto Balthor. "I need to step away. Can you oversee these puppies?"

Valri growled. "I am not your love, you red buffoon. Go with the Crow Man."

Balthor followed Maledic, chuckling softly as they found their way to a secluded section of the yard. "I just got a notice that I need to report to my father. I also need to check on an ongoing project in Slana. Can I trust you to keep her safe? Preferably in the realm of the living."

Balthor grinned. "She's not going anywhere; she doesn't want to. I have to ask—are you safe there? Darius isn't her friend. If he learns of your connection with her, it will become a liability."

Maledic mulled it over. "I worked closely with that couple the entire time she was gone, and it ended well enough. They never suspected me."

"Alright. I give you two days to clean up what you have over there. If you take any longer, I shall unleash your soul-bond. Trust me, you don't want to see her unleashed." Balthor clapped a hand on his shoulder, and Maledic chuckled.

"See you soon, Demon." He shifted without a second glance, launching into the air and heading for his father's study.

He landed with a thump, shifting back into his mortal shell. Surprise filled him at the sight of his father pacing in front of the fire. He approached with a smile that froze as he got a better look at his father's face.

"Father?" Kygoss turned and met Maledic's eyes, heartbreak shining in them. "Is it mother?"

"Oh. No, son, it's not. She is healthy and safe in Slana." He hung his head before whistling sharply. Two guards stepped into the small space, taking hold of Maledic's arms gruffly.

"Father? What is happening?"

"Mal, you need to just do what you're told, all will come out right. I will make sure of it."

Fear rose within him as the guards began to drag him out. *He knows.* The guards brought him directly to Darius' study, which was his next shock. He had expected a direct trip to the dungeon and Darius' famed pit. Darius stared up at him. "An interesting turn. I didn't see you as her match. In another life, we could have been brothers."

"Whose match am I?" Maledic played dumb, trying to buy time, knowing in his soul that he would never be able to stall Darius two whole days.

"Maledic, you are not a fool, and neither am I. You are Aurelia's soulbond, and if you want to live, you'll call her here so I can have an actual conversation with her."

Maledic leaned back, slightly stunned. *He doesn't want to kill her?* "What do you want to tell her? I know you had a conversation with her at the temple."

Darius let out a loud burst of laughter, looking as shocked by it as Maledic was. "You were there? Didn't see that coming. I mean to let your soulbond marry another. What a twisted place to be. You're darker than I thought. Faziel, the bitch, derailed that attempt. I need Aurelia's undivided attention."

Maledic rubbed his temple. "I won't do it."

"I didn't think so." Darius snapped his fingers, and Gerard stepped into the room. "You've always wanted to help me more; here's your chance. Make him see reason, or at least make him feel enough pain that she can't ignore it. You have full control; just do it in the Arena. Also, it would be best if he doesn't die until I can talk to her. We need the leverage, after all."

Maledic's throat dried up. Part of him had expected this, but in his mind it had been Darius doing it himself, ending in a swift death. *Would this stranger grant him a swift end?* Guards gripped his upper arms and pushed him through the door. Before he cleared the threshold, he heard Darius' parting words. "I shall see you soon, Maledic."

thirty-two

AURELIA

Tiv - Palion - Year 7568

Estrez circled her, a knife in one hand. The dampness of the dungeon coated her skin and sank into her bones. Aurelia tugged at her hands, but the ropes were cutting into her wrists, trapping her arms over her head.

Estrez sneered evilly. "How is my mortal pet doing today? Have you learned from your mistake?"

Aurelia refused to move or make a sound, despite her fear of the knife. A sweat broke out on her forehead. As the knife came closer, piercing her skin, there was a new sensation.

Panic.

It was the first indication that what she was seeing and feeling was a part of an intense nightmare. In her true past, she had never felt panic. What would have been the point? Suddenly, the vision shifted, and she was seeing a new male, one she was sure she had never seen before. The man blurred as a feeling of excruciating pain overtook her senses.

She jerked awake, her body covered in a slick sweat. Panic continued to course through her. She rushed out of her room, knowing Balthor was not on duty, and she headed to his room.

"Where is he?!" Her voice echoes off the walls.

Balthor, unsurprisingly, sat next to the window, methodically sharpening his blade, his sleep needs far different than a mortal's. Her hands shook as her braid swung violently, repeating in a steel tone. "Where is he?"

Balthor's hand stilled; he refused to lift his head, though, purposefully avoiding her gaze. "Who, Reli?"

"You know! Maledic. Where. The. Fuck. Is. He?"

He restarted his chore after a slight shrug. "He is on a trip. He will return in a day."

She pulled magic to her on instinct, her weapons having been forgotten in her rooms. "You need to start explaining, Balthor. What are you talking about? What trip?"

Balthor put his sword down, finally looking at her. "He needed a break from being ignored. His father gave him the excuse—he was needed at home. We should see him in another day."

Aurelia shook her head vehemently. "You're wrong! Something is off. I can feel it."

Balthor came to attention. "I shall go get him. You will stay here. It's undoubtedly a trick. I won't serve a Queen into the jaws of their trap."

"Balthor! You are the shittiest piece of demon ever. I WILL GO."

"You're the goddamn Queen now, Reli. You can't—otherwise you'll be seen as abandoning your post. Valri and I can get in and out quickly. He'll be winging his way to you swiftly."

She took a deep breath, recentering herself. "Balthor, I am going. Suzu will hold my place here and ensure the King and his minion do not go out of control in my absence. My issues with Darius go far deeper than him just holding Maledic. The day has come for him to pay."

Balthor groaned deeply. "Fine."

"Valri stays to back up Suzu. You and I will save Maledic and dispose of Darius."

Balthor shoved his sword dramatically into its sheath, clearly upset by her words. "Let's go then."

She returned to her room, dressing for battle, rebraiding her hair and fastening it in a crown around her head. Her sword made it onto her hip, and she secured as many daggers as she could in her corseted top, in her boots, and up her sleeves.

Suzu flew into the room, her night robe swirling around her. "How can I help?"

"Tell me what you know about Drakore and Darius. Do not send me in blind."

Suzu swallowed loudly before speaking quickly, extolling all the secrets she had gathered on Aurelia's former homeland.

Aurelia took it all in as she picked a basic leaf and vine motif crown, fastening it in her braid. "I shall return soon. Keep Lucian and the pet in check. If they veer too far, use some of that immense magic and do whatever is necessary to hold my throne."

Suzu grinned, tears glimmering in her eyes. "Always."

Aurelia stomped out of the room, pleased to see Balthor waiting for her in the hallway, similarly armed. They both headed up to the top of the tower in a silence so foreign to their friendship.

Once they reached the inky darkness of deep night, Aurelia sank into her magic, calling upon her shifted form. A form she had only really visited during her violent coronation. Some whispered it was an abomination, but she loved it and had waited twenty-six years for it.

Her wraith dragon gave her the gift of flight she had grown up wanting, while also embracing her full death magic.

She leapt into the air, letting it embrace her form, her

wings snapping out. She craned her neck, looking down at Balthor, taking in his leathery wings emerging dramatically from his back. Once he was in the air with her, she wheeled toward their destination, anger filling her, along with the pain that continued to flow down the bond with Maledic. Storm clouds formed at the tips of her wings, filling the sky she flew through. Thunder clapped, and lightning rained down as her wings continued to propel her to her destination.

May whatever God Darius believed in grant him a warning so there would be a chance of a decent fight.

thirty-three

MALEDIC

TIV - DRAKORE - YEAR 7568

The knife cutting into him ceased, causing any significant pain. Part of his brain flagged this as a huge problem, but he numbed it out.

Gerard leaned in close. "Come on, Maledic. Call her here I'm not allowed to kill you. Neither is he. Just give her up."

Maledic tried to laugh but all that came out was a bloody cough. He leaned over, spitting another wad of bloody mucus onto the floor. "I don't control her. Nor do I make the dire mistake of thinking I do." Gerard sliced down across Maledic's chest, shallow enough that he wouldn't die, but Maledic merely grinned. "I am an unshakeable tree. I will die due to my loyalty. What will you do to prove your morals?"

Gerard rolled his eyes. "She wouldn't die over her loyalty to you; otherwise, she'd be here." Silence fell, only disrupted by the dripping of his blood. A clanging sound echoed through the Arena. "What was that?"

Maledic grinned, touching the bond that was strengthening by the second. The sizzle of ozone filled the air, causing

185

every hair Maledic had to stand up. "You may want to reevaluate that last statement. Be careful what you wish for."

Lightning struck, and the blinding light cleared to show the Wraith Dragon Aurelia could now become. Gerard's mouth hung open as he took her in. Maledic realized Balthor stood by her side, tucking in bat-like wings.

A popping noise echoed in the room, revealing his storm-faced Aurelia. She moved seamlessly, without warning, flinging a dagger he hadn't even realized she had palmed. It found its home in Gerard's shoulder, his body absorbing the shock before collapsing in a heap.

Balthor turned away, clearing his throat, interrupting Aurelia's journey to his side. "We have company and—" Balthor sniffed deeply. "It's not mortal anymore."

Maledic craned his neck and saw Darius stepping out of the shadowed doorway. *Not mortal?*

thirty-four

DARIUS

TIV - DRAKORE - YEAR 7568

> *The majority of Avian shifters firmly believe in returning to the air once death reaches them. Thus, it's unsurprising that they do their best to dedicate their bodies to continue to aid future flyers. Their bodies are placed in a deep hole in the ground, leaving room for a sapling's root ball above them. Thus, their mortal form becomes one with a tree that will one day become a roost for an avian flyer.*
> *~Ancient Death Rites, Margoth's Journal*

Watching her kill Gerard without a second's hesitation infused him with an odd sense of pride. Gone was the timid, people-pleasing Aurelia, replaced by a foreign, highly powerful entity wearing her skin. Her companion's comment about him not being mortal made sense. He now had to feed on blood to curb some of his most violent urges. He stepped further into the room, arms up in supplication, showing he wasn't hiding a weapon.

She stopped a few feet from him, hands on her hips, staring intently. He could still feel the immense magic that had preceded her arrival. He bowed low, careful to keep his head angled to maintain eye contact. "Aurelia."

Her eyes flashed from blue to gray, and her companion began to speak quickly. "You had better explain what is happening here, Monster, before she releases her true gift."

Darius straightened. *Monster?* He was far from a monster —just a man striving to do the best he could. "Aurelia, I need to speak to you about what happened."

She glowered at him, anger clear on her face, but at least her eyes had shifted back to blue. "When?" Her voice was ice.

"Ten years ago." He took another step forward, his heart yearning to unload the truth after so long.

Her annoying companion's sword came out between Darius and Aurelia. "That is close enough, blood monster."

Darius raised an eyebrow, turning to meet the demon's gaze. "Blood Monster?"

"Yes, I can smell it on you. You will be unable to hide it from demons. We recognize our master's creations."

Master? Tixdarr? That answered a lingering question. "Alright, Mr. Demon." He turned his attention back to Aurelia, who was twirling a dagger between her hands. "You have to have questions. Cerial would want you to know the truth."

He watched her pace a few steps before stopping and pointing the knife at where his heart used to live. "If you lie to me, I will know—and there will be consequences."

He nodded, a euphoria rushing through him at the idea of loosening the burden that weighed him down.

"Why would Cerial want you to tell me?"

"She—She and I were soulbonds. She loved you more than

anyone. When she created the plan, you were meant to be protected." His voice shook. He hadn't spoken of her in any amount of detail since she died in his arms.

"What was her plan?"

He swallowed, unsure if recounting that would help. "Do you want her original plan, or what actually happened?"

"If you are going to this trouble, you will tell me what I asked. What was her plan? If I have to ask again, I take blood."

He rubbed a hand across his brow. "She wanted the throne. The easiest way to a throne was Palion, due to the existing betrothal, but she didn't want a pretend marriage. She knew that the only option left was the Drakore throne."

"Our parents would never have agreed to her ascension at eighteen." Aurelia flung the dagger at the wooden post next to Darius' head. He didn't blink.

"I know, and so did she. She sought counsel with my father, Rayner, searching for a way to get them to relent. She didn't know and neither did I, how far he had fallen down the hole of madness. He convinced her that your parents would never accept me, so she insisted we keep it a secret. He turned on her and stole her from me."

"So you expect me to believe that she sanctioned the death of my parents?" Another dagger flew, this one grazing his ear.

"She believed Rayner would allow them to live, merely threatening violence until your father surrendered the power of the throne to her. I never wanted to rule. But I would do anything for her. I was blinded by the bond." Darius hung his head, exhaustion flooding his veins.

"So Rayner killed her, because she stood in his way? Was I actually in danger? I remember that the rebels searched for me."

"Rayner killed her to punish me. He hated me, and anything I loved got ruined or destroyed. When Rayner was in charge of the coup, you were in danger. I searched for you to unload this story, to aid you. I never wanted to rule, I would have given you the power right then. Leaving the world to be with the only person who ever truly saw me."

He watched the wheels turn behind her eyes. Part of him wanted to know exactly what she was thinking; another part of him just wanted to give her the power and disappear.

She began laughing. "You have to be kidding me. The Gods are playing the worst joke ever. I went through all that, and you would just give me the throne. And all it comes with."

He nodded silently.

"The plan is that you will now--what? Give me your throne? Give me the Great Power of the Sky?"

"Yes."

She walked closer to him, getting right in his face. "Why do you think I want it? You've ruined what my family created. You think I don't know of the depravities you've committed?"

Darius flinched. "I did what I thought was best. I only injured traitors or those destined for early graves."

"EXCUSES!"

Darius growled. "I am not here for you to judge me. I am here to tell you the truth—and abdicate the throne."

MALEDIC

TIV - DRAKORE - YEAR 7568

A scream caused Maledic to jerk upright. His body still oozed from the various injuries inflicted on him by Gerard. Balthor strode to him, and Maledic shook his head, panic filling it.

"No." He groaned. "Save her."

"She's not the one screaming, my man. She would roast me if I let anything happen to you, so consider me your new shadow."

Maledic glared but turned back to Aurelia. She stood next to Darius, but they were both turned toward the open tunnel. The scream sounded again, and Darius stepped in front of Aurelia. *Thats a bit odd.*

"You can't give away my throne! You don't have the right. You are nothing but a monster!"

Faziel stepped from the shadows, and Maledic recoiled at the sight. Gone was the perfectly coiffed Queen. Instead stood a crazed woman, her hair hanging in lank clumps, her dress in tatters—what had once been a perfectly put together face of makeup—was instead streaked, colors smudged by tears, grime, and hands. He realized her wings were out, but one was nothing but a bloody stump, oozing beneath dirtied bandages.

His eyes flicked to Aurelia, noting that she was still next to Darius, far too close to Faziel.

Balthor gripped his upper arm painfully, forcing him to stand. "You need to be up. Ready to run. If," he smirked, an evil glint to it, "you can be quiet, we can watch the show. Otherwise, my job is to get you out of here."

Maledic stood, biting down on the groan of his muscles. "Your job is to ensure she stays alive. I will flee if necessary."

Balthor's smirk morphed into a grin. "You are about to witness why I am following her orders, not yours."

Maledic refocused on the scene unfolding in front of them.

"I can give away my throne whenever I choose, Bitch. But this opportunity is hard to pass up." Darius took a step away from both women, looking them up and down. "Fight for it."

Aurelia shot him a glare. "Seriously?"

"Kill her and you get what's left of your families legacy. You can leave the dogs and return home."

"I kill her and I'm still left with your sorry ass."

Maledic's heart stuttered at Darius' next words. "No, you won't. That I swear to you on your sister's memory."

Faziel took a few more steps into the room. "She can't kill me! She only took my wing due to luck! I am connected to the Great Power, and she isn't!!"

Balthor coughed. "Bullshit."

Faziel's eyes whipped to Balthor before settling on Maledic, a slimy, flirtatious tone filled the air. "Maledic Mercer Corvus. What is a man like you doing here?"

She took a step forward, but Aurelia sidestepped, firmly placing herself between them and refocusing Faziel on her. She brought up her sword, causing a whine to escape Faziel. "That isn't fair. I don't have a weapon."

"You want a fair fight?"

Mal's internal alarms started to sound. *She needs to keep her sword.*

"A fair fight for the kingdom would be best." Darius held his hand out for Aurelia's sword.

"Fine." She sheathed her sword and unbuckled the strap, pointedly ignoring Darius' proffered hand. Maledic's heart sank as she threw the sword and dagger belt onto the ground.

thirty-six

AURELIA

Tiv - Drakore - Year 7568

This was a stupid idea but her pride could not be quieted. She needed to win her father's throne, and if it cost one life rather than potentially an unknown number of innocents, so be it. She watched Faziel, her magic begging to be unleashed. Yet, she kept a lid on it, waiting for her moment.

"You were supposed to be my sister, Aurelia. You were supposed to care for your family but you left us all to die." Faziel pointed her hands at Aurelia. It took mere seconds to summon a shield of air in front of her. It did the job, dissipating the lightning that Faziel aimed at her.

"You are still alive, Faziel. We could both win—agree to stop the fight and take what we want from Darius." She circled, searching for an opening to maim, unwilling to kill her.

"My body still functions for the most part. That is not the same as being alive, Aurelia." The words hit deeper than

Aurelia could anticipate, weakening her block. The lightning fizzling against the wind shield.

"Have the dogs taken your power, you selfish bitch? Fight back—prove you can rule these people."

Aurelia threw some wind, but nothing with the intent to harm. "Faziel, let me help you! Let me—"

"Let you lie to me just like all the rest? I think not." Faziel's stumbling gate had her smashing into Aurelia. She knew there was a risk to touching her, but her heart ached with what she had endured.

"Faziel, I endured trauma as well. We can work together. They will pay for what they did."

Faziel took a deep breath, and Aurelia registered the gathering of power beneath Faziel's skin. She didn't have a chance to scream, merely took a fortifying breath as lightning soared from Faziel to her. Her skin felt hot, stretched too tight over her bones. Her head tipped back of its own volition, the scream finally ripping from her lungs.

"No!" The echoing male scream brought her head around.

She sent Mal a smile, hoping to reassure him. Her hands shook with aftershocks, and she gripped the dagger hidden in her corset. She sent Mal one last nod of acknowledgment before turning her knife on the panting Faziel.

"Why aren't you dead yet?" Faziel's voice was faint, her body panting, trembling with exertion.

Aurelia grimaced as she slid the dagger to its new home. Faziel let out a gasp, her eyes going wide. "Not. Fair."

"No Faz, this wasn't fair. You should have married your soulbond and lived a life of indulgence after all you endured as a child." Aurelia closed her eyes, tears gathering as she remembered the little girl in the nursery the day she had left for Slana. Innocent. Her mind was so full of memories she missed Faziel's movement slow as it was. She was jolted back to the present when Faziel's hands grappled with her face. Her nails scratching, blood oozing down.

"You'll join me." Power surged beneath Faziel's finger tips. Aurelia knew she should release her own power in response, use her death magic. But the idea of using it against her foster sister threatened to kill a precious part of her that still existed after all she had endured in Dodsfell.

The next moment, she had no control. As the searing pain erupted across her face, the last thing she saw was a bright white light, her control over her death magic snapping.

thirty-seven

MALEDIC

The light erupted through the room and Maledic's heart stopped. He couldn't get his body to move, mainly because Balthor had his arms banded around his middle.

His scream shredded his throat as the black fog he had seen once before erupted from her, extinguishing the light. Both women were slumped over, unmoving, but Aurelia's death fog still lingered among them. "Balthor, let me go. I have to know." He pushed halfheartedly at the demon's arms, desperation cresting within him.

Balthor loosened his grip, his head hung low, defeat escaping his every pore. "Be careful, Maledic."

Maledic stumbled forward, his legs not fully on board with suddenly walking, blood oozing down from his various cuts, but he ceased noticing or caring, his focus entirely on her.

"No. NO. NO." He hit his knees, sinking into the magic cloud still hovering around her.

His first realization that their life had changed irrevocably was the smell of charred flesh mixed with the salty tang of copper blood. "NO." He blinked rapidly, trying to clear his eyes, his fingers gripping her shoulders, pulling her away from Faziel's slumped form.

"Well? Who lives?" Darius' harsh voice came through the haze of panic.

His eyes danced over her still-smoking face, unwilling to see what would be left, his fingers shaking as they dug into her neck, his breath catching in his throat.

...nothing...

"No." Maledic stubbornly held his breath, forcing his heart to regulate so he could feel more. His fingers pushed harder, and shock filled him as something pushed back at him.

A steady beat.

Maledic collapsed over her body, completely overcome with relief and the overwhelming feelings of panic and anxiety. He let himself sob. The tears ran hot down his cheeks, pooling on her stomach.

"Seriously?" Balthor whispered, fear lacing his voice. "She can't be gone."

"No." Maledic sat up, shaking his head. "She lives." He choked on a sob and fastened an arm around her torso, trying to pull her farther from Faziel.

"Balthor, come help me. Please?" He heard Balthor get closer, but the demon hissed when he reached the edge of the dark fog that enveloped Maledic.

"I can't, Maledic. Her magic won't let me get closer. You will need to get her out of the fog."

Maledic nodded, doing his best to focus his mind, and more importantly, his muscles on dragging her. Darius joined Balthor on the edge of her cloud. It took ages to pry her shoulders past the dark fog; he did his best to not focus on the fact that she still hadn't woken up despite her body jostling and the gruesome injury on her face.

As soon as she was clear, Balthor—and surprisingly, Darius, each gripping under an arm, pulled her the rest of the way. Maledic stood on shaking legs, looking back at Faziel. She was lying in a puddle of blood. Shock and sadness warred within him. She wasn't a bad person—not truly—just the one always in terrible situations, never safe.

Sadness filled Maledic, but determination swiftly followed. He had to see Aurelia through whatever was to come. If anything, this situation proved he would not survive her loss. He leveraged himself up and forced himself to look at her face, examining what was left there. He started at her chin, where there were merely streaks of blood from the mess Faziel had left behind. Her perfect bow mouth remained intact, though now it was tensed and tight in pain. The tip of her button nose remained. As his eyes drifted upward, blood filled his ears, the ground started shifting beneath his feet.

Balthor shouted. "Maledic, you need to breath slowly. Through your mouth. In your nose and out of your mouth, forcefully. Do not faint. My Gods."

Maledic blinked frantically, doing his best to stay on his feet. Incrementally, the ground solidified once again. Between his blood loss and the shocks of the moment, he needed rest more than much else. He placed himself protectively between Darius and his soulbond. "What's the deal, Darius? Are you going to give her your throne, or are you going to finish Faziel's failed attempt at killing her?"

Darius glared at him. "I don't want the throne. She is welcome to it—if she survives."

Balthor stood next to Mal, the potent glare aimed at Darius. "She will survive, because you will give us a room and access to the best med witches in Drakore."

Darius smirked, orchestrating a low bow. "She will be accorded all that an injured Queen of Drakore would receive."

Balthor hefted Aurelia's still-prone form into his arms, "If you double-cross me, Darius, I will take great joy in ending you in very creative ways." Maledic nodded along, following behind Balthor as Darius led them out of the dungeons.

thirty-eight

SUZU

> *Humans bury their bodies deep enough to escape the useful root systems that could aid in breaking down the body and returning it to Baelia. They want their bodies to slowly deteriorate, leaving the soul plenty of time to stay in the vicinity, to watch over their loved ones.*
>
> *~Ancient Death Rites, Margoth's Journal*

Suzu paced the room, unsure how to keep Aurelia's throne safe as her tenure in Drakore lengthened. The days started out fine—Lucian ignored anyone who had backed her. Something had shifted, though. Tensions continued to mount between him and Zadon, and perhaps that was what led to the fancy envelope she toyed with.

Belvina put her arms around Suzu's waist, resting her chin on her shoulder. "Before opening whatever madness that man has brought to this room, have you heard anything from her?"

Suzu shook her head. "No. They left three days ago, but so far I haven't heard any solid leads on what happened. The silence is stifling."

"We can weather whatever comes. We have the power. If she's gone, Balthor will return. If she isn't, they will all return." Belvina squeezed her reassuringly.

Suzu nodded, tearing open the envelope. "We should do this like Ulfur did—except avoid an oath if at all possible."

The notice was written on thick parchment, the inked letters curling amongst each other.

King Lucian invites you and a plus one to join his court at a formal dinner tonight.

She sighed heavily. "Darling, do we have any formal gowns ready to wear tonight?"

Belvina stepped back. "I always have a little something up my sleeve."

They dressed in gorgeous gowns, both mentally preparing for the potentially painful dinner. As they entered the dining room Suzu was shocked to find only Lucian seated at the dining room table. Zadon and Ulfur were nowhere to be seen.

She sat down after orchestrating a small curtsy to Lucian. "Sire, thank you for the invitation."

Lucian sat straight, tapping the table. "I've been thinking."

Belvina settled next to her, gripping Suzu's knee. "Whatever you are thinking about, I am sure it is for the best of the kingdom."

Lucian hummed deep in his throat. "I keep thinking about the coronation disaster—and how my father's murderer was not only invited, but coincidentally able to help us subdue her dragon form."

Suzu stiffened and Belvina's hand squeezed harder on her leg. Sweat broke out on her brow, but she maintained eye contact, even throwing a smile at him. "It was rather convenient. I do hope one day we can all know who it was, so we can thank them."

Lucian smirked, his head shaking in a silent laugh. "It would be rather odd for me to thank the murderer, don't you think?"

Suzu gave a fake laugh. "Well no, of course not. I meant to thank them for helping on coronation day."

Lucian steepled his fingers in front of his face, but before he could speak, Belvina cut in.

"Where are Zadon and Ulfur?"

He shot her a dark look. "I have sent them on a mission to accomplish this conversation in peace." He turned back to Suzu, and she gulped. "You are the murderer, aren't you, Suzu?"

She leaned heavily into her ability to lie. "Me? I am a lady. How would I kill one as great as Harold?"

Lucian turned to Belvina. "Explain to your wife what happens when wolves share blood willingly."

It was Belvina's turn to stiffen before she woodenly replied. "Wolves who share blood willingly can inadvertently share memories."

Lucian nodded once, "I've been seeing bits and pieces from Ulfur, despite doing my best to block it. Imagine my surprise at seeing Suzu here, covered in his blood, my father's crumpled corpse next to her."

Suzu turned to Belvina, intent on saving her. "I love you more than life itself, but you need to go. He will let you go—because if he doesn't, I will fight back using the power in question."

"Now, now, little panther. I won't be killing anyone today.

I brought you here to show you that I know. At a time I choose, you will give me what is rightfully mine."

Suzu held Belvina's eyes and nodded once. "Alright, Sire. When you're ready, it's yours. At the end of the day, I didn't want the power, merely to release an elderly man trapped by circumstance."

She watched Lucian as her words hit home. He glared at her. "I expect you in attendance every day, or I release Zadon from his leash."

Suzu grabbed Belvina's hand, yanking her from the chair. "We shall see you tomorrow, my King."

thirty-nine

AURELIA

She woke to the feeling of bone-deep coldness seeping through her body, her limbs heavy. Her mouth was dry and crispy, the lingering taste of copper all she could sense. She moaned. A severe heat built on her face, shifting to the side, doing her best to find a comfortable position. Heat for her body, coolness for her head.

The comforting voice of Maledic sank into her mind like sand into water. "Don't move, Aurelia. Oh shit. Tell me that the med witches are here?"

Aurelia tried to open her eyes, needing to see. She wanted to comfort him while also comforting herself—that all was going to be okay. For some reason, that didn't fully sink into her mind; she couldn't get her eyelids to open. Her stubbornness reared its head, overriding the pain swamping her mind; she pulled her arm up, desperate to rub her eyes clear.

Balthor grabs her arms, his smell stark. She could hear Maledic's voice crack with emotion. She opened her mouth, desperate to speak, except nothing came out. Pressure built against her arms as memories flooded her tired, sore brain. She screamed, her feet kicking and digging as she fought her past as well as her present.

Maledic's voice sounded closer, as if he had moved. She jumped a bit as he pressed his nose into her ear. "You've got to stop fighting us. We are going to take away the pain—I promise."

A whimper broke free of her throat, and she gave her best nod. What happened next was a whirlwind of sensation; cool hands landed on her temples, which seemed to lower the heat building behind her eyes. Sounds became distorted, some coming in louder than she was fairly convinced they should. "I've stopped the magic from continuing to damage her, but there is no spell I know of that could even attempt to reverse what's been done."

"So its gone?"

"Yes sir."

"Will she live?"

"Yes. Though I can't begin to predict what type of life she will endure until the Gods call her home."

Aurelia wasn't sure how long the conversation went on, or who Maledic was talking to, but enough was enough. Her body seemed to agree because after a few coughs, she ground out, "Fuck the Gods."

The room went silent, so silent she could probably hear insects walking. All of a sudden, she felt Maledic crouching next to her bed, "Aurelia."

"No Mal. They've never cared for me, and I doubt they're going to start now. We just need someone to patch me up."

She sensed Balthor by the lingering smell of burnt ash filling the room. "That's the Reli I trained."

She patted around on the bed she was laying on, frustration building. "Someone help me to sit up! I won't get any better laying on my back." She could hear Maledic groan as he gave her his hand and pulled her up.

"Ma'am, you should really lie down. Your body needs to rest to heal properly. You aren't tied to the Power of the Sky or Land, and it isn't clear how deep the wounds go."

"No. I have said from the beginning I do what I decide. There will be no more dictation of my life. Balthor, get rid of her." She continued to push and pull, wiggling into an upright position until her back found a hard support. Perhaps a wall.

She could hear Balthor kindly ushering the healer from the room. Maledic's body sank on to the bed next to hers. "She may have been able to help you. Why can't you let people help you?"

She sighed heavily, unwilling to answer his questions. "How bad is it, Maledic?"

There was a long pause. "It's extensive. You won't be able to regain your sight."

Her hearing blinked out. Only a high-pitched noise reverberated in her mind. She tried to scrunch her face as the sound pained her, but the act of her facial muscles spasming had more pain crashing through her. She hissed and Maledic's hand grabbed her arm, squeezing firmly. "You aren't alone. I am right here."

She nodded jerkily. "Yes. I know. You are always here."

The image of his smile floated through her mind. She gasped realizing that she would never see that again. She shook her head, dismissing that thought. *What would be the use of dwelling on the loss?* "I will always be here. This doesn't change anything."

She tried for a smile but could feel that it wasn't genuine. "Where is Darius?"

"He is in the palace somewhere, waiting for you to be ready."

"Ready for what?"

"To ascend his throne."

Her mind reeled at that. "He was serious?"

"Yes." There was a heaviness to his words.

"What is it? What are you hiding?" She was desperate to know, to have him be honest with her, to know that she could still tell when someone was lying—that not everything had changed.

"He... all the things he has done and been through were all due to being blinded by love, by the Gods bond. It makes me wonder about every bond. Are we all blinded by the Gods?"

"I will never be blinded by the Gods, Maledic. That you can be assured of. There is an undeniable connection between us, one I never got to choose—not truly. But I decide what I do and why. I won't let them change me yet again. I have died twice now. There won't be a third time; they will have to come for me themselves."

Maledic squeezed her arm. "I won't let you die again."

"Go get Darius." Maledic squeezed twice before standing up.

Once he was gone, she sank into her mind, trying really hard not to drown in the loneliness that her lack of eyesight brought her. The blackness was so dark, it rivaled even the darkness she had endured in Dodsfell. It felt like a thousand years before she heard the door open again and the footsteps of three individuals entering the room.

She remained silent, stomping hard on the urgent question lighting up inside her. She wanted to demand who entered, to know who it was. Yet she waited. Maledic cleared his throat, and she let out the building tension from her body in a deep breath. "Aurelia. I have brought you Balthor, and Darius."

Aurelia nodded. "Darius. What are we to do now? I have killed your Queen as you needed."

Darius let out a short laugh. "Next is you take this

wretched power and the crown so I can disappear as I have always wanted."

Balthor's heavy footsteps came closer to her seat. "She can't take the Great Power of the Sky. She carries a Master Power already."

"WHAT?" Darius' outburst was loud and unexpected, causing her to jump a bit, her body flooding with embarrassment and annoyance.

Maledic interjected. "Technically, she could. Tiva cleared the way for that, according to Oba Aewenna. She can take on one Great Power. I thought at the time it was a reference to the Great Power of the Land, since she was going to be coronated in Palion. Yet, there was no power transfer at that coronation."

"Yeah because the Pup's an idiot who lost control of his inheritance." Darius scoffed loudly. "I knew that at the Marriage Rite. He didn't have that power, someone else in the kingdom does."

Aurelia remained quiet, waiting for the annoying males to shut their mouths long enough for her to get a word in edgewise. Balthor clucked his tongue. "She really shouldn't navigate a power transfer just yet. Plus it's possible her mastery of death will get upset over her attempt to secure more power. Death is a snarky creature."

Alright, enough is enough. She cleared her throat, the conversation drying up. "First of all, I can take whatever power I want. I don't know how to explain this any differently, but at some point, everyone needs to just accept my words. I do not care about the Gods, not what they say, not what they feel, not what they decree. That being said, I don't want the Power of the Sky. I am already coronated in Palion; they are my people by circumstance, as much as Drakorian people are mine by blood."

"You have got to be kidding me! I have been waiting for this for ten years and you won't take it!? I don't want this job.

I never wanted this job." Darius growled, and from the sound of it, he was stomping around the room.

She leaned her head back against the wall. "I never wanted to be blind, I never wanted to go to Dodsfell. What I did want was to meet my soulbond, marry, and rule in peace in Drakore while my sister ruled happily from Palion. I wanted to grow up and find love with my family. To come into my powers fully before having to navigate the inner workings of politics. No one has shown much interest in what I wanted. I don't see why I should care about what you want, Darius."

"Cerial would be ashamed of you for not caring. She would want you to rule when she could not."

Anger spiked in her blood, and she tried to control her impulses. They didn't want to be controlled, though; she had controlled enough for one day. She slipped a hand up to her corset and snagged a dagger, honing in on Darius' continued complaints. His voice took on an annoying whine; with her heightened hearing, she flung the dagger, a satisfyingly wet thunk met her ears, her mouth curling into a satisfied smile. "Don't speak about her anymore. She may have been your soulbond and died in a gruesome manner which makes you feel a certain way. It's important to remember, though, that she was first and foremost my sister, and as my family, she will be given respect. I may not believe that she would choose me over you in the end, because I think the actions of ten years ago speak for themself. I will, however, choose myself over you or her memory. You are dismissed from this room."

Silence descended as the knife struck home in Darius' shoulder. She knew it had been his shoulder, sparks had flown from the dark void she had stared in, directly where his voice had come from—sparks that had settled on his form, high-lighting the edges, giving her almost something for her sight-less eyes to see.

Interesting. Why did spilling his blood elicit sparks? What was showing them? Was it her magic? She didn't give voice to her questions, opting instead to wait, to see what else would happen.

Balthor and Maledic, by the sounds of it, were escorting a very angry Darius from the room. She could make out a few words as they manhandled him. "Just take the power. Make her take it. I can't keep living like this!"

She closed her eyes—or at least she tried to. She had no idea if they remained. Her next task would be to make Maledic explain in great detail just how grotesque her appearance had become.

forty

DARIUS

ANIT - DRAKORE - YEAR 7568

The feeling of sun on his face brought him around. Orange blossom scent filled his nose causing confusion to filter into his barely waking mind. That scent hadn't been strong since Cerial had been alive, wound around him. He stretched, and then his hands encountered something that shouldn't have been on his bed—silky strands, strands of hair. He never let anyone sleep in his bed, not even Faziel when she was alive.

He cracked his eyes. Blond curly hair spread across his pillow, the owner of which was turned away from him. *Who? How?* His mind raced over the night before, but nothing made sense.

The woman stretched and turned. His blood stopped in his veins. A pair of gorgeous blue eyes met his, a coy smile on her face. "Cerial?"

A look he hadn't had any hope of seeing again. "Darius." She nodded, her hand coming up to stroke his face.

His other hand came around, pulling her into him. "How are you here? How are you real? What is this?"

She smiled wider. "You made a deal with Tixdarr. He honors his obligations, and now you can see me. I've been with you this entire time."

"I thought souls moved to Dodsfell or the Void." He stroked her hair, his eyes not even wanting to blink for fear she would disappear once again. Her body was solid, even though he knew she was dead. He had wrapped her corpse himself, preparing her for Dodsfell.

"I stayed behind. It was hard, but only manageable because of the chaos caused by Aurelia's entering Dodsfell. A mortal entering the realm caused enough mayhem that I could stay here. I will always be here. I told you that once, and I meant it."

Tears formed behind his eyes, hot and prickling as they dripped down his cheeks. "I did my best to not be him. I did try."

She nodded, her own tears flowing. "I know love. I've watched. I cheered on your victories. I am here now, and I can talk to you—answer when you have questions or when you seem unsure. I will help you."

"Aurelia needs to *see* you. She needs to talk to you so she knows what you've done and why."

Cerial pushed herself up, and he marveled at the way she moved, so familiar to what she had been like when she was alive. "I can't show myself to her yet. Once she fully masters her magic—death itself—she will be able to see more."

Darius scoffed. "No she won't. Her eyes have been fried out of her skull. Its honestly hard to look at."

Cerial shot him a look of no-nonsense anger. "You know I didn't mean literally! She has been through an extreme amount of trauma, yet you forced her to fight again. I am disappointed in you for that, Darius. You will respect her from here on out. She didn't choose to lose her vision. The power of Death will provide a solution, once she accepts her fate. She will open the door to new levels of power. Once that happens, she and I will meet again."

Shame flooded him. "I didn't have a choice, Cerial. I had no control over her going to Dodsfell—that was the dogs. As to the fight with Faziel, I couldn't kill Faz without being compared to my father; someone else had to remove her."

Cerial shook her head. "There were other ways. But that's done now. There is a caveat to you being able to see me, Darius."

Dread swamped him. He pulled himself upright so they were sitting in front of one another. "What could be worse than living without you for ten years?"

"When your time comes, Darius, and your life is taken, we won't be able to meet again. Our souls will forever be separated. I don't know what will happen with me, as I am stuck here in Baelia, but you will be sucked into Dodsfell, where you will be forced to choose. Either be recycled back into the world through the Void or stay in Dodsfell." Her eyes lowered, sadness filling her.

His brain raced. "I just won't die. I'll disappear to a place where I am safe, and you and I can make a home that we should have had all those years ago."

Cerial smiled through the tears. "First, let's see Aurelia through this and learn more about your newest issue. Tixdarr made you something new—a blood slave of sorts."

"I know. So far it's being kept in check. I killed Notus, and that kept me going. It was once; it'll be fine."

Cerial shook her head, her hands coming up to caress his face. "Darius. Deep down, there's a hunger. Do you feel it? That is what needs to be controlled, and can only be done through the consumption of blood. You'll need to find a way to consume that regularly."

Darius dug into his soul, finally feeling all the things he had locked behind dragon-ore-laced doors. She was right, there was a hunger in him, one that didn't ache for food but instead something else. "How do I consume it without being like Rayner, killing the innocent all the time. Killing Notus was so hard, I can't keep doing that."

Cerial worried at her lip, her mind working. "Perhaps animal blood would work. Perhaps we could capture something and bleed it, allowing you to drink it in a glass. Then you only take a little bit, allowing the creature to live on."

Darius absently nodded along as he sank deeper into the feeling of hunger. It had been so long since Notus. To long. As the hunger crested, he ceased being able to understand exactly what was happening or what was causing the hunger.

A knock had his eyes focusing on the door, his head cocking to the side as he picked up the sound of thumping.

...ba boom...ba boom...

Cerial's voice drifted through the fog, "You can't open the door, Darius. You'll kill her. Let her leave the food."

Her voice was faint, though as if in a tunnel, and the need for what waited outside the door became too great. His hand shook as he brought it to the handle.

forty-one

MALEDIC

Watching Aurelia struggle had to be the hardest thing he could have imagined—a bloodless form of torture.

She had survived, but he wasn't sure how. Now it was time to make a change to ensure her safety. He had no doubt she was still capable despite her new difficulties, yet he would do his part.

He ascended the well-worn steps to the disused tower. His father's study was alight with a cheery fire in the hearth. He stepped into the room, his eyes instantly finding the hunched form of his father collapsed over the desk.

A small part of him worried about the man who had raised him. He ignored that pull, though, slamming the door behind himself. His air magic could register the even breathing, which spoke to the fact that the man lived.

The sound of the door reverberated around the room, causing Kygoss to sit up, his eyes swollen and drool leaking from his lip. A survey of the room revealed the cause of his deep sleep: a bottle of ale rested with only about a quarter of it left on the desk.

His father rubbed his eyes, staring, disbelief shining out. Maledic refused to engage with it, though. "How are you alive?"

"That is one question. I have another. How did you get to the point where you sold out your own son to your known enemy?"

"I had no choice." Kygoss rubbed harder at his head. "They threatened your mother."

Maledic stepped back, feeling the words like a blow. His mother was innocent in just about everything, always the one to help. "Did you consult her? Did she approve of you using me?"

"No."

He nodded once. "What do you expect to happen now, Father? Are we supposed to welcome you into Aurelia's court? Are we supposed to allow you in on her inner secrets? After you so willingly worked for Darius."

"I took an oath, Maledic. It was to support the holder of the throne of Drakore. It wasn't for Darius. I haven't become his lackey, no matter how it looks."

Maledic met his father's gaze, his gut roiling with an unknown feeling. "I can't trust you. You set me up with Faziel. You set me up with Darius. I would be a fool to give you a third chance. If your oath truly was to the throne and not Darius, then you will be able to see that through in Slana. You are not allowed to set foot in the palace again. You will no longer represent the crown. Your authority is done."

Kygoss stood, his mouth hanging open. "It's my life's work. You can't take everything from me."

Maledic leaned against the window frame, facing his father. "You have two options. Option one: you take me at my word and go home, spending the rest of your days with Mother. Option two: you spend your days in the dungeon, slowly wasting away, leaving mother to navigate life without you."

Kygoss groaned. "I can't lose you either. The plan was to do my best to keep both relationships together."

"How?! By praying to the Gods that I'd be saved while continually offering me to the ones that caused this torture and trauma? You were bound to lose me, and you'll be lucky if mother ever talks to you again." Maledic held the door open. "You have been banished. The guards have been notified, and if you are found here after an hour, you will be locked away."

Kygoss stood slowly, his head hung low. As he made his way toward Maledic, he squared his shoulders. "Someday you will face a decision such as I did, and perhaps then you will understand me better."

As he crossed the threshold heading toward his private quarters, Maledic muttered, "Absolutely not. I would put my child first, as Aurelia would expect me to. As impossible as that decision would be, there is a right and a wrong. Ultimately, you chose wrong."

Kygoss walked away down the hall, his head shaking. Maledic ignored him, turning away—choosing to move forward and leave his misaligned father in the past.

It was time to organize the information at his fingertips and get a concise report to Aurelia in time before she made decisions on this kingdom's future.

forty-two

BALTHOR

ANIT - DRAKORE/PALION - YEAR 7568

> *Elves have built a giant place dedicated to their dead. It stands tall and proud, each room holding shelf upon shelf of urns adorned with a plaque naming the person resting within. The community forever united in death as in life.*
> *~Ancient Death Rites, Margoth's Journal*

"Balthor, you need to go to Palion and make sure Suzu can handle it. I am going to have to be here for awhile, figuring out how to run Drakore without Darius and with this new development." He watched her gesture halfheartedly at her face. "Zadon will take advantage of a long absence."

Balthor paced, trying to figure out how to argue with her when she was so clearly correct. "I will go. But I will return shortly. You need me here just as much. I will ensure Valri stands strong with Suzu."

Aurelia cleared her throat. "I think there's more to Valri and Zadon, and while she has a compelling argument to hate him, I think he might have the upper hand there. We need a more sure plan before you can return."

That halted Balthor mid-step. "You think there's a binding between them?"

"Yes."

"I shall find out. Be safe and lean on the Crow Man. He cares for you more than you are willing to acknowledge." He watched her mouth twist in discomfort before she nodded.

He bowed to her before backing out of the room. Maledic was waiting anxiously in the hallway. "Keep her safe, Crow man. I will return soon."

Before Maledic could really question him, he strode quickly toward the courtyard.

———

As he landed in Palion, he could feel the tension in the air—similar to what had been the case when they arrived in Drakore. He rolled his shoulders; they needed both kingdoms to find their calm rhythm. He glanced at the waning sun and realized that, if old patterns held, Lucian's court would be getting ready to sit down for a formal dinner right about now.

He strode to the dining hall Lucian enjoyed using and took a seat, gracefully draping himself across the chair, waiting. He schooled his face to neutrality as he heard laughter and talking in the hallway. He twirled one of the knives between his fingers, looking downright bored.

As the door opened and the party filed in, the words died off, echoing silence in its wake. He looked at all of them, taking in the fancy dresses on the women: Suzu, Belvina, and

Valri. The formal dining suits of the men; Lucian, Zadon, and Ulfur. He grinned openly. "It's about time you all decided to join me. I am so famished I could eat an entire person."

He didn't know which of the women it was, but one of them stifled a laugh with a cough, causing him to grin wider. Lucian strode to his place at the table. "I don't recall you getting an invitation. The only person in this palace who enjoys your presence is Tiva-knows-where. So slink off and enjoy your food elsewhere."

Suzu stepped forward, the slightest of inclines of her head. "Sire, give the poor demon some food. He knows he isn't welcome in your court, but its more torturous to make him sit among what he can't have."

Zadon spoke next. "I vote he can stay, but he is not allowed to talk. After all, in this setting, it's he who is the pet and pets don't talk."

Balthor barked a laugh, taking the water glass and toasting the air with an eyebrow raised. He would remember this.

Lucian grumbled. "Alright, fine, if you think its best."

"Well, someone faithful to the bitch should see how a court should run. We all know she doesn't have any idea."

Balthor's eyes darted around, taking in everyone's expression. If they wore masks, they were damn good ones. Suzu and Belvina wore warm smiles. Valri remained her stoic self, but Ulfur had tightened his fists threateningly. *Interesting. Does anyone truly support Lucian?*

The meal moved forward, and everyone talked around Balthor, who bided his time waiting. As the meal wrapped up, Balthor leaned toward Suzu, seated nearest him. "I have found an interesting novel in the market recently. Perhaps after dinner, you'd allow me to steal some of your time so you can review it. In fact, I am fairly sure Valri would be interested in it as well." He raised his voice to be heard by the other demon.

Valri cocked her head, giving a small nod of assent as Suzu made a ridiculous cooing noise. She clapped her hands, "I do love books. My favorite time, when King Harold was alive, and we had our charities, was the time spent in the library before-hand. What, pray tell, does this book discuss?"

"Oh. Well, this book discusses all kinds of topics but most importantly, the topic of resistance in the face of severe medical maladies." He watched her eyes widen as her brain jumped to conclusions.

"Why, that sounds like a fascinating read. I would love to have access to it when you all are done." Zadon leaned over, plucking a bunch of fruit from Balthor's plate.

Balthor looked at him and smirked. "If you're sure you can read such big words, I would love to spread the message." He sent Zadon a wink, settling into his seat.

Lucian sat up, tuning into the conversation. "You will not address my spymaster in such a disrespectful way."

Balthor stood and offered Lucian a deep bow. "It would be an honor to address your spymaster. I wasn't aware that one had been appointed. Demons wouldn't be my first pick, after all we have a tendency to deceive, focusing only on one thing, ourselves." He sent a calculating look at Zadon before turning his eyes to Lucian.

"What I do is none of your business. Leave before I throw you out of the palace entirely. Your mistress isn't here; there's no reason for you to be."

"As you say, Sire." He walked out, heading for Aurelia's conference room, waiting for Suzu and Valri to extricate themselves.

It took a few hours but Suzu arrived dressed in all black, slinking in through the doors. "Is she dead? We had heard a rumor Faziel had killed her in defense of Drakore yesterday."

Balthor raised his eyebrows. "How intriguing. She lives—most decidedly. She will however, carry the scars forevermore. She lost her sight but gained the kingdom. The biggest issue is she will need time to secure the kingdom before she can return."

"Why have you returned? It merely adds to the rumor that she is dead." Anger rippled in the air.

"My darling girl, while you hold the Power of this Land, you need some back up to make sure you can keep Lucian and his pet on a secure leash while she is busy." Shock crossed her face, but he continued. "Valri may be compromised, and you need more backup than just your power, especially if you are going toe to toe with Zadon."

Suzu sighed heavily. "I don't need help. I can manage this on my own."

Valri strode into the room. "I think you forget that I can hear you even from the hallway. The joys of our demon nature. Why do you suspect I am compromised?"

Balthor turned his attention to her. "Aurelia thinks you're somehow deeply connected with Zadon, and thus you can't be trusted. At least not fully."

Valri sighed. "I am connected to him, though I hesitate to say deeply."

A look of confusion crossed Suzu's face. "How?"

"He has a favor with me. He can cash in at any point. So if we step too far over the line, I am sure that he will intercede."

"That puts a wrinkle in the plan. I need you to have a powerful backup just in case Zadon decides to play demon level tricks." He rubbed his temple, concerned that he would need to stay after all.

A soft knock sounded on the door that had all of them stiffening. Balthor strode over, opening it, ready to do damage to anyone interrupting them. An elderly woman whom he had never seen before stood there. She was hunched and rigid with age but her eyes glinted with mischief.

"Well hello, there my boy. You have certainly gotten larger since I last saw you."

Balthor's mind raced. He knew that voice, but it had been a few centuries since he had heard it. "Margo?"

She grinned and shoved, showing just how much of an illusion her mortal frame was. Her strength shifted him a bit back into the room. He stepped back, ushering her in, scanning the hallway uncertainly. *How had she arrived here? Where had she been?*

Closing the door, he grinned at the other two women. "The answer we need has presented herself. May I introduce you to Margoth."

Valris' eyes widened in shock. "The Margoth? The rumors were that you were killed when the dragons were."

"Dragons? Margoth? What is all this?" Suzu stepped warily away from the group.

"My dear, do I look threatening to you?" Margoth hobbled closer to Suzu. "In fact, one of you younglings get me a seat; these old bones need a rest."

Balthor laughed, "Margo, you've never needed a seat. However, I learned the lesson well to treat family reverently." He bowed deep before offering his arm to her and walking her to the nearest armchair. "Suzu, this is my mentor and matriarch. The last time we were together was when she trained me to be impervious to the soul crystals. She's the oldest demon that is known."

Margoth laughed a crackling coughing sound, "Yes boy that I am. But I am fairly certain at that time I did teach you to not speak so of a woman. We don't appreciate our age being widely discussed."

Valri cleared her throat. "How did you get past Zadon at the gate? He can smell demonic nature."

Margoth smirked. "Why my dear. I can hide everything about myself if I wish. I have been around so long no one can find me unless I wish it. Do you forget, child, that as we age, we gain more power. At my age, I have become quite adept at choosing the power carefully when the opportunity arises."

Suzu stepped closer. "So how will this work?"

Margoth grinned. "I'll be the long-lost-grandmother of someone in this cabal, and when the boy acts out of turn, I shall show him how to behave. Ask my big lad over there, I can be quite convincing."

Suzu nodded. "Well you will have to pretend to be my wife's grandmother. I don't suppose you can smell like a wolf shifter? Why do you want to support Aurelia? Or are you just backing up Balthor?"

"I have been watching that girl since she met her soul-bond. I know more of her fate than you, little panther. Though my time in this kingdom has shown me your fate will be quite intriguing."

"My fate?"

"You shall see, I shall say no more, though, because then they could claim I tampered."

Balthor couldn't suppress his smile, "Any issues should get reported to Madam Margoth. She will decide how to move forward. When we head home, I shall send a note to Margo so you all know to be prepared. Things may get a little tense."

"Oh no, Althy, it won't be tense, it will be quite exciting. It's been ages since something this interesting has come along."

Balthor laughed. "You would find this all rather exciting, you twisted old bat."

She crowed with laughter, her deceptively frail looking body shaking with mirth. Suzu walked over, sitting next to Margoth. "Come, teach me how to weave a good enough story for the King."

Balthor left them, excitement for when they finally returned. Margoth and Aurelia would be a formidable team.

forty-three

AURELIA

BYR - DRAKORE - YEAR 7568

Maledic walked her to the council room, a cloth tied around her sightless eyes. He situated her at the head seat. She didn't know what they had picked for her to wear—only that it was something from Faziel's closet. It unfortunately still stank of her nauseatingly sweet hair oils.

They couldn't hide her deficiency; the scars reaching past what the cloth covered. Yet the council of her father's kingdom didn't need to see her struggle to find her seat. She listened as they all filed in, the silence thickening as they noticed her. Maledic had explained the order he would settle the lords, so she had half a chance of knowing who was speaking to her. She could smell the tears and baking coming from her left and knew Maie sat there. She tightened her grip on her own fingers, to resist reaching out to the one familial person who still lived.

Instead, she cleared her throat. "Welcome back to the

council room, Lords and Lady. It comes down to me to tell you that Darius has relinquished the throne in favor of me."

There was a moment of silence before a scraping of chairs preceded the entire table standing, clapping, drowning out even her own thoughts. She merely tightened her fingers and waited. After long minutes, the councilors returned to their seats. "We have much to attend to. First and foremost, we need to plan my coronation."

Krooth the eagle lord stood. "Your Majesty, first I must exclaim at how gratifying it is to see you in the flesh. I have missed the even temper of the Berrid rule and relish seeing you entrusted with your family's power. The eagle clan will gladly step back into its role as royal executioner and arrange for the end of the traitor Darius' life. Thus clearing the way for you to acquire the power your father wielded."

Aurelia couldn't help the smirk. Some men would need to learn quickly that she wasn't what they expected. She straightened her shoulders, raising a finger, trusting Maledic that he would see her gesture. Satisfaction flooded in as Darius was ushered into the room. The council inhaled sharply, hands going to sheaths by the sound of it.

She cleared her throat and stood, both hands splayed on the tabletop. "Thank you for that rousing speech, Councilman Krooth. Now is time to listen, however. Darius is giving up the throne, but he is keeping the power for now." She paused the dense feelings of disapproval laying heavy. "What you don't understand, Councilors, is that I already wield more power than anyone here. When I find someone deserving of the Power of the Sky, Darius and I will find a way for him to relinquish it. I do not wish for him to die—at least not at this stage."

She sat, pleased at the sense of anger. "You must accept that I am not the meek daughter of your King any longer. She died long ago, forced to endure atrocities that the majority of you would crumple under. Drakore will change. I am not abandoning Palion. Instead, we will create a unified border kingdom accepting of everyone."

She could hear Darius' heavy footfalls as he took up his place behind her chair. Maie cleared her throat. "Aurelia—I mean Your Majesty. How will we unify with a kingdom where we have had, let's call it, tense relations?"

"Councilwoman Mercer, I have a unique relationship to the King of Palion. I am his wife."

She heard Maie gasp sharply and knew in that moment that Maledic hadn't told his parents of their connection. "As the wife and crowned Queen of Palion, I will forge the path. On to business, we need to arrange a coronation for me here. As agreed upon with Lucian, Drakore is mine first and foremost. Since you are all in town, let's get this done tomorrow."

Councilman Gossek, the meek, stood, pushing his chair with a shaky hand, the legs wobbling. "Your Majesty, I watched you grow as a child into a teen burgeoning with untold power. I would be honored to stand next to you tomorrow representing your father's court. He would be proud of you."

Councilman Gossek returned to his seat and the reports began. Aurelia wasn't surprised at just how far the kingdom had fallen. She began to make lists of all the things that she would need to address after the coronation. Projects that would need to be in place before she returned to alter the fabric on which Palion functioned.

Maledic touched her shoulder gently, his pine smell reassuring in her nose. His lips descended to her ear as he whispered, "Balthor has returned and is waiting to report in." She straightened, alarm floating through her. Balthor was supposed to be gone for a week or more, fully securing her spot in that palace.

"Councilors, I apologize for cutting this short. Tomorrow,

meet at the throne room where we will perform the coronation. Then I have a requirement of a final council meeting the next day. We will begin making strides towards the better kingdom we all want. Peace will come someday, but we will work hard to get there. Send notes on what you need. Before I return to Palion, I will be visiting each of the clans. Any further questions?"

"How will we all be united? You will forget those of the air when you are once again ensconced in the land of the wolves, panthers, and assorted animals. You will get distracted, and we will fall once more to the side." demanded Councilman Wulfric, the Flightless clan leader.

Aurelia rubbed her temple, her eyes beginning to ache. "We will all have to work on trust. While you may not understand this, I am already showing you trust by having this conversation in a room with people who supported a coup."

"We didn't!" The shouts rang out, but her patience had snapped. She slammed her hands on the table.

"YOU ARE HERE!" Her voice rang out so loudly the Councilors fell silent. She stood slowly, the wind beginning to be released. "I am no longer a child. You can no longer hide behind excuses. There is no way that the entirety of this room had no inkling of Rayner's moves or Cerial's missteps. Yet you stayed silent. Otherwise, you'd be dead." The wind began to whip. "I have gotten rid of one who should sit in this room. Perhaps it'd be best to demolish the entirety of the council and begin again."

She could sense Maledic behind her. Maie's energy filled the room, attempting to appease her wind magic. "That won't be necessary, Your Majesty. We will see how things develop and trust that you will remember us."

Aurelia sighed deeply, choosing to allow Maie to calm her. "I shall see you tomorrow."

She walked to the door, allowing Maledic to discreetly lead her with a hand at the small of her back.

forty-four

DARIUS

Byr - Drakore - Year 7568

Cerial sat on the foot of the bed watching him fasten his shirt in preparation for Aurelia's coronation. "You are so handsome, my love."

Darius smiled at her as the odd sensation of joy and warmth flooded through his body. "Are you sure I have to attend? The kingdom would prefer if I just disappear. You heard them at the council meeting. They want to kill me."

Cerial stood, patting down his collar, a sigh escaping her lips. "They don't understand you, love. But yes you do have to go and support her."

He sighed deeply before striding to the door.

As he entered the throne room, he did his best to tamp down all the memories this space held for him.

Aurelia was standing, dressed not in the stately gown like her sister would have insisted upon. Instead, she was garbed as a fighter. Her hair no longer bore the Palion crown; all that encircled her head were her long braids. The eyes that had reminded him so much of his beloved's were now covered with a lace-patterned fabric, adding a feeling of fanciful whimsy to her stark pain.

Her demon was stationed next to her, lounging almost bored by the entire process, while Maledic strode around arranging the various council members. Darius was shocked to see the Oba Aewenna hovering to the side, her veil of office fluttering. She hadn't been seen in the kingdom for years. One person who was oddly missing was Kygoss. He had been a second father to Aurelia, and with both Maledic and Maie here, his absence was a loud void.

Darius stood by the door, doing his best impression of the wall when Aurelia's voice rang through the room. "Darius, your place is here, not being a wallflower."

He gulped and schooled his expression as the entire room watched his progression toward the soon-to-be Queen. He bowed despite her lack of sight, as a silent way of trying to get the crowd to accept his change. "You requested me?"

She pointed to her side. He shrugged and took the position she wanted. Once he was there, in a low tone that only he and the demon would hear, she spoke. "You killed the maid, Darius."

His mouth thickened as if his tongue was swelling. She could end him, order his death or imprisonment, ending his reconnection with Cerial. She crossed her arms, leaning back against a small table. "She died in such an odd way. My magic could feel her lose all her blood."

Balthor leaned over in front of her. "I told you he's a blood monster."

"What does that mean, Darius? What is a blood monster?"

Darius blinked. She was so calm, he didn't hear anger or concern, merely a tinge of curiosity.

"I made a deal with a God, and this is what I was left with. I didn't want to kill the maid but I couldn't stop. The hunger over powered everything."

Balthor nodded. "Margoth warned me about this once. You must be careful in your deals with that God. He is chaos and death incarnate."

Aurelia scoffed. "He thinks he is. We shall see. One day, he and I will see who death truly obeys. I have a few guesses that, with some training, it will come to love me more."

"Why not just take my power now and leave the Gods out of it. Embrace the Power of the Sky and free me from the burden."

A sly grin unfurled on Aurelia's face that shot true fear into his gut. "You have a price to pay, Darius. Ten years of pain lay at your feet. A bit longer holding immense power won't kill you. Plus, it means I get to keep tabs on you."

Maledic chose that moment to interrupt. "Aurelia, its time."

She sighed, muttering, "At least this coronation won't be quite so violent." *What had happened before?*

As she walked away, Cerial appeared next to him. "Her shifted form emerged in a cataclysmic way. A few innocents were lost, much to her dismay."

He nodded, the only acknowledgment he could give her in public. Her admission did little to quell his frantic mind. *She was going to make him pay for something he never intended to happen.*

He watched as Maledic walked her to the center of the room, where Oba Aewenna stood waiting. She raised her hands up towards the ceiling. "The Goddess Tiva smiles down on this development. Will there be a sacrifice in order to secure this throne?"

Darius' blood froze. Perhaps that was why she wanted him front and center—she had changed her mind and would sacrifice him. Aurelia, however, laughed. "Much to the dismay of my new council, no. There will be no need for a sacrifice. The previous king is stepping down."

Oba Aewenna nodded once. "Alright. Is the crown here?" Maie stepped up with a crown Darius had never seen before, resting on the cushion.

From Darius' vantage point, he could almost identify the crown. Part of it was an old Drakorian one, the spears of the sun stones jutting out triumphantly. Cerial gasped sharply. "They've taken the true Drakorian crown and melded it with her Palion crown. The vines and leaves intertwining with the sun spears is not the original design. It must have taken all night."

Darius shrugged, but Cerial whispered on. "Darius, this is huge; both kingdoms are finally wholly united through her. The first time since the Gods split them."

Oba Aewenna called everyone's attention. "Tiva grants Aurelia the complex job of ruling both the land and the air, but she still waits for you to choose which power you will use to aid in your rule."

Aurelia merely waited, an eyebrow raised. Oba Aewenna cleared her throat and continued. "Do you accept this responsibility?"

"I accept the responsibility of ruling both."

"Do you accept the responsibility of bringing both kingdoms to the true Pantheon? To believe in them as much as they believe in you?"

Darius expected her to do what most would-be rulers did. Yet silence and shock met her simple answer.

"I do not."

A sense of pride filled him as he watched her relaxed state. Oba Aewenna blinked, obviously unsure how to move forward.

Aurelia grinned. "We've done this dance before, Aewenna.

The next part involves placing the crown on my head. Then there is some blood, as all ceremonies have."

Maledic cleared his throat once. Aurelia inclined her head in acknowledgment. "Oh Mal, I am merely reminding her of the routine. I would never dare to tell her what to do."

Oba Aewenna drew in a sharp breath before beckoning at Maie. "The crown, please."

Maie placed it within reach as Oba Aewenna dictated. "If you could kneel, Your Majesty."

Aurelia lowered herself, only a slight wobble betraying her lack of sight. Darius watched as the crown was lowered onto her head. He had never known anyone to be coronated twice, so it was anyone's guess as to what would happen to her.

As the crown settled onto her head, tension began to build within the room, as if the magic held in the very stones of the palace was begging to be released. Aurelia held out her hand, knowing what was coming. Oba Aewenna took the ceremonial knife and slashed down.

Darius' breath came fast, Cerial stepping up next to him. "Just breath. Do not focus on the blood."

Balthor stepped into the space Cerial occupied, forcing her to disappear. "Blood monster, if you move against her, I will take you to meet Tixdarr once again."

Darius breathed deep through his nose, choosing a speck on the floor to focus on. As the smell of blood hit him, his hunger swelled.

"I ... can't..."

Balthor placed himself fully between Darius and Aurelia.

"I'm sorry... Tell her I'll come again once it's under control."

Darius turned, fleeing out of the room.

forty-five

AURELIA

Byr - Drakore - Year 7568

After the coronation, training took all of their time. A few weeks had gone by in a blur, with Balthor being more and more demanding of her magic. They had only recently started refocusing on her combat skills.

"Sword really won't work as effectively for you anymore. There is a higher likelihood that you will cut yourself by accident. I want you to work with a staff, and perhaps we can grow into using a spear." Balthor's voice moved away from her in her perpetual darkness.

A thump began to accompany his footsteps, nearing once more. "Hand out, please."

Aurelia sighed heavily, extending her hand, a wooden pole meeting her seeking fingers. As they encircled the polished shaft, she realized just how weighty it was. "How long is it?"

"You want the staff to be about as tall as you, though it could be a bit taller. If you feel to the end, you'll feel that the ends taper off. It will give you range and help disguise your ability through your disability."

She smirked. "How in the hell am I disguising anything. The scarf clearly shows anyone paying attention that I am blind."

Balthor chuckled. "Well. When you return to Palion, walking the streets with a stick guiding your way, they will think you helpless and humbled."

Catching on to his thoughts she laughed. "I see. Me, helpless."

"Yes. Now you can see my plan. At some point, you will show them just how deadly you still are."

She nodded along, seeing the logic and just how she could play into it. She took a deep breath and began swinging the staff slowly, feeling how her arm and wrist responded to the new weight.

"Let Crow Man continue his work with the intelligence while you and I sink into this skill. Your powers will pave the way for you to absorb the techniques more easily after about a week of intensive study. We will practice for a few hours every day; you need to be flawless." She nodded. "First lesson. Feel the impact when you make contact with something. Swing to your right."

She swung and felt the impact before she heard it. It was the oddest combination of soft and hard. As the staff made contact, her brain registered something, a light—bright highlighting of where she made a connection.

But that couldn't be.

She pulled back and swung again, this time waiting for the vision to return to her. His left shoulder lit up as the staff impacted, and Aurelia yelped, immediately dropping it, its clattering causing a second yelp to escape.

Balthor laughed it off. "It's fine. We will have you anticipating movements despite your lack of sight in no time."

"Balthor, I could see you."

It was his turn to drop the staff. This time, the clattering indicated it rolled away from him, forgotten.

"What?"

"It was like your outline vibrating away from where I hit you. The first was the upper right arm, and just now I hit your left shoulder. Right??" She was excited and desperate.

He hummed in his throat, his tone carefully neutral. "Has it ever happened before?"

"Once, but I thought I was losing my mind. Right after my sight was taken. When Darius came begging me to take his powers and I threw that dagger—I could see his shoulder."

"Before or after it made contact." His lack of emotional register in his voice was starting to make her skin itch.

"After."

"You didn't have a great handle on your magic then, but you do now."

She could hear him come closer but couldn't place whether he had gone behind her or in front of her. "Balthor..." She didn't hear anything after he stopped moving, just the sounds of her own breath and erratic heartbeat. Suddenly his hand appeared bleeding in front of her.

She sobbed. "You're bleeding." Her knees felt weak.

"Interesting. One more experiment." It took all of her self-control not to stomp indignantly for an answer or an emotion from him.

He took her by the hand, dragging her from the room, ignoring undeniable stares they were getting. She struggled to get her breathing under control as he directed her where to go. She could smell the outdoors as they came to a stop in a breathless pant.

"Alright." He shifted her shoulders a bit. "What about now?"

As if a switch flipped, she saw a flower floating in front of her. Glancing down, she could even see the stem where it had come from. "How can I see this?"

"Not here. Lets get Crow Man and talk. I have an idea of what's happening."

They went directly to Maledic's cave. He had purloined her father's old study and from the whispers of the staff, had redecorated. Opting for a much more serious and streamlined aesthetic—it didn't sit right with the Maledic she knew. He used to be cozy, with soft edges, but since she lost her sight, those had been hidden from the world.

She heard Maledic gasp as they came to a halt in his study, rushing to her side. "What happened? Are you alright?"

Balthor shushed him. "No, Crow Man. It's better. She can see!"

Aurelia blanched, taking a step backward, shaking her head in denial just as Maledic exclaimed, "Really! A miracle?"

She fumbled, taking another step back, her magic rising with her panic. As it rose within her, the room seemed to sparkle with odd flashes of light in strange corners. Maledic and Balthor were visible purely because of the negative space they took up. Yet as Maledic scratched his head, the place his fingers touched sparkled gold.

"Balthor, you need to explain, because I am so close to losing it I can taste the madness." Her voice shook with her suppressed emotions.

"You need to embrace your magic, Reli. That is the key." Balthor's voice was calm and centered as she fought to listen.

Maledic must have clued into Balthor's train of thought because he excitedly began rocking on his heels. "Everything dies! All the time, things are dying around us—insects, plants. When someone falls, ill that's a form of death, I'm sure. If your hold on death is that precise, you would be able to see at least the shapes of most things."

It clicked, and mentally she opened her arms to the dark

magic that loved her so much. Her eyes felt hot, and if she could have tears, they would have flooded down. Instead, her breath came in pants and hiccups. She forced deep breaths, and the truest smile she had ever felt since childhood adorned her face. "I can finally hold my own, truly. We can return to unite the kingdoms."

"Give me another week of training with your staff. It will get you stronger and give you time to tour Drakore before returning to Palion. I am sure Lucian needs rescuing from Margoth."

Aurelia nodded, her grin beginning to hurt. "Yes. We shall. Mal, make the plans—we will spend a day in each clan. That will be your seven days, Balthor. Each day we will spend several hours talking to the leaders, and the afternoons will be dedicated to training."

Balthor groaned a bit but nodded. Elation filled her as she realized she could see him nodding.

forty-six

MALEDIC

> *Centaurs dwell in the desert of Baelia and fully embrace the little oasis pockets that exist. Their dead are brought out to the harsh desert winds, each community having their own sacred place to leave loved ones for the Gods of heat and wind to take them.*
>
> *~Ancient Death Rites, Margoth's Journal*

He waited eagerly outside her room. During the night, Feginth had visited his dreams and requested that he bring her to the cave to meet the eggs. On his way to her room, he had stopped to notify Balthor that her training would have to happen in the evening in Slana, which was the destination of the day anyway.

His heart rate jumped as her door cracked open. There

was a pause before she asked, "Mal?" She sounded unsure, but it was miles better than before they unlocked her powers.

"Yes. I wanted to catch you when you first woke up. It's finally time I showed you my biggest secret. It's a very secret slice of Drakore. It'll be an adventure, but one I think you will enjoy."

She looked rather taken aback, but slowly she nodded. "Alright, Maledic."

He led her outside to a terrace balcony. "We will need to shift. Can you see when you shift?"

"To be honest, I haven't tried, since the incident."

"No time like the present, then." He waited, wanting to be able to talk her through it if he needed to.

She seemed to turn toward the new sun barely waking in the sky, drinking in the rays, before a deep breath escaped. As her exhale ended, she was in her dragon state. A marked difference between her last dragon shift and this one was the eyes that were now whitened, scars jagged and full of echoes of pain slashed from the sockets.

"Are you going to be able to follow me?"

She nodded her regal head, and he grinned easily, shifting into his crow form. He flew to the cave, the path so familiar after all the years of visiting. He could feel her awe through their distant bond as the vastness of the inner cave registered in her mind.

As they neared the ground, he shifted back, a small pop echoing through the cave. She stayed in her wispy dragon form, her head looking around. Suddenly, she nudged the sand piles gently with her nose.

"Yes those. When you were taken, I came very close to dying myself. When all seemed to be ending, I met Feginth—a magnificent dragon. The one from the legends. She was locked down here for centuries by the Gods. However, she was intricately tied to your family. When your family perished, she became tied only to you."

Aurelia flew over to the farther hidey-holes as if she knew exactly where the eggs were. It seemed she could see more clearly in her dragon form as she circled the piles.

"Can you sense them somehow? Feginth could always sense you. She was able to keep me motivated and interested in life. These butterflies are pieces of her, I think."

Dragon-Aurelia did a slow spin in the air, tracking the curious insects.

"I'm pretty sure it's a death ritual from long before the Gods. When she died, she became this torrent of butterflies. Some have left, but the eggs have never been without her in some form."

Aurelia dropped, shifting to stand next to him. She wobbled her feet, acclimating to the uneven ground. "How many are there?"

"There are six. We can't tell anyone. She warned that the Gods may come hunting for them. There is also one that keeps growing, which I had to move off by itself."

He wandered over to where the black egg lay. As he dug in the sand, he could feel Aurelia stepping in behind him. "The butterflies are.. somehow.. helping me see.."

He half-turned, the note of wonder in her voice drawing him in. The pain was quick—then gone. Just a flash across his palm.

"Ah shit." He glanced down, noting the blood beginning to well up and drip onto the sand.

He watched as one lone drop beaded up and slid down the sand to splatter against the shell of the black dragon egg.

forty-seven

AURELIA

Byr - Drakore - Year 7568

She could feel tiny wisps of feet covering her arms almost as soon as she shifted into her mortal form. In her dragon shape, she could see the butterflies; she was still bound to the muted tones of grey and black but the shapes were clear and concise.

As they landed on her color seeped into her vision again, the colors more vibrant than she remembered pigments ever being. "The butterflies are helping me see!" She repeated, her voice taking on the panicked tone of excitement.

In front of her, Maledic was crouched, staring into the sand mound. "Mal, what is it?"

A cracking sound met her question as he scrambled back away. "I think its hatching!"

"What? Wait! That's possible?"

"I don't know, I was just told to protect them."

"Go help it! Dig it out!" She watched the shape of Maledic coming in and out of color as the butterflies fluttered on and off her. Maledic dug deeper into the hole, unconcerned by the cut on his palm.

As the egg came into view, Aurelia gasped at the size. The egg was easily two feet around she couldn't tell how deep into the ground it lay. "Aurelia, theres a chunk coming off. What do I do?"

"It may shock you to realize this, but I have never met an actual dragon! You have though—use that knowledge!" Panic and excitement crested in her mind as she picked up a cry from the creature emerging.

Maledic leaned down, and as he scooted back, he had something in his arms. The butterflies swarmed her. Her vision returned for a few moments as the butterflies landed. She could see the spiny creature, membranous wings draped open, the head crying piteously against Maledic's chest.

The dragonet was white, almost silver. As awe and shock ebbed reality crashed around her.

"Mal, what are we supposed to do? How can you care for a baby dragon? It won't be a secret from the Gods if we walk around with it."

Maledic stepped onto the more solid ground, away from the sand. He placed the dragon on the ground, letting it test out its own legs. He sat next to it on the cobblestone and Aurelia felt out of place.

"Aurelia come here and sit next to me."

"If I move too much, the butterflies will leave and you will both just be shades of grey and black again."

Maledic looked up at her and sent her a smile she hadn't seen since childhood. "Feginth will help you. Come here."

He held out a hand and she took it allowing him to aid her in sitting down next to him. The dragon stumbled toward Maledic, crying. It's sharp taloned wings dragging painfully behind it. The horns of the dragon had begun to sprout leaves and flowers, that quickly shriveled and died to be repeated once more.

"Mal what are we going to do?"

Maledic hissed out a breath. "I'm not sure. I do know with us both, this little man will be fine. We may have to protect him, though."

"How do you know it's a boy?"

"You can't hear him? He speaks in my mind. His name is Bashi." - there was a pause before he continued - "He is the death dragon reborn. Long ago, he was killed to give Tixdarr the power to build the Realm of the Dead."

She felt like a small explosion had gone off in her mind. "If he's the death dragon, why is he white or silver? My magic is a black void."

Silence reigned. Just the fluttering of wings and small creaks as Bashi moved.

"He says he knows the beauty of death, just look at his horns. At times, for those sick or in pain, death can be a wanted release. He says in time you may even learn how to see souls that wander this world and help them find their ultimate rest. Death doesn't always have to be the scary monster."

"Oh." She sat stunned, unsure how to move forward or what to say.

"Bashi can feel our connection, and if you want to let him in, he's willing to bond with us both."

To bond with the dragon would open her up, make her vulnerable. As if reading her mind, Maledic grabbed her hand. "He isn't asking to pry. He claims he can help you and that the process is simple and can be done later. I know you aren't ready."

She sighed deeply. She wasn't ready. So much of the time she still gripped onto her sanity with her fingernails. She couldn't even bear to have Maledic experience her mental weakness. She couldn't taint the first dragon in Baelia.

She turned toward Bashi, giving him a seated half bow. "Thank you for your offer, Bashi. I can't do that at this point."

Maledic cleared his throat. "Bashi understands and will be here when you're ready. As to what to do next, he said Feginth's soul can help this one time. Once we are out of the cave, we will have to own his existence. He said long ago, Queens used to beg the dragons to have their rule blessed by their existence." Mal laughed. "He wants to be perched on your shoulder as you walk to your Palion Palace."

"I see. That would put him in danger, though. Does he realize he's not a full grown beast?"

Maledic chuckled. "He has more power than we know, apparently. Plus, apparently he will grow quickly."

Aurelia rubbed her temples. "Let's do this. We certainly can't leave him here and there will be no mention of the other eggs."

She looked at Maledic once more, relishing in his handsome face. Sorrow pierced through her heart at the bags under his eyes and the slight hunched nature of his shoulders; life was weighing on her soulbond and it was her fault.

She sighed silently, thanking Feginth for her gift in allowing Aurelia to truly see him once more.

She shifted, the legions of butterflies taking flight as her body once more became that of the wraith dragon. From this form, everything took on shades of gray. She watched as around twenty butterflies swarmed Bashi, landing on him. In two breaths, the dragonet became a small crow hopping around on its two taloned feet. Maledic laughed and shifted, teaching the crow/dragon how to fly with the feathered wings.

Aurelia laughed at the comical display. Once Maledic had Bashi up and flying, they all winged their way toward the Slana manor house that haunted her dreams.

LUCIAN

Byr - Palion - Year 7568

Lucian rubbed his temples, a migraine building behind his eyes as those in front of him fought.

"Its time he started changing things. Really step into his role as king and show his people how he intends to rule." Zadon banged on the tabletop, causing Lucian's heart to jolt with the noise.

"He is showing his people. He's stable and calm and kind —even to Aurelia—aiding her in returning to rule her kingdom of Drakore. Together they are the uniting couple, destined to go down in history as the only ruling pair to manage it." Suzu triumphantly argued, setting aside what Lucian was beginning to suspect was fake knitting.

Lucian sat straighter, preparing to once more council Suzu and Zadon to be civil, when Belvina's voice rang out. "Suzu, my love, are you tormenting Zadon again? At this rate, that scarf will never be completed."

Lucian held his breath, hoping that the elderly voice that so often accompanied Belvina would stay silent. He carefully let out his held breath as silence reigned. Zadon sulked against the wall, and Belvina calmly re-instructed her wife in the intricacies of knitting. Just as his body began to relax, the migraine becoming fuzzy along the edges, an elderly hand gripped the edge of the chair next to him.

"Hello, young Princeling."

"He's a King now, Granny, remember," Belvina called out kindly, shooting an apologetic smile to Lucian.

Lucian sent her a microscopic nod, swallowing his complaint. Deep down, watching Margoth and her granddaughter elicited strange feelings within him. His grandparents were long gone, well before he was born, having chosen to abandon Palion completely when Harold took the throne. He turned to Margoth, a pasted smile on his face. "Greetings, Margoth. I hope your accommodations are suitable."

"Ah yes, about that."

Belvina stood, rushing to Margoth's side, shaking her head emphatically. "No. No. No. We don't need to bother the King."

"Granddaughter!" Margoth slapped the table much harder than Lucian expected. "He is the Princeling and he inquired. He should know how his palace runs when he is distracted."

Lucian's curiosity was piqued beyond the need for the correct title.

"Grandmother, he's the KING."

"Oh Pish. Princeling, Kingly—the difference is minimal. He still should know."

Lucian cleared his throat. "Belvina, it is fine. I did inquire after all."

She met his eyes before nodding. "As you desire, Sire, but she still will be respectful despite her fading mind."

"Did she just say her loving grandmother is crazy?"

Margoth leaned close as if whispering, but instead she was speaking loudly for all to hear.

Everyone chuckled while Lucian did his best to keep her on track. "Miss Margoth, you implied something was wrong."

"Ah yes, young Princeling. The room is so dusty. My humors are all misaligned by the accumulation, and I fear grave consequences. When I was much younger, I had the joy of visiting the palace of your father. This was never an issue then."

Lucian's head began to throb in time with his heartbeat. "I am sorry you are experiencing this, Miss Margoth. I will personally speak to the maids and see this rectified."

Margoth clapped. "Excellent. Now one more thing. The eggs in the morning are being served rather cold."

"I see, well, I shall speak to the chefs as well."

Margoth nodded once, a toothy smile on her wrinkled face.

Zadon groused from the corner. "Those tasks and complaints are far below the purview of a King, as you well know."

Belvina straightened, ready to defend her grandmother. Lucian held a hand, staying her reaction. "Zadon! You have been told to keep your opinions to yourself unless asked to share. I asked Miss Margoth, and she shared with me."

Margoth leaned in, her sickly sweet scent clogging his nose. "Don't be too hard on him, Princeling. This youngling just needs to grow up a bit. There is plenty of time for that—one can hope."

Zadon dramatically rolled his eyes, but Lucian was just glad he kept quiet for once. Belvina cleared her throat. "Anyway, we were at the marketplace and heard some disturbing rumors about Aurelia. Has anyone heard from her directly?"

Zadon sat at the table. "All we've heard is that she is now disfigured and licking her wounds. We expect that once she's accepted her new reality, she will return. She's going to struggle not doing as much as before."

"Oh now." Margoth sat straighter. "You can't underestimate anyone." She leaned in conspiratorially closer to Lucian. "Perhaps he needs some social training along with growth. He looks old enough to have learned that lesson."

Lucian sadly felt inclined to agree. Every day, it seemed Zadon grew more erratic and less calculated.

forty-nine

AURELIA

BYR - DRAKORE - YEAR 7568

They landed in Slana, and Aurelia was shocked that Kygoss wasn't waiting. Instead, Maie stood as the leader, with Balthor next to her, the staff he had bequeathed her in his hand, ready to pass it off the minute she shifted.

She watched Balthor, better able to see his facial expressions in her dragon form. His eyes were glued to the small crow that was tucked under her wing. Maledic shifted and held out his hand. "Bashi, the time is never going to be better than now."

There was a pause, and Maledic turned to Balthor, assessing. "He is, as of yet, a friend."

Bashi bumped her in a friendly way, almost like a crow hug, before descending down to Maledic. She waited in her more powerful form to see just how Balthor would behave.

Balthor cocked his head at her and planted his free hand on his hip. "You've been keeping secrets, Reli, but this one takes the cake. The damn death dragon! Come on down. I won't eat him; I'm fairly certain he could eat me if he was motivated to." Balthor's head shook in disbelief.

Aurelia shifted next to Balthor, aiming so she could take her staff. Feeling more comfortable with a weapon in her hand.

"I didn't keep this secret; he did." She pointed at Maledic.

Maie cleared her throat, her eyes ping-ponging around. "What are you..."

Bashi's disguise popped away, his body growing and becoming his reptilian self. "Mother, I have the honor of introducing my new friend Bashi, Dragon of Death. He would like to assure you he is newly hatched and one day he will be very impressive in size."

Aurelia swallowed her giggle, instead directing her attention to Maie. "Councilwoman Maie, it is time to discuss your clan's issues. What do the crows need?"

Maie lingered on Bashi before formally bowing to Aurelia. "Yes. If you'll follow me, we can settle into the study. There's room for everyone to get comfortable."

Aurelia used her staff to guide her through the hallways and around the staircase. She paused by the stairs, memories crowding her mind.

Maledic came up behind her, his smell crowding in. Gently, he placed his hand on her lower back. She nodded once before following his gentle guidance to the study. Maledic leaned over to her ear and whispered, "He won't be here. He betrayed us for the last time."

"He doesn't need to be this thoroughly banished. I can handle a traitor."

"You may be able to, but I am still on the fence."

"So long as you are doing this for you. I won't carry the burden of this decision, Mal."

His hand traveled over to her hip, squeezing lightly. "Understood." Bashi licked her cheek before Maledic moved away.

He stopped short at the doorway's entrance. "The table is straight through to your left."

She nodded, adjusting her grip on the staff as she moved forward. She found the table easily. Maledic, right behind her, sat. She crossed her hands on her lap, the staff resting across the arms of her chair, ever at the ready.

"Councilwoman?"

Maie's shape nodded as she cleared her throat. "May I speak frankly, Aur... I mean, Your Majesty?"

"Yes." Aurelia held her breath; something big was coming, the tension in the air building to it.

"Drakore as a whole is an open, oozing wound. There are food shortages to begin with, and communities such as Slana have come together to try and aid everyone. However, I fear for places such as the proud eagle clan. Councilman Krooth runs a tight ship with a self—first mentality."

Aurelia had expected this problem and could have guessed at the prideful eagle clan's additional issues. "What else?"

"Hunger makes for anger. Anger in some is expressed physically. In the past, families reached out and clan leaders protected the innocents, and turned in the guilty to the crown."

"I don't need a civics history lesson, Maie. Get to the point."

Maie stuttered. "Its families. Those with violent members have nowhere safe to report it. Added to that, soulbonds were unable to be recognized, so it's hard to track everyone."

The implications of what she said hit home for Aurelia. Living in fight-or-flight with no say in anything.

"We will issue a proclamation by end of day. I'll need your

fastest messengers. Soulbonds are to be celebrated if all parties are walking into the relationship willingly. If anyone is seeking a dissolution of a mating, I will make it a priority. Safety will not be a gamble in my kingdom any longer."

Silence met her proclamation, and then Bashi squawked. "Yes, you're right, Bashi." Maledic seemed to be making notes as Bashi's talons clicked on the table.

Maie cleared her throat. "There's one more very important area we need help with."

Aurelia tapped her fingers on the staff, waiting.

"Medical help. Med witches have disappeared with the last administration. I'm guessing they fled, but people die everyday of treatable sicknesses. I've done what I can with herbs and tonics for Slanians, but the issue is wider spread."

Fury ignited hot and heavy in her veins. If she still had access to Darius, he would be at the end of her staff receiving some much—needed punishments; however, that wasn't possible since he fled. She couldn't afford to do much more of anything, at least not yet.

"Balthor, we have a meeting to attend. Now." She ground out the words, trusting Maledic to figure out the announcements.

She used her staff and pushed herself up, relying on it and her sense of hearing to find the door where Balthor's smell awaited her.

She followed him, using her nose as he led her out of the house to a small field next to the stables. Balthor came up in front of her and lowered his tone. "You sure you want to do this right now? I can sense your magic jumping beneath your skin."

She took several deep breaths, pulling her powers tighter. "I won't lose control. Not like at the Palion coronation—but training happens now."

"Alright." He moved the staff in front and placed her

hands in the best position—one third of the staff above her top hand and one third below her bottom hand.

"I'm going to move your staff; let your body follow as you learn the drills. Tomorrow I'll have a staff, and you'll practice returning hits and blocking."

She nodded, the buzzing in her head preventing her from talking. The process was tiring, but by the end, she felt like perhaps she had a handle on her powers.

Balthor stepped away, stretching slightly. He leaned back, in whispering, "Turn around and bow."

Huh. She stiffened. All the calm that the workout had given her was ebbing. She didn't argue, though, just turned and bowed. A cheer erupted from the crowd she hadn't sensed. She muttered out of the side of her mouth, "Let's get back to the manor house. I need food and a bed."

"As you wish, my Queen."

She settled into her room after a good soak and clean clothes. Her mind raced with the problems Drakonians faced in her absence. She would have a fight on her hands with Lucian to get the resources she would need to pull this off.

She fell into a restless sleep, the stress of what was to come mounting. In the morning, she skipped breakfast, heading instead to the balcony. Maledic waited there for her, Bashi roaming the floor, his talons clacking.

"Which clan will we visit today?" His tone held forced positivity, leading her to question who he had gotten into a fight with overnight.

"Let's go to the Eagle Clan. They need to understand that their pride will have to take a backseat, just as I had to when she took my eyes."

Maledic nodded once. Before he could speak, Balthor's voice rang out from her room. "Reli, it's wake up time!"

She chuckled. "We are out of here."

"We? Who is this we?"

She heard his footsteps and then his dramatic gasp. "Oh. You and Crow Man."

She laughed as Bashi squawked. "Bashi would like his presence acknowledged as well." Balthor bowed low. "Actually, Balthor, we need your help today. When you shift, your hands are free. So you'll have to carry Bashi for this tour."

"Oh. I can do that if Bashi agrees."

Maledic leaned over, picking him up and walking toward Balthor. "Bashi agrees but has declared that by the fourth morning, he will be flying on his own."

Aurelia laughed. "Humble."

Balthor took the dragonet, and everyone shifted. Aurelia was ready to get going, clear from the heaviness of the past.

As they took to the air, surprise filled her. The sound of hundreds of crows cawing filled the air. She spun in a circle, searching for the shifters. The trees around the manor were full of the blue-black birds. They appeared as black balls on the trees. She roared to the sky as she climbed, leading her small group toward the Eagle Clan.

It wasn't until they reached the Eagle's tree top villa that she realized fifteen crows were flying behind them.

<hr>

Maie had been right: Krooth's people were suffering just as the Slana people were. They were also extraordinarily prideful.

After settling into the council room, she got right to business. "The time of putting your clan before the betterment of the kingdom is over. Pride has no place here."

Krooth grumbled a bit, grudgingly nodding.

Their complaints were all the same. When she had heard enough of the tragedies, she would order Balthor outside where their training would progress each day.

They went to the Owl Clan next, followed by the Ravens, Falcons, and Flightless, all of which were more of the same. Each morning, when they rose to move on, bird shifters of that clan would send them off. Then, as they flew on, fifteen to twenty shifters would join the entourage.

T heir last day was in Gossek's land of the Sparrows. After their sparring, which had developed into something much more intense, Maledic, Balthor and Bashi met her in the small sparrow council room.

"Tomorrow's the day we actually unite with Palion. We need to decide how we want to return," Balthor stated.

Aurelia strummed her fingers. "I won't hide. Yet I am not sure that we should shove this newfound popularity in Lucian's face."

Maledic chuckled. "You should shove everything in his face. It's time he chose a side—his pets or uniting the kingdoms."

"How would that even look?"

Bashi squawked, "Bashi envisions you walking up the palace hill, Bashi on your shoulder with your staff in hand, Balthor on one side, me on the other. The sky filled with your people. It will show him you are serious." Maledic paused his translation. "He also wants to remind you that you could bond with him and make this process much easier."

Aurelia debated. She would need every advantage, at least at first, while she finally established her rule in Palion. "Alright, Bashi, how does this work?"

Mal grinned. "He says, as everything does, a bit of blood and a dash of magic."

She groaned a bit but , pulling a dagger from her corset. Quickly, she slashed her palm, holding it out in front of her.

Bashi leaned down, licking the slice. A searing pain started in her hand and scorched through her body. She curled in on herself and moaned.

A deep, calm voice resonated in her mind. "Hello, Aurelia. It is much nicer to speak to you through this method. We shall have you arrive in style."

part three

PANTHEON BEGINS

GODS HISTORY AS SEEN BY MARGOTH SEER OF BAELIAN HISTORY

The Gods appeared overnight, introducing themselves boldly. Tiva was the first, the bold pixie woman walking through what would one day become Longspire.

"Hear me, humans! It is I, the Goddess Tiva, the purveyor of the female arts."

The humans didn't react in any particular way; rather, they nodded at her and moved on with their days. Tiva as expected, was highly insulted. Poofing back to her husband, the God Oxius, in the Void.

The next day, they both appeared, anger and entitlement radiating from them.

"Humans. You refused to listen to me. Perhaps your barbaric race needs to listen to one hung with a cock and balls to believe." Tiva was a pretty picture, sitting primly on her massive minotaur's shoulder.

He glowered, a grumble coming from his chest.

An old man, hobbled with age, bowed to them. "We need no Gods. Feginth, the dragon of Life, protects this area. She is all we need."

Tiva threw her hand out, a blue sparkling cloud swarming the man, freezing him in place. "Oxius, my love, we must make an example if we are to gain followers. Should it be a positive or a negative one?"

Oxius appeared to consider the now—gathering crowd, but before he could speak, a younger man pushed to the front.

"Please release him! He's my father and the village elder. We need him."

Oxius laughed, cruelty dripping from him. "And she is my world, yet he insulted her. As did your entire village yesterday. This shall be a punishing example, my darling."

Tiva cackled. "As you say, my love."

Tiva stood tall, using her hand on his horn for balance as her wings twitched. She waved her arms wide and spoke loudly. "Humans will no longer be able to be blessed by magic —not until all the dragons die and the second coming arrives. Until then, you shall be dirty, magicless parasites. As for you two," She pointed at the Elder and his son. "You will be cursed to live to watch the downfall of your meager people."

"No! I have a family! I can't live beyond them!"

"Perhaps you'll spend your centuries teaching your people manners!" Tiva snapped.

Then they were gone. Longspire heard rumors of temples going up in honor of their tormentors not long after. It made sense that soon they closed their borders to any magical species, thus making the history of humans difficult.

The Gods grew quickly, Tiva and Tixdarr loving to spend most of their time in the Baelian realm.

fifty

LUCIAN

Byr - Palion - Year 7568

> *Minotaurs are a unique species because they don't have female minotaurs. A dead Minotaur man gets dressed in his warrior's best. They are then paraded through the city, where the citizens would stand silently in honor of their sacrifice. Then, at the end of the parade, they would be hoisted onto a pyre and sent to their ancestors through ash.*
> *~Ancient Death Rites, Margoth's Journal*

"Lucian, you have to stop her!"

Lucian rolled his eyes so hard it hurt. "She's not doing any harm. Margoth is an old woman who needs her family. I won't stop that from happening."

He stormed to his office door, intent on leaving the conversation behind, when Zadon moved faster, blocking his way.

"No! There is something more afoot. I just don't know

what. She can't be allowed her own rooms in the palace. Someone needs to keep an eye on her."

The paranoia shocked Lucian. Zadon had always been so steady, but since Margoth's arrival, he was unraveling at the seams. "Are you afraid of an elderly wolf? I can assure you her wolf side has long gone dormant."

"NO!" Zadon's shout had Lucian stepping back.

"Move aside, Zadon. You don't get a say in this. It is harmless for an old lady to take up rooms in the residence wing."

Zadon stiffened, his face taking on a look of pure fury. "Fine. On your own head be it."

As he stepped aside, the door slammed open, shocking them both into reaching for their swords.

A serving lad stumbled in, a look of wonderment on his face. "I've been sent to fetch you! Come see, milord! The Queen has returned!"

Indignation flashed through Lucian's mind. Why would she return without warning him? Added to that, the fighting with her and Zadon would only worsen, especially with how he was acting.

"Zadon, you are under orders not to provoke her. If she pushes you first, I will handle it."

A low growl emanated from Zadon before he jerked his head in assent. "Fine."

He made his way to the front doors, Zadon hot on his heels. They were thrust open, the sounds of cheering and shouting just reaching him.

As he stepped out, looking down the steps, he noticed he was not the first palace resident to arrive. The women of the court were all decorated in their court finery. His eyes snagged on Margoth, positioned the closest to him, oddly holding a cat in her arms idly scratching it.

As if feeling his gaze, she grinned. "Say hello, Little Princeling, this is Niamh."

He nodded absently at her. Why was everyone dressed up? Did they know she was returning?

He turned his attention to the mayhem coming up palace hill. She was dressed in fighting gear—a hearken to her past, perhaps because the staff spoke truth to the rumors she had lost her eyesight in securing the throne. She was even wearing some sort of covering over her eye sockets. Her hair was different, finally let down, a crown he'd never seen before gracing her proud head.

His eyes shifted, catching and holding on the reptilian figure clinging to Aurelia's shoulder, its wing getting tangled in her hair. Somehow, she had found a dragon. *How? Where?*

Despite her issues, this woman had brought what appeared to be half the Drakore kingdom. He straightened his shoulders as his mind rolled through how to handle his wife.

As she ascended the steps, the women, one at a time curtsied low before stepping in behind her once she had passed. He watched, his mind blanking in disbelief, as the majority of his court peeled away, joining her.

Zadon stood behind him, and Ulfur rigidly stood to the side. That was all that was left for him in his own palace. He squared his shoulders and affixed a welcoming smile.

Something needed to change in his kingdom, and he was more convinced now than ever that he would have to push the change despite his constant struggle with the monsters in his own head.

She stopped in front of him, cocking her head to the side, a smile on her face. "Lucian."

"Welcome home, Aurelia."

"Home." She seemed to be tasting the word. "That remains to be seen. I am pleased to see the kingdom still stands."

He nodded, doubt creeping in; perhaps she retained some vision. "I noticed you have quite the entourage."

"Yes, I am told the ranks have grown quite large. They needed to see their Queen to her destination—proof that I am shown respect here."

Lucian nodded wisely. "Of course, we offer respect, as you were crowned here as well." She leaned against the staff, putting more weight on the wooden tool. "Who is on your shoulder, Aurelia?"

"Oh him?" She half-shrugged, careful not to dislodge the silvery beast. "I got jealous. You had a pet. I wanted one too. Maledic did what any decent soulbond would. This is Bashi, the Dragon of Death."

Lucian bowed deeply as the dragon roared. "Welcome to Palion, Bashi."

Aurelia seemed to be studying him, but before she could say anything, Margoth had stepped forward from her retinue.

"Bashi? I never thought I'd get to see your scaly face again." The cat she had been petting was now sitting on her shoulder, much like Bashi was on Aurelia. She pushed Maledic out of the way, threading her arm in Aurelia's. "Let's go catch up, Miss Queen. My, have you grown."

Lucian's mind stuttered. She knew Aurelia? She knew Bashi? That wasn't possible... Unless. The words "Miss Queen" played on repeat. He was never the King to Margoth, only ever Princeling.

As the women all entered the palace heading to Aurelia's wing, Zadon stepped up behind Lucian hissing. "Margoth is a demon. She's been toying with us this entire time. It's the only explanation."

He swung his eyes to Ulfur, who shook his head. "They don't tell me. Suzu is well versed in secrets, and Belvina is, as you have well known, sworn to Aurelia."

Lucian turned to Zadon, glare ready. "Perhaps if you had treated her like a fucking innocent from the beginning, she wouldn't have felt the need to bring Drakonians to aid her in returning. Nor would she have needed to befriend extremely powerful individuals." Zadon opened his mouth, but his wolf surged, as if standing up to Zadon was beating back his own monsters. "She has a fucking dragon, Zadon! It changes our entire approach."

He turned, stomping into the palace, heading for his study. The time had come to wake up and take charge of his kingdom. He could no longer afford to give his grief his full attention. Instead, it would now have to be shoved to the back of his mind to molder while he worked double time to save what he could.

fifty-one

AURELIA

DUELE - PALION - YEAR 7568

They settled into her rooms relatively easily. The process of getting to the palace had sapped at her energy. She had poured much of her power reserves into being able to see the flickering lights of death and the dying, thus aiding in her journey.

The result, though, was pure exhaustion. She settled into an armchair, safe within her suite of rooms.

"Suzu, Margoth. What's been happening?"

Bashi had hopped off her shoulder, gliding to perch on the back of her chair, overseeing all.

"The pup and his pet are at odds. It won't take much effort to break that bond permanently." Margoth's voice was gravely with age.

Aurelia nodded and waved her hand, encouraging more.

"There really wasn't much happening here except the fighting. He's snapped several times, even siding with the feisty Margoth over Zadon. Lucian found out about my role in his father's death, but for some reason he hasn't acted on it." Suzu's voice was tentative but pure.

"Mal, go secure a spot for Bashi within your quarters. Once he's big enough to protect himself, we can move him outside."

"I will be hard to kill even as my tiny self, so rest easy when it comes to my well-being." Bashi's deep voice resonated in her mind, causing her to smile.

Maledic walked over to them, a smile in his voice. "I appreciate that sentiment, Bashi, as I am sure she does as well. I do believe that was our Queen's subtle way of asking us to leave."

Aurelia didn't lie to them; it was exactly what she was doing. Once the door shut, and she could feel the faint ribbon around her heart that she knew belonged to Maledic lengthen, she turned to the rest of the room. "Balthor, I need a guard on those two until it feels safe here."

There was an elongated pause. "Bashi can care for both of them. He won't appreciate you assuming otherwise."

"I don't really care. We aren't at the point where we can afford to risk the reality if you are wrong. Or do you want to be responsible for the death of the only dragon." She kept the reality that she was truly protecting Maledic to herself.

Margoth cleared her throat. "The monthly council meeting just so happens to be tomorrow."

Suzu hummed. "It is, but we've never had a queen sit in a council meeting here. It won't be received well."

Aurelia grinned. "Yes. That will make it interesting. But if we are truly united, it's time to show it."

S leep was well spent, refreshing her magical reserves. As she strode to the council room, Maledic, Bashi, and Balthor ranged around her, the glimmers of death sparkled in her darkened visual field.

Margoth's energy met them outside the council room. "Be gentle with the pup, girlie. He's on the verge of a mental leap."

Aurelia contemplated the words, nodding once before replying. "Yes. Perhaps he will be amenable to change, but a fight will still be on the horizon—especially if Zadon has any sway. I will be in on that meeting. Change must begin."

Margoth hummed, staying outside with Bashi. Maledic and Balthor stayed by her side. She settled into the only available chair left in the room, silence falling at her entrance.

"Gentlemen."

Lucian cleared his throat, tension filling his voice. "Aurelia. Did you need something to help you settle in?"

"No, thank you for the concern, Lucian. I am exactly where I need to be."

The harsh tones of Zadon cut through the room. "Queens are not welcome here. Council meetings include the spymaster, King, and the city mayors, along with the head of the army. None of those titles are ones you bear."

She waited, giving Lucian the opportunity to prove Margoth's assessment. Surprisingly, he did. "Zadon, you were warned. As you do not hold any of those titles in an official capacity yourself, you were only here as a guest. That privilege is now being revoked."

More stunned silence greeted them. She heard Zadon as he slammed something against the table before stomping off. The door slammed, splintering. Awkwardness reigned.

Aurelia gestured to Maledic—or at least her best guess as to his location. "This is my spymaster." She gestured to Balthor, "He is my head of the guard. As you can see, I have brought only the required people."

Lucian's shadowed form nodded shortly. "Let's carry on with the meeting."

Aurelia listened in depth, as much to her surprise, Lucian carried himself with poise and thoughtfulness, allowing everyone—including Maledic and Balthor, a chance to report.

At the end, he turned to her. "I am guessing you have joined us because there is something you need my help with."

"I have several orders of business. Firstly, the crowning at Drakore has happened, which you may have guessed at. I did not take the great Power of the Sky, however. Darius is free, wandering Baelia, having relinquished his hold on that throne." She paused, letting the reality that the man who had been seen as a villain for so long roamed free.

Lucian's voice was tense as he asked, "Is that all?"

"No. We should station a guard unit at the Tixdarr temple. It is the only way, as the united kingdom that we are, to ensure the Dodsfell realm remains right where it belongs."

There was a pause. "I understand where your concern is coming from, Aurelia. Yet I don't think that is a wise use of our resources. Your concern is no doubt rooted in your tragic past. Dodsfell has remained solidly closed for this entire time. There is no indication that there will be a change to that circumstance."

Heat flashed across her cheeks. He was saying no, dismissing her experience.

"Balthor, how many guards do we have at our disposal?"

"Around twenty."

"Well then, if the palace is unwilling to help in something for the greater good, we will make it work. Issue the needed orders."

"Yes Ma'am"

Lucian slapped his hand on the tabletop before growling. "If that's all, then I call for this meeting to be concluded."

Aurelia grimaced as she stood, not bothering with formalities, striding swiftly from the room; the door slam echoing around her.

fifty-two

MALEDIC

Duele - Palion - Year 7568

A few weeks had passed since they'd returned to Palion, and the tension hadn't relaxed in the slightest. The bond that had flared to life all those years ago felt somehow stronger now, as if Bashi bridged her half-mortal reality. He needed to make her see it was there. She had yet to really acknowledge it—undoubtedly, due to the complexities of her marriage with Lucian.

Suzu had worked hard on passing over the details of how she ran things as spymaster. Maledic had been shocked; she had been the one running things under Harold's rule. Now they would work together to ensure the much larger kingdom remained safe.

Through her, he had learned of the Festival of Duella happening throughout lower Palion. He had debated which way to go about their adventure—disguise her, or wander the city allowing her to actually connect with her people. Ultimately, he decided to give her people a chance to show their love of their queen.

He wandered through the residences in Aurelia's wing until he reached Balthor's door, and was surprised to hear Valri's raised voice through the crack.

"Absolutely not! Margoth, you can't be serious. He's a disgusting man. Why would I entertain the idea of actually being tied to him? I've had my soul connection, if we ever really even get them as demons."

Balthor's voice cut through. "I know, love. You've fought long and hard for him and your youngling. It's time to find your new purpose."

Margoth interrupted, cutting off the rest of his words. "Crow Man? What are you doing lingering in the hall? Girlie didn't make you a spy—merely a master of them."

Maledic pushed the door open, facing the three demons spread throughout the room. Valri strode to him, angling herself so that she could intercede on his behalf if needed.

"Huh. Further proof of my point, stubborn child," Margoth scoffed as she limped to the nearest cart holding drinks, pouring herself a hearty amount. Balthor stared him down silently, clearly angry at being overheard.

"I came to inquire if Balthor would guard Bashi today from the snake that we all know Zadon is. However, I'm now wondering if I should leave him to his own devices."

"He shall be safe." Valri spoke, her tone not allowing any arguments.

"Does Aurelia know the demons of her court have some sort of different agenda that must be discussed privately?"

Balthor took a step forward, his face unreadable. "She would understand the reasons. After all, we are demons—and we have business elsewhere."

"Right..."

Margoth sighed deeply, hobbling over to Balthor. She whacked him with her walking stick faster than Maledic had ever seen. "Hush. You're breaking the trust *you* built, you dolt.

Perhaps the girl has a point—you are just another man at the end of the day. Though I thought I beat that out of you all those years ago. Perhaps you want round two." She wagged her wrinkly finger under his nose as he paled. "Crow Man can know what's afoot."

She paused, staring down Balthor the challenge clear. Once he took a step away, she continued, returning her attention to Maledic. "The rules state we cannot touch Zadon in this realm—not that we can't explain our plans to those we trust."

Balthor grunted. "Fine. Though you are risking a lot on a technicality, Margoth. I've worked for centuries on this deal." He turned back to Maledic. "The goal is to have a ruling couple in Dodsfell to control the demons. At some point, opening it up to trade and commerce, as it once was."

Maledic mulled that over. "The communities would need to to be coaxed into working with demons. I don't understand why you're hiding it from Aurelia."

"There are rules to making this happen."

"I see, you should be aware that, I am taking her to the festival in the city center. One of you needs to keep Bashi away from Zadon. We all know that Bashi can protect himself, but Zadon has proven to be slippery."

The trio of demons all nodded. "You can be sure of it," Valri stated. "I am uninterested in Dodsfell's potential throne."

Maledic nodded halfheartedly. "Alright then Bashi can reach us mentally if something happens."

He headed up to Aurelia's room, waiting for her to exit, giddiness at the possibilities about their future. Hopeful that she was feeling something similar.

She strode out, stopping just short of running into him, her staff clunking on his boots.

"Woah there. Good morning, my Queen. I am hoping I can convince you to join me on an adventure today."

She cocked her head a bit. "What kind of plans?"

"The kind where we're responsibility—free and encouraged to enjoy ourselves."

Aurelia rolled her head, causing him to grin widely—her new version of the sarcastic eye-roll brought him so much joy. Proof that his Aurelia remained, buried deep down.

"Come on, Spréach give us a shot to be ourselves again— the version where we get to eat cake and indulge in drinking chocolate in Slana. Together, we can learn what Palion's version of that is."

She sighed, clearly mulling over the alternatives. "It can't hurt, I suppose. Plus, a good Queen has to know all of the Kingdom's traditions."

His grin faded a bit. He wanted her to come for him, but ultimately he would accept her wherever she was. He almost missed it as he turned to lead them toward the main doors. She reached up, tugging on her eye covering, vainly attempting to cover more of her longer scars.

Reacting on pure instinct, he reached up and touched her hand with the barest brush of his finger tips. "Aurelia." It came out as a pained whisper, which had her stiffening. "You look fine. It will be fine. I promise."

Her answering inhale was shaky before she shook out her shoulders and snapped. "Of course it's fine. I survived after all."

He bit his tongue, not wanting to push; instead, for them to find joy and happiness.

"Lets go. Today your people are celebrating, and so should we."

He led them both down the hall, heading out.

P alion's lower city could have been an entirely different realm. The atmosphere radiated lighthearted joy, children screeching and shouting their excitement up and down the road. He spared a glance at Aurelia, joy filling him as he caught the small smile on her face.

Musician's played lute and harp on street corners. Women sold baked goods at tables sporadically down the road. Each pastry representing a part of the Goddess Duella's realm. Oatcakes of various varieties represented the bountiful harvest, along with various fruit and vegetable—filled delicacies.

As more people exited the dwellings, the crowds swelled, forcing Maledic and Aurelia to stand shoulder to shoulder. More musicians joined in, and dancing began as young couples joined hands and swung in circles, men twirling the women and dipping them low. It didn't take long before Maledic and Aurelia were swept into the fun as well. Maledic grinned as an endless giggle began escaping from Aurelia as she was swung around from person to person, and he followed along, participating with the fun. After a bit, they both exited the crowd breathing hard, grins wide. Together they walked to the nearest food stand.

"That was the most fun at an event I've ever had. I don't think I ever got to fully engage with the public in Drakore." Her voice was a bit breathy.

"I don't think I did either, I usually avoided large gatherings of people. I wonder if the food is as good as the dancing is."

When they reached the table, the vendors eyes widened in recognition. "What-? Umm... What can I give you?"

Aurelia's expression didn't falter as she reached into a pocket, pulling out some silver coins. "We shall take whatever you think is your finest treat."

The vendor's mouth fell open slightly, shocked that the Queen would deign to talk to her. "Right away, Your…"

"No. Today, right now, its just Aurelia." She waved away the formalities.

Maledic grinned, his heart glowing at the feelings of joy and relaxation emerging from the bond they shared; she had never felt this light, free from burdens.

He glanced over her head and noticed in the greenery near Duella's small temple there were tables covered in buckets of flowers.

"Excuse me?" He leaned down to the vendor. "What's happening over there at the tables?"

The flustered vendor glanced to where he pointed. "Oh, that. It happens at each of Duella's festivals. Men and women still looking for their soulbond create flowers chains, choosing flowers that the Goddess tells them is correct. Those who have a soulbond work together to create matching flower crowns that they wear through the night."

Mal looked around, his eyes now registering the flower crowns speckled through the crowd. "What do those with chains do?"

"They wear it as a scarf, hoping their soulbond finds them so they can turn the scarf of flowers into a crowns of flowers."

"Thank you so much for telling us." Maledic placed his hand on the small of Aurelia's back, steering her as she juggled her staff and the goodies the vendor had given her. As they approached the tables, the atmosphere shifted from frenetic energy buzzing to calm determination.

Aurelia took a huge bite, handing the other end of the honey-apple oatcake pastry out for Maledic. He bit into it, an explosion of apple sweetness lighting up the sensors on his tongue. A unique blend of tart and sweet melding together.

He opened his eyes to take another bite but instead noticed the look on Aurelia's face.

"Maledic. Is that woman crafting a scarf or a crown?" She pointed to a brunette whose hair was cascading down her back in becoming waves.

He took a few steps to clearly see the project in front of her. "It looks like a scarf. Why?"

Aurelia ignored his question, her head swinging to the left, gaze narrowing. "Do you see a man standing just next to that far table, all alone? He's staring at her."

Maledic looked as he took another huge bite of pastry. There was no one standing there. "Aurelia, there isn't anyone there." He spoke through the chewing, glancing back at Aurelia.

Her face scrunched as she glanced between the woman and the empty area.

"What is it?"

"I think he's who she's searching for, but I think he's gone."

"Gone?" He asked, to the air as she had moved over to the woman scarfing down her last pastry. Maledic followed staying out of the way, keeping close enough that he could still hear her.

Aurelia approached her directly, a warm smile at the ready. "Hi. I don't mean to interrupt, but I was hoping you may be able to help me."

The woman startled, clearly being pulled from a deep concentration, "Of course. Is this your first year building with flowers?"

Her smile widened a bit. "Yes, but the main problem is my eyes aren't great, I can't see colors anymore. Perhaps you could point me to the correct ones."

Maledic noticed the woman's hand hesitate over a pink lily as she refocused on Aurelia.

"Of course! What colors do you need? Do you have a flower preference?"

"I want white flowers. I suppose I'll just use my nose to pick which particular smells I want."

They both giggled, and Maledic leaned back against a table, thoughtfully munching a pastry. He watched as Aurelia's fingers flew.

"How do you weave them so quickly?" The woman gaped as Aurelia took another white flower, interweaving it with the rest in just seconds before requesting the next. He watched her fingers feel out where the last flower ended, before securing the latest acquisition.

"When I was a child, my sister and I made flower crowns in the garden. It was a favored activity in the summer. I forgot to ask, what is your name?"

The woman smiled shyly. "Hura Dreuger. I know who you are, though."

Aurelia paused, measuring with her hands before accepting a few more white flowers. "Hura, can I ask you to get me a peony, make it your favorite color."

Hura found the correct bucket filled with flowers that were all the same, peonies apparently, though Maledic wouldn't have been able to tell anyone that. She plucked a purple one, returning to Aurelia and handing it over. Aurelia wove it in, then did the necessary work to weave them all together into a crown.

"Hura, I have some news for you." He could hear the hesitancy in Aurelia's voice. "I don't know how much you've heard about my powers, but I can see the dead."

Maledic straightened, moving closer a few steps. *Seeing the dead was a new development.* Hura stood confusion filling her face.

"Did you know white flowers are considered the best way to honor the dead? Peonies, in all their glory, represent life. Hura, you've searched so long for your soulbond. Its important to know he looked for you too. This crown is for you from him. He wants you to try and find a second-chance soulbond."

Hura's eyes grew wide, her hand traveling up to her mouth as tears began to drip down. "He's gone?" The quiver in her voice broke Maledic, his own pain echoing hers.

She gripped the flower scarf, then slowly reached out to take the crown Aurelia held out.

"Do you know his name?"

"Yes. He wants you to know it was Finn. He lived in the Fae realm, which is why you never crossed paths. He's eternally sorry for not traveling and finding you." Aurelia chuckled. "He claims he was quite a worker bee, and never wanted to leave his library, always convinced there would be more time."

"He loved books? I do as well!"

Aurelia grinned. "He claims it was more than books, sounds rather complicated, to be honest. You should know he's always with you, but he wants you to find true love. Love the two of you didn't get to experience."

Aurelia walked up to Hura, and enveloped her into a hug. Maledic closed the remaining distance, wanting to show his support. Hura let go of Aurelia with a sniffle placing the crown on her head. "Thank you, Aurelia."

"Of course."

Hura straightened and walked away, twisting a lock of hair as she disappeared into the crowd. Maledic slipped an arm around her shoulders. "You can see the spirits of the dead now?"

"Apparently finding joy within myself opened more of my magic. He just appeared in my vision, and then I could hear him."

"It's an interesting skill. Do you think she'll find another soulbond?"

"I've never heard of it, but Finn's spirit was adamant that it is possible. Time will tell."

"Will we ever find that idea of true love, Spréach?"

"I'm half dead, Mal. I'm married and forced to find common ground with someone I don't want to. Love isn't guaranteed for anyone, but we have an even tougher road to walk. How about we try to just be friends."

Maledic kissed the top of her head, nodding. "Friends first. Always."

fifty-three

AURELIA

Osi - Palion - Year 7568

The feeling of hands swinging her round and round as exhilaration bubbled up around her filled her mind. A laugh escaped her throat, exiting on a breathy exhale. She could feel Maledic close to her, reveling in his own joy. The scents of sweat and sunshine filled her as another giggle burst free. She could feel the sensations of warm hands gripping hers—squeezing and pulling her toward the next person. As she rounded the third turn the hand began to change shape, the fingers elongating, turning smoother and sharper—that of talons.

Fear gripped her chest. Icy sensations stabbed downwards. The feeling was so visceral it forced her mind back into consciousness. She sat up, white knuckles gripping the sheet around her body. Sweat slickened her nightgown as she sent her death magic through the room, determined to find whoever lurked meaning her harm. It returned having found the room empty. Satisfaction didn't flood in to quell the terror running in her mind. As her feet made contact with the icy cobbles, she heard it. Bashi was roaring.

She forgot her staff in her haste to get to Maledic's room, sprinting haphazardly, tripping and banging into furniture as she went.

As she ran down the hallway, her magic swarmed ahead of her, trying to find the danger that was ricocheting around her heart.

"Maledic!" Her scream ripped from her throat, only to be echoed by a fresh scream from Bashi.

A door slammed just ahead of her. "Aurelia!" She crashed into his arms, breathing hard.

"What happened? Are you hurt?"

"No, we are fine."

"THE WALL IS BREAKING," Bashi's voice was deep with concern.

Aurelia straightened in Maledic's hands, sensing Balthor and Margoth.

"Balthor—mobilize the Palace. Everyone. Ours and his. We need to head to Tixdarr's Temple. There needs to be an army there before it falls."

fifty-four

LUCIAN

Osi - Palion - Year 7568

> *Pixies are the tiniest of creatures. They pick the largest tree in the fae lands to be their death cradle, the tree hollowed out and filled with their precious dead.*
> *~Ancient Death Rites, Margoth's Journal*

He awoke to loud shouting and hundreds of boots stomping around his hallway. *Were they invaded?* He sat up and noticed that Zadon was sitting in the doorway, eerily watching Lucian sleep.

"Zadon? What are you doing here? What is happening?" A prickling sense of foreboding eased into his chest.

"That Queen of yours." He stressed Queen with a sneer. "Has mobilized the entire place. She is forcing the army to gather at Tixdarr's temple, claiming that the wall is breaking."

Lucian sat up in a rush, his blood draining as the sheets pooled around his hips. "That's not even possible."

"It's time you finally do what I've been trying to do. Put her in her place. I have tried time and again with women in this court, but they just don't seem to listen or respect me."

Zadon paced his room, getting closer to the bed, his body radiating anger. Lucian's mind flipped into pleasing mode. "Its fine, Zadon, I'll talk to her."

Zadon halted, staring at Lucian intently. "Right. Always talking."

Lucian nodded, his mind buzzing with too many inputs. For reasons he didn't understand, Kasria's face floated into his mind.

Zadon stomped away, slamming Lucian's door as he left. Lucian quickly got ready and exited, shocked by just how many people were moving under Aurelia's orders. He strode toward the main doors, anger rising with every step.

He found her standing with her pesky soulbond behind her, the dragon roaring in the gravel road. Aurelia was barking orders and brandishing her staff like an orchestrator at the symphony.

"Aurelia!" His tone was loud and harsh, spurring those nearest to them to run and hide. Maledic stiffened behind her, aiming a glare in his direction. "What is the meaning of this!"

Aurelia spun on her heel facing him. "The wall is coming down, and we will be prepared."

His patience finally snapped. He swallowed many of his internal thoughts when it came to his wife, but this was the end of it. "You don't know anything. You are a traumatized girl stuck in a woman's broken body. Time to grow up and not drag our people into the mess of your past."

He registered Maledic's movement as he took a few steps toward him, but it was Aurelia who ended up in his personal space. She moved so quickly, reminding him that she wasn't entirely mortal anymore. Her staff was jammed against his sternum.

"You are just a bully. A misguided, weakling of a man who lost his soulbond. That loss doesn't give you a reason to give up. I lost mine. Even now, we don't get to experience a true bond because of what I've been through. Despite it all, I push on. You rely on the snake in the grass to run the kingdom for you. What you don't understand is he's trying to destroy your people—those same ones who look up to you and need you to survive."

His wolf whined in his mind as her words struck true. He took a step away from her. "Why do you think you are always correct?"

"I ceased caring what anyone else thinks. Instead, I do my best to make decisions for the kingdom. I don't matter. Your horse is being saddled, and I expect you to either show up and lead the charge with me or disappear while I stand for Baelia, as is our task."

She turned on her heels, not stopping for a response. She continued on past Maledic, past Bashi and beyond.

Maledic strode to him, murder on his face. "She's died at least twice in her life. Stop making what she has left so miserable. You fucking won. You got her, and she will rule with an expertise that will put you and your father to shame—if only you'd get out of her damn way.

"You are stepping over the line, Maledic."

"I don't care. I will step in the way whenever I can after what she's been through. She's strong—we've all seen it—because she's still fucking choosing to stay and breathe, working for the betterment of us all. Now you step up and show her that she is no longer alone."

"She's not alone! There's an entire palace of people here. You don't leave her side! She doesn't need me."

"Bullshit!" Maledic got right into his face. "She needs you

a hell of a lot more than she needs me. You are her ruling part-ner. You make the important decisions. I am doing my best to make room for you. Show me my own torture is worth it!"

Lucian took three steps back and stared, open-mouthed, at Maledic.

"If I thought it would have made things easier, I would have slit your throat myself." On those parting words, Maledic turned away, approaching the still—screeching dragon.

Osi - Palion - Year 7568

Everything moved so quickly; it was mere moments after leaving Lucian that the horde of fighters, led by Aurelia, down to the Gates of the Kingdom—Bashi, Margoth, and Maledic bringing up the rear.

"We wait here, Crow Man." Margoth threw an arm out, her wrinkly skin slapping against his chest.

"Margoth, we've barely left the city gates." Bashi echoed his frustration.

"Yes, boy, and if the demons actually get the wall to break, we can escape back into Palion to fortify the city."

"She's down there! No one down there is focused on saving her; they're worried for the kingdom. I need her!"

Margoth grumbled a bit. "Lets clear the first stand of trees. You should be able to see the battle in your crow form from there. I will not risk you or Bashi closer, though."

"Now that he's here, it's fine if I go. You will care for him until he is his adult size."

Margoth took a few steps, placing her fragile form in front

of him. "You tied yourself to Bashi, and if you die, he will feed you his life source to keep you alive. The world needs the dragons. I have waited over four thousand years for someone to be deemed good enough to bring them back into Baelia. You will not selfishly destroy that!!"

His frustration exploded out of him in a loud roar, his heart shuddering under the weight of anxiety. A butterfly flew into his eye line fluttering a few times before stopping and landing on Margoth's forehead.

"It appears Feginth agrees with me." Margoth snorted at the insect.

Maledic couldn't articulate a response, merely shifting into his crow form and flying to the furthest tree in the stand.

He could see the army, under the orders of Ulfur and Juro, being organized into units of ten ranged in front of the gate. Shouted words carried through the air, though he couldn't make it out.

Valri and Balthor had shifted into their demon forms. Balthor stood around nine feet tall, fully red, pebbled skin gleaming in the sunlight. Valri's demon form was smaller but she was multi-colored. Her lower half looked to be a light purple, clearly beginning to transition to the bright red that her upper body gleamed with. They were positioned right next to the gate, clearly assessing the walls magic through their connection.

His eyes caught on a russet wolf with blonde streaks running through her fur, standing next to a panther. Sitting behind the army, they guarded Aurelia. She sat on the ground her staff next to her. He knew from the hasty conversation in the hall, before she had gotten dressed, that she would be deeply accessing her power throughout the battle, only resorting to her staff if the army line was broken.

Maledic wasn't surprised to see that Zadon and Lucian

were missing. Stubbornness would take more than harsh words to change minds.

Clouds began to roll in, the wind whipping around all of them. Belvina's wolf whined shrilly right before a gong sounded. It was similar to when Aurelia was released into the world.

The army ranks began to shift like a wave as creatures emerged. Wolves, panthers, serpents, and more flooded the area where once mortals had stood mere moments before.

The air became full of the first wave of owls, the closest clan to the neutral lands. The sounds of animals all restlessly waiting for something more to happen was interrupted by the ground beneath them all rolling and turning. The trees swaying and bending to such dramatic angles that Maledic himself had to hold on to the branch firmly.

Bashi screeched so loudly that Maledic had to turn to assess. Margoth had transformed into her demon self, a white pebbled skin glowing across the field. She hissed towards the gate, echoing Bashi.

"They come. May we survive to see the dawn of a new day." Bashi's dark voice rumbled through Maledic's mind. His caw echoed out in a lull of noise, causing Aurelia to glance at them.

"We will, Bashi. For today we defend, and tomorrow we plan." Aurelia's solid tones sounded in both of their minds, doing nothing to soothe Maledic's nerves.

Balthor let out a battle cry—the only warning they had as the wrought-iron gates, signifying the temple's importance and the realms official entrance, crumbled to dust.

Shock ricocheted in his chest at the concept that an iron gate would just dissolve. He didn't have long to contemplate that as demons began to stream through the hole. His heart crept into his throat as the first five or so dissolved into pink mist. His eyes flitted to Aurelia, sinking her hands into the ground, her head down in concentration. The panther in front of her shifted back to Suzu's willowy form as she held her hands out, beckoning the meadow grasses to grow, entrapping more wayward enemies.

Balthor and Valri focused on the trapped demons, cutting them to bits as the grasses held them still.

Ulfur stood to the side, yelling his orders as his warriors moved. Some had shifted back to their mortal shells, preferring steel to tooth and claw.

Belvina howled as a demon neared her. She launched herself at its throat. Suzu half turned, anguish and concern in her face, yet she stayed focused on the gate. Maledic could see tears flowing down as Belvina let out a few yelps of pain but battled on.

Lucian strode up to Maledic's post, stopping and surveying the battle. "I had a love that saved me. She brought light to me and gave me the strength to fight my inner monsters. Then she left me. No—that's not true. Someone stole her from me. In doing so, they also stole my ability to care for the larger picture. You were right, Maledic. I need to grow up. I know you're stuck up here, so I shall go protect our Queen and show the both of you that I learn from my mistakes."

Maledic bowed low, a murmured caw escaping as Lucian unsheathed his sword, descending the hill. His eyes fitted back to Aurelia, still hunched over on the ground, sparks now dancing on her body. A loud rumble occurred right before six precise lightning strikes landed on invading demons.

Maledic tore his gaze from her back to Belvina, who had gotten her opponent prone and was attempting to tear out his throat. If he hadn't been in his crow form, he would have missed the mice swarming over the entangled demon, stabbing it with sticks.

Everyone was here, ready to fight for their land—the big and the small.

Margoth stole his attention from the battle, screaming, "Crow Man, fly. Right now."

He trusted her, leaping into the air with ease. He shifted his body, glancing behind to where he had sat. The branch was now gone, drifting to the ground. He flew higher soaring in circles, trying to figure out what had happened. He couldn't see anything so he soared back to his tree settling on a higher branch.

He refocused and saw Lucian had taken a spot next to Aurelia, aiming to protect their Queen.

She continued to channel massive amounts of power, dissolving their enemies in batches and shooting down lightening bolts without pausing. Her focus so intense, he was sure she had yet to notice Lucian had engaged in battle, taking out one, then two demons that neared her.

Maledic glanced back to the gate, fear rushing in as the waves of demons seemed to just grow larger. It was in that moment he heard a shout. The voice was oddly familiar, but one he hadn't heard in a few months. "Aurelia, behind you!"

Maledic refocused on her, his breath caught as his mind struggled to process everything in front of him. Darius was on the other side of Aurelia, but somehow he wasn't close enough to intervene, as Zadon materialized a shiny knife in one hand. It was clear his target was the kneeling Aurelia.

Lucian, however, was moving as Aurelia half turned toward Darius, Lucian threw himself in the way of Zadon's blade.

"Zadon, NO!"

LUCIAN

Lucian heard the male voice shouting at Aurelia, his charge. His brain couldn't truly process what was happening.

He glanced at her, but she was still working her magic. Out of the corner of his eye, he saw a flash of blue that had him moving. He saw Zadon in his entirely blue demonic form, the most evil expression on his face. His mouth twisted in a gruesome grimace, the knife glinting in the sunlight.

He moved without thought, shifting his body to shield Aurelia. "Zadon, NO!"

He felt the hot, searing pain as the knife entered his abdomen, causing him to gasp. He dropped his sword, his mouth opening in shock. His hands went reflexively to the knife.

"Why?" He asked it through the pain, his mind spinning at the idea that his best friend just stabbed him.

"I killed her, Lucian, and I'll kill Aurelia as well. Now get out of my way." Zadon pulled the knife out, his flesh squelching on the release.

Lucian moved on instinct, his mind stuttering over the words. "Killed her?" He stood over Aurelia, only allowing one hand to drift down and cover his wound. "Who is dead, Zadon?"

Zadon leaned closer, his teeth snapping in front of his nose. "I killed that pub whore who disgraced you from your potential."

A ringing took over his hearing, and he threw himself on Zadon. His mind not recognizing the danger, only seeing the need for vengeance.

He half-shifted his hands into claws, his mind reeling with waves of pain.

Aurelia screamed a warning, but he could no longer hear her. His ears still rang, replaying Zadon's declaration.

His last sight was of Zadon's demonic sneer. "Ever the weakling, even in death, Lucian."

There was a searing pain, and then Kasria's face floated in front of him. "Kas. My love? I trusted the wrong person. Please forgive me."

She blinked at him, but slowly her face faded away, disappearing into the blackness. "Kasria?!" The world faded to black around him.

fifty-seven

DARIUS

OSI - PALION - YEAR 7568

Lucian slumped against the ground as Zadon disappeared again. Darius moved quickly, placing his back to Aurelia's. She now stood crouched, spinning her staff in a circle, waiting.

"You slimy little pet, it's time to stand for what you want! You want me? Come and get it, bastard."

"I don't think taunting the currently invisible, murdering demon is exactly what you want to be doing."

She let out a short laugh. "Darius. Your refreshing take on the world has been almost missed." She raised her voice. "What the pet doesn't know is I can still see him. Demons never lose the touch of death."

Darius braced himself, thinking it meant the demon was heading his way.

"He's heading deeper into Baelia. Ever the coward, that one. A problem for later."

Darius stepped toward the road leading to Baelia—and the innocents beyond. "I shall find him."

Aurelia didn't respond, which caused him to turn around. She knelt once more. This time, she pulled Lucian's limp body across her lap, feeling around searching.

"He shouldn't have died! Not really. These cuts would have healed eventually." Desperation tingeing her voice, blood still pouring from his wounds. "I've had worse then this so many times before."

As Darius watched her hands try to close Lucian's wounds and stop the blood oozing from them, a silvery form peeled itself from Lucian's body.

Aurelia took a deep inhale, a whispered, "no" escaping.

Lucian's spirit blinked at both of them, causing the raging battle to fade from their attention.

"Lucian?"

Aurelia jerked and looked at Darius. "You can see him?"

"Yes. Tixdarr's manipulations have caused this, I suppose."

"What happened?" Lucians spirit asked. "Where is Kasria? I saw her, but I couldn't get to her."

Aurelia sighed softly, stroking Lucian's hair from his face, blood staining his blond locks. "It doesn't matter any more. She must have chosen to stay in spirit form in Dodsfell, hoping to reunite with you. You'll have to go to Dodsfell and hope to find her. Or choose the Void for a new life."

"Thats not entirely true, Aurelia. If she chose to wait for you, she was taken by Tixdarr upon your death as payment for the extra time she had watching you. She's gone now, and you will have to chose for yourself what you're going to do next." Darius whispered the words, not wanting to disrespect the now dead.

"Next? What do you mean?"

Aurelia cleared her throat. "Either you spend eternity as a spirit trapped in Dodsfell, or go to the Void, where the Gods decide your fate."

An increase of yelling brought Darius' head up as he

scanned the vicinity. It seemed the endless stream of writhing bodies had stopped flooding through the gate.

A woman with red hair was collapsed, a wolf licking her face. The mortals—be they land or air—were all strewn in various heaps of exhaustion or injury. He closed his eyes, the pain of this moment sinking into his mind and soul. "Has it ended?"

"That was merely the beginning. It all falls to me. Always me." She let out a wry laugh, that hinged on manic. Darius looked back at where Lucian's spirit had been and realized he was gone. "How did you know about Kasria?"

"Cerial told me. When I die she will disappear."

He couldn't read her expression, but concern grew the longer she sat, playing with a dead man's hair.

"Right." She slowly, gently, shifted Lucian's body into the mud, standing up with the aid of her staff.

Darius scanned the treeline, picking out Maledic's crow and the silvery sheen of Cerial. "Lets regroup with your people. I shall help while I can, but this blood will get to me soon."

"No. You should go back to wherever you've been hiding. Cerial needs you. I already have a plan."

She strode away toward the temple, leaving him stuttering behind her, unsure what to do next.

Maledic's angry caw sounded directly above him, causing him to duck as the crow's taloned feet grazed Darius' scalp before winging after Aurelia.

fifty-eight

AURELIA

Osi - Palion - Year 7568

> *Once there were plenty of dragons—so many, in fact, that they existed much like any other species. That being said, they did have a death ritual. The reigning death dragon, if available, could be used to ease an elderly or sick dragon into death. On occasions that the death dragon couldn't partake, each creature had the choice to either break their souls into living beings or slip peacefully from the world. Everyone knew if they saw a horde of butterflies, someone had chosen to stay behind to watch their family and friends.*
> *~Ancient Death Rites, Margoth's Journal*

Aurelia strode forward, her mind curiously blank. The temple doors had wolven guards who parted for her as she topped the steps. She didn't bother to acknowledge them, merely slamming the doors open. Striding in, she ignored the mutterings of the maroon-robed acolytes.

"Where is Kana? I imagine if Aewenna is still the Oba, then Kana is as well."

A small bowed head appeared at her elbow. "This way, Your Majesty."

Before following, Aurelia raised her voice. "You have an hour. Pack the essentials and get out. This temple now belongs to me."

The acolytes all looked at her, mouths open in shock. Her guide cleared her throat, and Aurelia fell into step behind her. They ascended the stairs, navigating a warren of rooms— which had Aurelia's mind planning for their uses.

The acolyte opened a door, curtsying deeply. Aurelia strode in again without acknowledging the robed figure. Kana was draped upon a throne of bone—or at least something designed to look an awful lot like bone. Her Oba veils matched the color of the robed acolytes': red veils draped in layers, hiding the face of the woman who represented Tixdarr in Baelia.

"Kana."

"Aurelia, or should I say Queen of both Drakore and Palion." Kana stood slowly, deliberately taking her time. "What can the order of Tixdarr do for one as illustrious as you?"

"The Order of Tixdarr is being dismantled. You have an hour to get whatever is important to you and get out."

Kana took a step back, assessing the seriousness of Aurelia's statement. "Out? To where? This has been Tixdarr's Palace since the dawn of time and the creation of the Gods."

Aurelia dug into her magic, filling the floor with the death-bringing fog. "Tixdarr declared war on Baelia, and I will not allow him to maintain his foothold in the mortal realm. Your acolytes will be given the same choice as you: rejoin the people of your home as a regular citizen, or try your hand in Dodsfell. Test Tixdarr's mercy yourself."

"I won't go. You can't make me! I am untouchable! How will the mortals of Baelia dispose of their dead without me?"

Aurelia envisioned a searing chain, one that would burn on contact with the prisoner forced to wear it. "On any other day, I would have had patience. I would have tried to reason with you."

She raised her arm, pointing at Kana's neck and wrapping the chain around it. "Today, I don't have it. Call me a monster or a villain. Spread lies of the atrocities I have done to you. I shall survive this. You will not."

Kana gasped sharply as the chain tightened. Her hands went up to the magical chains, a scream loosening from her throat. Aurelia tugged, beginning to pull her out of the room.

Acolytes halted whatever task they were working on to watch in horror as Aurelia, with a cloud of death magic preceding her, dragged the Oba out of the temple.

Kana gripped the chains, her veils having been ripped away, revealing her snarling face. "You bitch! You can't remove the Order of Tixdarr, the Order of Death, from our world! We are needed!"

Aurelia laughed. With each step, Kana let out a yelp and moan. "There is very little I can't do. Such a shame you won't be here to watch it happen."

She kept walking, dirt and debris flying up as Kana kicked and flung her body, trying to free herself from the magical chains. She deposited Kana in a heap right on the edge of the opening to Dodsfell. She turned to her now extensive audience.

"The war on Baelia has begun, and Tixdarr and his minions are responsible. I will not allow his Order to continue. Kana has refused to leave willingly, so I will be removing her."

Balthor strode closer, his arms crossed. Aurelia continued. "The temple will be our home while we move forward as a united front in order to protect Baelia."

"You will never succeed! You are condemning everyone to be cursed to wander Baelia, haunting the inhabitants for the rest of time."

"Ah Kana. Have you gotten it all out? Yes? Good." She turned to Balthor. "My friend could you scoop up the trash and toss it out."

Balthor grinned. "Absolutely."

She could see him scoop up the sniveling mass that had been the proud Kana.

Kana screamed shrilly as Balthor launched her into the air into Dodsfell. Aurelia turned back to the acolytes, who were all standing, staring in horror.

"You are not forced to follow her. You can take an Order with a different god or goddess, or choose to return to your home."

Maledic's presence popped into existence behind her, his anger registering for the first time since she'd been home, in her mind and heart.

fifty-nine

MALEDIC

Osi - Palion - Year 7568

Maledic watched with detached interest as the acolytes slowly disrobed, revealing fighting leathers. His anger was unable to be harnessed. Once more, Aurelia had acted without concern for him or their bond. Perhaps he was just delusional in thinking there was a bond to begin with.

Once the acolytes were disrobed and off to the city to regroup—perhaps to find their families—Maledic stood just behind Aurelia. "We need to talk, Spréach."

"There's a lot happening, Mal. Can it wait?"

"No, it can't."

She finally turned to him, seemingly assessing. "Alright, let's go back to the temple, it should be empty now."

He nodded, not trusting more words in the already volatile mix of emotions. Maledic noted that Valri followed them, stationing herself outside the temple, guarding the doors. Silence reigned as he studied his soulbond and the one responsible for his intense emotional pain.

"Well?" She had a hand on her hip her body speaking the words for her: dismissal, defense, and false innocence.

"Why did you leave me behind?"

She startled. "What do you mean?"

"You almost died. Darius and Lucian protected you, and yet you acted alone. You didn't even glance back to make sure I was there. You just left, intent on your own vengeance?"

"Maledic..."

"No. No excuses. Answer one question." He walked up to her, closing the distance. "Is there a connection to fight for? I can feel it! I feel it when you walk in the room and my eyes see only you. I sense it when my blood turns to fire with a need to protect you. Yet I won't stay and continue to torture myself. I will leave to save my sanity if I have to."

Aurelia turned away, trying to put space between them. "It's really hard to know if the bond exists. The death magic stifles internal connections and makes it hard to keep my mortality in check. The urge to snap to the other side—to eliminate those who don't serve me—is stronger than I let on."

He swallowed. He'd seen her power in multiple situations, and for her to unleash any restraint terrified him.

She stopped in front of him. "You keep me grounded in this reality and not in the one that lives in my head. I never considered that you need me. I am a burden of responsibility, and I can't remove my problems."

"If you let me in, you cease to be a burden. We become partners instead." He hesitatingly stroked a finger up her cheek.

She inhaled sharply, leaning into his touch. "Alright. You may have to help me stay mortal. The line is so blurred."

He stroked down her cheek to her neck. "Deal. Now, what is the plan."

"Destabilize Tixdarr. In so doing, destabilize the Gods'

hold on Baelia. If they are real, they cannot toy with our lives —we are not their dolls. But on the off chance that I am right and they aren't real, I am merely dismantling the corrupt system. I want to unite the kingdoms, pulling down the walls, and build a giant palace here. This palace—this temple—will be dismantled stone by stone and replaced with a symbol of unity. Drakore and Palion will be renamed."

Maledic stroked down her neck to her shoulder. "Perhaps we name it Alore—a combination of both names, melded together as the people will be with time. Your take on the Gods and your plan makes a lot of sense. Feginth claimed something to the effect that they were corrupt, power-hungry beings."

Aurelia expelled another breath, the tension finally releasing as their hands entwined. "After all, what is a God?"

sixty

SUZU

Xita - Alore - Year 7568

She watched with a mingle of awe and disbelief as her mate kneeled down in front of Sarina, Culgan's Oba. The words boomed magically across the moonlit field.

"Lord Culgan was saddened when the last Alpha of the Palion pack fell to his own paranoia. His final act of sacrifice will be forever remembered and honored. It is an old tradition that the wolves had Alphas of either gender. One he is certain will be accepted without complaint."

Suzu could hear the undertone of threat, as could the rest of the wolves, as they all whined. Belvina even though she kneeled, kept her head still, looking on proud and strong. Ulfur took to his knees next to her, ever the stalwart protector, but as a panther shifter, Suzu was left to watch on the side.

Sarina cleared her throat before reaching behind her to an awaiting acolyte. A crown of woven willow passed between them.

"Belvina Feo, you have been selected for your strength and

adherence to old pack traditions. Lord Culgan believes with you at the helm, all will be mended."

Slowly, Sarina placed the crown on Belvina's head. Suzu clenched her fist tightly, her nails digging in as power flooded her mates. An echo of thousands of voices filled Suzu's mind, faint but powerful.

Suzu struggled to keep her feet as she was rocked with the feelings of the Alphadom flooding their bond. Blood dripped down her palms as her knees locked, body swaying. Pride swelled as Belvina merely inclined her head, unwilling to crumble.

"Culgan has one last gift for you, Alpha." Sarina curtsied slightly as Belvina met her eyes. "Your wolf, while powerful in its own right, has the option to become God-touched. Thus squashing anyone's potential false narrative that you don't deserve the title you have earned."

Belvina rose to her feet, silent for a moment before nodding her assent. Sarina leaned forward whispering instructions, but before Suzu could formulate a guess, her beauty had transformed into her wolf, russet in color, the blond streaks shining in the moonlight.

Sarina hit her knees, her head and arms laying flat in front of her. It was the only warning Suzu had that something major had begun to happen.

A larger-than-life black mass slowly emerged from the surrounding trees. Suzu reached instinctively for her power over the Land and was distressed to find it gone. The black shadow solidified into a great wolf, as a deep voice resonated within her mind. "Never fear, child, I am here to do as your mate has asked. No more." Suzu's instincts screamed at a God taking what wasn't his to take, distrust seeping into her bones. A voice sounded at her elbow as she helplessly watched on.

"He will treat her well. He's one of the few Gods who cares about mortals and their ways."

Suzu tore her eyes from Belvina's kneeling form; they widened as she took in the ghostly figure standing next to her. "Lucian?"

"Yes, Suzu, it's me. With the wall being down, I can wander as I please." He gave a ghostly shrug. "I needed to stay close and make sure *she's* doing what she swore."

Suzu turned back to Belvina, blinking back tears. "We are doing our best. Aurelia cares for everyone before herself, just as she always did. Your people became hers."

Belvina's wolf whimpered as Culgan advanced. Lucian's voice continued. "He will give her powers, and then she will be untouchable. Though she already was, we never really got to the bottom of why you did it. Why did you kill him? My father always admired you, you were his favorite."

Suzu swallowed, remembering the moments she had spent debating whether to take Harold's life. "Zadon was torturing him, keeping him drugged and starving for some unknown reason. I had no other option but to do it myself. I couldn't risk someone else finding him, or Zadon returning and torturing him more."

"You could have claimed the throne."

Suzu let out a short laugh. "No, I couldn't have done that. Zadon's entire goal was to put you on that throne, and if I had deviated, he would have murdered my loves as he did to yours."

She risked a glance at Lucian, noting his reserved expression. "Perhaps it happened how it had too."

A bright glow brought Suzu back to watching Belvina. Culgan had placed one giant paw on her head, glowing ichor of the God gushing forth to cover her wolf's coat. The pack whined in unison as Suzu felt white-hot pain emanating from her soulbond connection, both Ulfur and Belvina in immense pain.

Culgan removed his paw, licking at the cut and sealing it.

She watched in silent horror as the blood soaked into Belvina's body. The blood settled, changing her fur from russet tones to black as the night around them.

"It is done." Lucian's voice intoned a note of awe. "She will rival even Aurelia for power if my guess is correct."

Suzu grimaced, trying to keep her mind in a positive place, despite how difficult it was to see the positive when their world was enmeshed in a war with the demons and potentially the God of Death himself. The wolves began to howl and prance as Belvina stood up on all fours, shaking out her fur.

"They will run."

Suzu sighed heavily, wanting to dismiss Lucian and join them, even if she would be merely a panther among wolves. Instead, she steadied herself, letting the cuts in her palm heal. She dusted her skirts off, sending love down the soulbond to her mates, taking her time to reach the new headquarters of Alore.

Aurelia and Maledic had claimed a half-built shack with Bashi. The demons—Balthor, Valri, and Margoth—took turns manning the area where Tixdarr's gate had once stood, protecting the half-created base of operations.

Suzu, Belvina, and Ulfur had claimed a chunk of land, placing a tent down while they all waited the complex's creation.

Time would see Alore prosper. After all, Aurelia mastered death, Suzu the Land, and now Belvina had the wolves. What could possibly stop them?

epilogue

THE VOID

"How dare you go against me! I am your Queen!!" The small, pixie sized glowing figure stomped angrily.

"Whatever are you referring to, sister dear?" The large demon shifted back in his chair, amusement bubbling under the surface.

"If we ever want to be released from the Void, we need the mortals to crave our presence! All you have done is get your order officially removed! That chit will stop at nothing other than to erase you."

"She can't erase me. She will try. She will fail."

"So says you! You are gambling with my life's work, Tixdarr, and if you continue, I will unleash Oxius on you."

A sly smirk unfurled on the demon's face. "There are oaths yet to be called in, members of my realm to beckon home." His eyes gleamed in the dark. "The battle may be lost, but the war has just begun."

FAE CHRONICLES BOOK 1

Unsurprisingly, nothing was as it seemed.

Niamh leaned her back against the cool glass. *How had she gotten here?* A shiver went through her whole body as her mind whirled, ignoring the strain on her wings as she pushed herself harder against the curved surface. She had started her day as any other, opening the Archive's new acquisitions wing. It had been a miracle in securing the position at all. She was notorious for breaking things; her family even joking about her being cursed as a klutz. Somehow, against all the odds, she passed the background check.

Though they did start her off very simply, merely cleaning the artifacts deemed non-dangerous every morning. Three weeks of working, and amazingly, she had only broken three items.

The first dusting brush—its handle snapped after too much pressure. Poor craftsmanship, really. The second incident had been less defensible. No one had clearly specified that she shouldn't brace herself against the colored panes of glass inlaid into the wooden doors of the entryway. It became obvious, though, after one ill placed hand coupled with enough force and it splintered into a million glittering shards. After that, all doors were retrofitted with a clear designation on where it was safe to push.

The third casualty had been a set of shelves in the employee lounge. The staff was allowed to utilize the room to store their personal belongings safely while at work. On a random morning, during her first week, Niamh set down her bag and the whole shelf collapsed into a heap of dust, nails and splintered wood. The groundskeeper declared the shelf old and simply made a new one. Since none of these actually affected the artifacts, she had gotten away without getting punished. Today had been normal. She had been dusting carefully, the feathered brush dancing around various bottles, books and sparkling trinkets when her hand spasmed uncontrollably.

She rubbed the offending appendage as her mind raced over what had happened next. The bottle—a small round bellied glass simply corked with a bit of paper inside—popped off the shelf.

Niamh lunged on instinct, desperate to catch the bottle, her entire goal to keep it from breaking open and perhaps damaging the delicate parchment inside. It had never occurred to her that something else could happen.

The moment her fingers touched the glass, her body went wispy—shrinking, folding inward, yanked painfully through the mouth of the bottle. She glanced up and noted that the cork had disappeared.

Perhaps her presence had caused it to fly off?

The parchment rested on the glass opposite of her, small enough that she didn't actually touch it with her feet. She turned, looking out, surprise filling her at the realization that the bottle seemed to be back on its shelf. She could just make out Master Eoin walking through the room, scribbling in his notebook. She whimpered with frustration as she tapped her forehead on the glass. He was going to be so mad.

A whisper filled the small space as her breath fogged the inside of the bottle. "Do you want free, little bug?"

She inhaled sharply, insult and concern warring within her. She was small even when she wasn't trapped in a bottle, but the term 'bug' was an insult to any pixie. Then there were the rules. She hadn't been working there long, but the rules had been clear from the beginning. The first and most important:

Do not interact with the artifacts directly.

In fact now that she thought about it, she was only allowed to clean certain shelves—those deemed safe enough, so how had this come to pass? Master Eoin was unlikely to have mislabeled the bottle, so something else—an unknown entity—was at play.

"Niamh, where did you get off to?" The distortion due to the glass did not hide the aggravation in his tone.

The odd whisper once more filled the bottle. "Little bug, your task master is looking for you. The only way out is by reading the words I hold within."

A deep sense of foreboding filled her. Both sets of her membraned wings fluttered in unison, betraying her nerves as she glanced up to the corkless opening. She just needed Eoin to hear her, then he could fix her latest mistake.

"Eoin! Master Eoin!! Please hear me!!!" She hammered on the bottle's glass, her fists hurting with the impact. The desperate need to escape this unknown prison without dabbling with the parchment creature bubbling up.

The High Fae's Archive of Antiquities held magical artifacts that had been appropriated from all over Baelia through the centuries. She had learned of it as a youngling at her grandmother's knee. There had been many evenings where the Elder pixie would tell stories about all the items the High Fae held safe for the rest of the world. When questioned about the uptick in appropriation when the Pantheon of Gods over-threw the Dragons of Legend, her grandmother had shrugged it off as coincidence. After all, Fae of all kinds truly only cared about themselves.

Due to the vast possibilities, there was no way of knowing what would happen when she touched the paper. One thing that Master Cain had not deemed necessary for her to know was where everything originated before their imprisonment in the archives. Another round of fruitless banging on the glass, and she watched Eoin's distorted figure walk out of the room. Her blue skin flushing lavender as her options narrowed to the parchment.

"What are you?" She demanded from the roll.

"An escape of course."

"Out of the bottle? Back to the world I came from?" Her voice shook, but she knew she had to keep all deals with magical entities clear. They had reviewed that on her first day.

"Oh my darling little bug. I would never dare to deposit you anywhere untoward." The voice held a silky quality, coiling around her thoughts, drawing her in. She fought the urge to step closer as it continued. "It could be quite a treat to send you somewhere colder. The Fae realm is always so humid and hot. If temperature does not tempt you, perhaps I could find somewhere that would use your unique qualities far better than Mr. Grump out there."

She took a deep breath. "No. I want to go back to where I came from."

"How positively boring, little pixie. Your kind were once adventurous little gnats—I mean creatures."

Niamh crossed her arms, anger overcoming common sense. "You are a bit of a bully aren't you? Is that what got you locked away?"

A chuckle sounded. The glass seemingly reverberated

around her, her body feeling the vibrations. "There are many reasons I was locked away, but this is just a slice of my true magic. You can't truly believe such a small container could hold one with my vast power. The world is going to see the entirety of my prowess soon enough."

Niamh glanced between the room beyond, the glass, and the parchment, debating how to get what she needed without falling prey to the creature locked within. "How can someone be locked in ink? You aren't a real person are you?"

"Darling bug. Who said my entire being was trapped in here with you. I am but a piece of a larger masterwork."

"What is the price of your assistance?"

"Why freedom of course. We shall both be free."

She groaned a bit. Her curly brown hair swishing from side to side. She threw her hands up exasperated. "Fine!" She took a shaky breath gathering up her courage. "I have no other options apparently."

She brushed the tip of her pointer finger against the rough paper. A smell of sulfur escaped into the air, as her vision faded to black.

The next moment her eyes filled with the glowing runes of a language she didn't recognize. Her body felt pushed and pulled morphing into a new shape, a foreign one. The air shifted as well, the familiar smell of the archives filling her lungs.

A dark chuckle permeated the air, "Silly little bug. You should have clarified what form you came back as. This shall be great fun. I will enjoy watching you try to explain away this development. As is common with the Fae, nothing is as it seems."

notes

Thank you so much for reading Aurelia's story. I poured a lot of myself into her creation.

This concludes her story, but it doesn't conclude the adventures in Baelia. As Tixdarr pointed out, the war of the Gods has just begun. The next Baelian installment will be a standalone book that delves into the past of Balthor and Margoth.

Then the next major character in the war will be revealed sometime in 2027. I hope to see you then.

Never fear—You will see Aurelia, Maledic, Suzu and her mates again. They will just play side characters to someone else's story.

P.S Zadon's story has not been forgotten. While he disappears here, he will reappear with explanations provided in future. After all, one must remember he is a pawn in the war of the Gods.

acknowledgments

We live in difficult times. I also know my world I have created isn't full of sunshine and roses. I appreciate any and all who read my words. I fully believe reading fantasy—even the dark stuff leads to deeper thinking, which is needed for our real world selves. Aurelia's story has been in production for five long years, and I can't believe it's here for others to consume. I wouldn't have had the strength to write this if not for the following people.

My husband: In the darkest times of our life together, he is the one who encouraged me to write adventures. The specific adventures he has requested are still in production but without his belief, I don't think I would have picked up the pen. I am beyond grateful to have had you to ramble bits of this book to.

To my chaos gremlin: You won't read this for MANY years, but I hope I do you proud.

My mom: You raised me. You taught me all the ways to survive, and without you, I simply wouldn't be. I am lucky to have you as my best friend and helper to get this out into the world.

To my sister: You are my biggest cheerleader and have been there for every plot hole and twist. I hope you enjoy this.

To my one faithful BETA reader. Your comments made me brave enough to push through this process.

Koja Kalos: You know what a gem you are. You contribute more to the writing world than you realize. Keep writing!!

To Maventhoria: A huge thank you for the complimentary BETA read. I have never won a contest before, but it was such an amazing experience working with you. I also utilized them as my editors for this book and they did not disappoint! I look forward to working with you all again!

To my ARC readers. Thank you for taking a chance on this Indie Author!!

author bio

Mave Hathaway is a writer of many genres. While writing takes on the majority of her time, she still strives to ARC and BETA read for fellow Indie Authors. Mave writes for all ages, having both kid and adult books in her backlist. When not writing, she is kicking ass in martial arts and spending time with her family.

Check out her website and socials to fall in love with reading.

www.loftywingspress.com

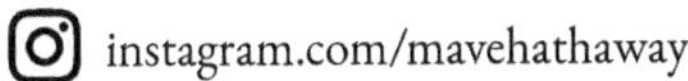 instagram.com/mavehathaway